AND THEY WILL SUFFER

RICHARD BEAUCHAMP

All Rights Reserved

Cover design by Marta @ GetCovers

Edited by CD McKenna

First paperback edition October 2024

Paperback ISBN: 978-1-959396-66-6

eBook ISBN: 978-1-959396-67-3

Please visit us at

www.anatolianpressllc.com

For my grandmother, one of the greatest story tellers I know.

"Look at a relief map of The United States, and you will see the Ozark country standing out like an egg-shaped excrescence in a vast central plain— The only mountainous region between the Rockies and the Southern Appalachians. The Ozark Hills are rugged in places, and extremely beautiful, but they are called mountains only by grace of contrast to the interminable prairies which environ them."

-Vance Randolph

AND THEY WILL SUFFER

By Richard Beauchamp

ACT I: THE SURGEON

June 14ᵗʰ, 1863—somewhere in the Saint Francois Highlands, Missouri.

CHAPTER 1

Charles can't decide which sound is worse, the bestial cries of the man thrashing underneath him, or the grating sound of the surgeon's saw against the soldier's femur. A sound so much like a tree saw against a stubborn hardwood, like winter-hardened hickory, that bone saw made. Sweat stood out on the surgeon's face, dripping from the long black curls of hair into the open valley of gore at the man's leg, where it ran with his blood. Charles sweated too, for the triage tent was a sauna, hot with Ozark summer and human suffering.

"Hold him down, damnit!" the surgeon, Dr. Hanz Fischer, barked, but his tone was neither reprimanding nor angry. It was *jubilant*. Charles could see the feral glee in his eyes, plain and naked now. He remembered when the surgeon used to try to hide it, his excitation during times of duress like these, the cots full of damaged and moaning meat, his patients livid with agony seeming to act as a sort of aphrodisiac for the big man. But now, his lips crushed into a thin line against his teeth and curled up at the edges like a wilting flower, that grim sneer was on his face as he tried his hardest to make the dull bone saw do its job.

A deep furrow was gouged out of the white bone, the saw about halfway through the femur, with bits of gristle and marrow sticking to the almost completely rusted blade. An inch below this was the spot where the musket ball found purchase in the man's shin. The man, a private named Josiah Standridge, must've been from hardy stock, for his shin stopped the bullet's journey into Missouri soil and instead found a home within the man's body, the nickel-sized lead ball lodged neatly into the bone and gristle.

Josiah, who'd been given a watered-down opium tincture and a swig of Colonel Phelps's private reserve whiskey, was blessedly losing consciousness from the pain, his eyes rolled up to peak at his noggin, his twitching body slowly going limp. Charles then looked at the surgeon, who gripped the leg in one large, hairy hand, the unceasing blur of the bone saw frozen as he saw his patient was finally spared his agonies. A look of profound disappointment crossed over the huge German's face.

There it is, Charles thought with a sour gut sensation. He watched as Fischer's features slackened into that of disappointment, a child who has just been denied the succulent confectionaries his eyes fall upon at a drug store counter. He threw the useless bone saw aside, and instead gripped the man's leg in both hands. Fischer turned upon his assistant, his eyes, viper's eyes, cold, calculating, the pupils dilated obscenely, bore into the diminutive dutchman.

"Herr Wagner, if you would, please grab our soldier's foot, assist me," he said through gritted teeth.

"What? Why not proceed with the manual—"

"By the time that bloody saw cuts through this leg, the secessionists will have won the war entirely. That saw is about as dull as a confederate's brain. We must wrench the leg off. The bone is already compromised. Just pull and twist, ja?" he said, the grin pulling his lips back once more as he saw Charles's face turn the pallor of the dead.

Charles knew he must. As battlefield protocol dictated, Fischer was in a way his commanding officer, and to deny him would be insubordination. Feeling his breakfast of salt pork and coffee curdle in his stomach, Charles released his bear hug on the man's upper body and instead went down to Josiah's feet. Fischer made a violent ripping motion with his hands to demonstrate how Charles must do the job, before firmly placing both big hands on Josiah's upper leg to hold the nearly sundered limb in place.

Grabbing the hot, slippery limb, Charles squeezed his eyes shut and, with both hands wrapped around the thin shin, wrenched it upward, the sound of the bone cracking like that of a green tree branch unwilling to yield its fresh fibers. Josiah let out a low, gargling moan, stirred once, and then went limp once more.

"Again! It's almost free." Fischer breathed, the exaltation back in his voice now. Charles looked down and saw that the bone had broken somewhat cleanly at the sight where the saw had cut in, but several strands of hardy gristle and flesh saw the leg still attached to its body. Wanting to be done with this, wanting to be out of Fischer's insane gaze, wanting to be out of this fetid hell of human misery, he yanked hard at the leg a final time, the tendons and connective tissue separating with wet snaps, and there Charles stood, holding the calf of a union soldier.

It wasn't the first amputated body part he'd held, and he knew it wouldn't be the last. Charles placed it gingerly on the waste travois that sat in the corner of the tent, where a blanket of flies covered the corpses of two Union boys who died of shock just as they'd entered the tent many hours prior. Charles never thought he would miss the winter campaign, that first brutal slog through the highlands that saw men succumb to frostbite and hypothermia on their long marches toward death, but at least winter held onto the bodies better. The summer humidity saw anything without a pulse set rapidly to putrefaction.

There came the sizzle of meat to hot metal, the sound of pork fat spitting in a skillet. Except it wasn't pork fat. It was Fischer, who'd taken the red-hot paddle iron from the coals that simmered next to the bed, and set the hellish glowing metal to the exposed bone nub and flesh, cauterizing the wound. Even Josiah's shock and the narcotic nostrums he'd been dosed with weren't enough to numb him from that particular agony as marrow sizzled and exposed nerve endings fried. He managed one more feeble yell as his flesh cooked and his bone charred before collapsing back against the bed, the doctor's hellish ministrations finally concluded.

Charles helped Fischer take Josiah to one of the cots. Cots that at the start of the war were eggshell white and clean with their linens, but now held a ubiquitous brown hue from so many feeble washings in various creeks and rivers. The unending letting of blood, bile, shit, and vomit upon the linens, marking campaign casualties, had permanently dyed the once white sheets a congealed pus color.

"Next patient," Fischer said, his grin back, his operating table eagerly awaiting more wailing gristle, his veiny hands eager to wrench, cut, abrade, and rend. All under the guise of medicine.

CHAPTER 2

Charles Muller rose with the sun, finding a rare moment of solace in the bruised peach sky, the sun yet to drool its hot, blistering light onto the world, the early morning mist giving serenity to picturesque fields and meadows that would soon be the sight of so much spilled blood.

Only the overnight pickets were up with him, the men standing half asleep, using the long bodies of their Springfield muskets to lean upon as they wavered and groaned like ancient birch in a high wind, doing their best to remain vigilant. Charles and Fischer were one of five medic teams assigned to the 3rd Missouri infantry regiment, the band of some 1200 men camped out on a crowded knob that overlooked the valley they sought to hold from the Missouri State Guard. They were once 2000 strong, but between hit-and-run skirmishes with the Jayhawkers to the west and the rebel guerillas to the southeast, both of whom liked to fight dirty and use unconventional tactics, that number was slowly whittled down to the 1200 some souls that remained.

As Charles hiked down to the hollow at the base of the knob where the latrine sight was designated, he thought of how different this war was when the draft was first called as he squatted and had his morning push. Lincoln had put in the call for some 70,000 volunteers to help quell the traitors to the south, and like Fischer, Charles was one of the many German immigrants in the state who happily took up arms fighting for the north. Originally transplanted to Missouri to take part in the booming lead industry in these hills, abandoning his life as a brewer across the sea, Charles was immediately drafted to the Union medical corps when the federals saw he'd had experience as a doctor in Germany. He tried to explain that his medical experience was quite negligent, doing a short stint as a field medic in the Austro-Prussian conflict before becoming a brewmaster. The army didn't care. They needed men, pure and simple.

At first, Charles was enamored with his role, saw himself as a guardian angel to those upholding the doctrine of a free America, liberators of the enslaved, all that naïve romanticism. He'd also been an assistant to a wholly different surgeon then, as well. Back then, he was part of the 1st infantry regiment, Price's division, and a meek but soft-spoken Yankee named Hap Givens was the senior field surgeon for Charles's detachment. Givens was the very antithesis of Fischer, his bedside manner almost feminine in its tenderness. Of course, that was back when Union losses were small, as they were able to squash the poorly equipped and disorganized rebel pockets in the southern part of the state. Back when they had the time and the supplies to fully tend to each victim. Back when the war was still in its infancy, and the feral side of conflict had yet to rear its ugly head. Before the triage tents were transformed into rotating charnel houses full of leaking and groaning meat.

Givens had been killed during a nighttime raid on their camp last year. Charles remembered that night clearly, because from that night on any time he heard a branch break in the great eternal darkness that swallowed these never-ending hills each twilight, his heart would pound and his body would break out in fear-sweat in anticipation of great violence.

Charles had been sleeping deeply next to a smoldering campfire, the cusp of the autumnal equinox bringing with it pleasantly cool nights that allowed a man to sleep comfortably in his uniform and tattered bedroll. The sound of gunfire, which until that evening he'd only heard in diluted, distant waves, muffled by the hills and hollers that separated the main camp from theatres of battle, was loud and godlike as it shattered the serene night.

Charles shot up immediately, and felt a meteor streak past his head at the moment he did so, felt a bright burning on the tip of his nose as something sheared off the cartilage there.

"Ambush!" one of the colonels had yelled, blowing the muster horn before a stray Minié-ball cleanly truncated the warbling note off right at its soprano apex.

Charles rolled and hugged the ground as if it were his *mutter*, only daring to move his eyes as he watched men scramble to load their muskets and return fire. He watched great crimson coronas explode out of the backs of Union uniforms and heard their death rattles quickly swallowed up by the hellish cacophony of gunfire as bearded specters danced through the wood, whooping like sirens and throwing lead from the safety of the trees. Gun smoke and blood tickled his nose and angry hornets buzzed inches above his body as he fought back a sneeze. Then a corporal fell a foot away, his bayonet-affixed musket falling within arm's reach of Charles, blue eyes staring wide at the assistant surgeon. Time slowed momentarily as he watched the death-glaze shine those eyes into a permanent, vacuous stare.

He half entertained the idea of grabbing the rifle, but couldn't bring himself to. He was here to *heal* men, not *hurt* them. He then felt a hand pulling him to his knees. He turned and saw it was surgeon Givens, his balding, glistening head and crooked spectacles glinting off the various pockets of light erupting from the trees that surrounded them.

"Come, boy, we must run! We're surrounded, we're—" He turned to run when one half of his skull suddenly blossomed open like a sunflower on its first spring morning. He collapsed unceremoniously to the ground, and Charles fell with him, forgoing dignity for a chance to breathe again as he cowered by the dead doctor, hoping any stray bullets would be caught by the corpse of the man he considered a protégé.

It felt like whole lifetimes had passed as the fighting went on. Charles lay fetal, listening to whooping war cries and agonized howls and return fire, his ears ringing something fierce as the fighting eventually died down, a few brazened men sprinting off into the woods to counter-ambush the jayhawkers who'd preyed upon them, hoping to run off with a few horses and muskets despite being allies of the Union.

Eventually, someone was yanking him up.

"To your feet, dutchman," one of the captains barked as Charles blinked stupidly, saw that it was no longer pitch black but a peach-purple early morning, the first rays of dawn revealing the massacre he'd narrowly avoided. It was then he got his first taste of true war. All noble aspirations and thoughts of honor evaporated as he saw firsthand how efficiently the tools of man could rend and ruin flesh.

A month later, Price's decimated regiment joined with the Illinois regulars from the east, and they became the 3rd Missouri regiment. It was during this joining of forces he first met Fischer, whom despite being from his homeland, quickly set himself apart as a strange and peculiar man, soon to turn frightening and aberrant as the heat of war brought out the grinning, abhorrent ghoul that lurked within

#

"Ah, nothing like a morning *schiesse* to set the body right, yes?" Fischer's voice floated to him out of the mist, and Charles felt all the sphincters on his body tighten, truncating the runny stool he'd been depositing onto the dew-flecked grass. Fischer, who was huge, over six and a half feet tall and a trunk built like a whiskey barrel, squatted next to Charles, his trousers already around his knees. "Do you think we'll ever come down off this hill? I hear the fighting is really picking up down south. Engagements in Tennessee and Kentucky territories on a grand scale I hear," Fischer said, his heavily accented voice strained slightly as he moved his bowels.

"I'd be just fine never seeing another day of combat. This war has turned savage, doctor, and I'm beginning to doubt the efficacy of our roles here," Charles said as he quickly wiped with a handful of grass and hoisted his trousers up. Fischer farted and then let out a laugh.

"Efficacy? My dear boy, you see things all wrong. What war *isn't* savage? It is the nature of man to be savage. We are but emissaries of mercy, simply repairing those who wish to fight again. Take pride in your work, Herr Muller, for it is all you have," he said, switching to their mother tongue to say this last.

"That is not true. I'd like to start a family someday. Have a wife, children. I don't want to die on this goddamned hill, only to be carted off on a waste travois," Charles said, wishing to be done with this conversation. All attempts at palaver with the surgeon unnerved him deeply, for Fischer had the outlook of a wild beast constrained by the niceties of the society he was forced to live in. "Don't you have family?" he asked, not sure if he wanted to know more about Fischer than he needed to.

"No. A wife is but a burden and a child is but an 18-year commitment of debt and for what? I have no need to pass my bloodline on. The Fischer name is ancient and unending. I have no need for an heir," he grunted.

Charles walked back up the hill, unsure of what Fischer meant by that. The nebulous aroma of shit wafted to him on the morning breeze.

#

They ate a breakfast of boiled potatoes, bacon, and hard tack made somewhat malleable by bacon grease. Charles ate alone, the Union soldiers did not take to dutchmen such as himself, or the few colored soldiers who'd escaped their owners to come fight for the cause. They were allies in a common enemy, but that was all. Warm bodies to further the cause. Many in their company saw Fischer as a madman and a devil, and by association, Charles too. So, he ate alone, trying to savor the rich tastes of the pork, and wishing for some of the colonel's whiskey, or even more so, the bold, smoky flavors of the stout he used to brew by the barrel. That was one thing Charles missed about his homeland; the beer was *much* better.

The usual subdued banter of the men during breakfast time was cut off as two riders came up from the hill, their horses ran hard and frothing at the mouth.

"Colonel Phelps!" one shouted. "We have news for Colonel Phelps!"

Phelps, who was tall and rotund, his jowls whiskered by thick brown muttonchops and his hair slicked back in a ducktail, appeared flushed and befuddled from his tent.

"Who summons me? Speak plainly, for I do not like being interrupted," he called out. The riders came to him, the men of the company following their advance with great intrigue. Charles could see by their yellow armbands they were forward advance scouts, but from where no one knew. They dismounted and quickly followed the colonel to his tent.

With that, the men resumed their eating, though conversation was null as some attempted to eavesdrop on the news as they could hear animated shouts coming from the colonel's quarters. Charles was intrigued, for it was rare that the colonel allowed council during his usual morning libations of strategic planning and drinking, mostly the latter.

Finishing his meal, Charles made it toward the medical tent, where he began to check up on those who'd survived Fischer's brutal ministrations and re-dose those with opium tinctures that needed it, cleaning wounds and changing wrappings where appropriate. He was in the middle of draining an infected abscess from a man's thigh, doing his best not to look at the thick yellow discharge that erupted like curdled milk from the bulging pocket of flesh when an officer came into the tent.

"Doctor Muller, your colonel seeks an audience with you, on the double," the officer said. Charles blinked, looking at the young man, whose nose was crinkled up at the smell of human rot that constantly permeated the medical tent.

"Me? I don't—"

"Now, doctor."

Charles perfunctorily cleaned his hands on his trousers as he followed the officer toward the colonel's tent, feeling curious eyes upon him. He saw Fischer, Captain Lewis, and four corporals advancing toward the tent, as well. Fischer saw him and winked. Anxiety caused the recently masticated food in Charles's gut to bubble into an acidic bolus that found a home a few inches below his throat. He'd never been in the colonel's quarters before, the canvas tent spacious and of much sturdier build than the thin lean two tents the rest of the men were forced to bivouac in.

The officer held open one canvas panel and stood sharply, saluting the colonel as he nodded for the men to come in.

CHAPTER 3

"Like madmen, they just started turning on one another, they—" one of the scouts was babbling as they came in, but the colonel held up a hand to silence him. Charles saw Phelps favored his right leg today, could see how the leather of his left boot was pulled taught by the no doubt swollen foot within. The only time the colonel had spoken directly to Charles was when he was summoned to see to the man's recurrent gouty arthritis. Charles had told him several times that there was nothing to be done for the throbbing big toe and excruciating pain except dose him on opium, which was dangerous with the amount of whiskey the colonel consumed. He'd tried to explain that the man's painful condition was a consequence of lifestyle, that if the colonel were to cut back on his whiskey and bacon, his agony would be gone. But the man was stalwart as he was stubborn and would not hear of such modifications.

"Gentleman," he said, his face pulled taught with pain as he limped over from his map table. "I've summoned you here for an important operation."

"This is all you're sending? You—"

"Damnit boy, let me speak!" Phelps snapped at the leftmost scout, a young man who didn't look a sight over sixteen, whose face was gray and glistened with sweat. His eyes had the glazed-over, hollow look that Charles had only seen on men who were close to breaking bread with the reaper. The boy must've truly seen something terrible. Both scouts stood trembling but remained silent. "Now, as I was saying. I've called you here for a search and rescue effort. I've been informed there was an ambush on the nearby township of Poplar Springs. Apparently, those mongrels had the foresight to dress in stolen Union uniforms and make their way into town unmolested. They then proceeded to ransack the houses, try to steal some horses, and then, well, erm—" The colonel cleared his throat and looked at the scouts, granting them permission to speak.

"We arrived right at sundown, having gone to report on Poplar Springs to check the status of the picket placed there. When we arrived, it was . . . madness. The townsfolk just started throwing themselves at the soldiers, screaming and howling and biting . . . The soldiers fought back, but they were overwhelmed. Couldn't tell who was friend and who was foe. And . . . and—" one of the young men blabbered, unable to finish his thought.

"We had a small detachment sent down there to set up a picket and provide protection for the people. That's what we're here for after all, our state being contested as it is, we have to secure these secluded enclaves from all manner of enemy, . These isolated communities up in the hills, their loyalty will flip like a fish out of water. Whatever buys them safety for their farms and family. Hell, some of them don't even know there's a war going on! It is to be assumed that detachment was wiped out. I'm sending a small group back with the scouts to survey damage and find any survivors. You're also to requisition any materials you may see: food, weapons, horses—" The colonel went on.

"Sir," one of the corporals spoke up. Charles didn't recognize any of them except for the black man at the very end, knew his name was Gerald something. One of the few from the company to actually treat Charles like a human being, probably because he too was a pariah among the ranks. His face was a blank slate as his fellow corporal spoke. "Shouldn't you send a full company for this? I mean—" The man looked at the squadron assembled before him.

"There will be no need of that. For one thing, these scouts make it sound like no one was left alive, so resistance should be minimal, if any. That being said, arm the doctors just in case. I cannot afford to split my men up, however. I've been given reports this morning of heavy troop movements to the south, rumor has it a faction of the Missouri Guard is meeting up with the Arkansas irregulars to form a brigade and plan raids throughout the highlands. They think we are spread thin and ill-prepared in the foothills. I will prove them otherwise. Take the caisson with you and bring back all that you can. Save any that can walk and hold a rifle. Those gravely wounded and cannot . . . Let the sawbones send them off. Report back here with utmost haste," the colonel said, waving a hand to dismiss the men.

#

"All right, Dutchy, try not to shoot yer pecker off," Corporal Sanderson said as he showed Charles how to operate the Colt revolver. His hands shook so badly he'd dropped the thick bullets as he tried to load them into the cylinder chamber, much to the amusement of the men around him. Fischer on the other hand was given a Spencer repeater, and the intimidating weapon looked right at home in his meaty hands.

"You fight back at home, hoss? You and that gun look married to each other," Corporal Mayfield asked Fischer. Fischer grinned and shook his head.

"I hunted with my father back in the motherland. I was also a volunteer marksman for the Prussian legionnaires before I went to medical school. Firearms are no stranger to me," he said as he deftly loaded the gun.

14

After a few tries, Charles demonstrated he could load and reload his weapon without fumbling, whereupon he was vehemently instructed to keep it sequestered on his person unless otherwise told. Charles could do that, for he did not like holding guns, nor did he like knowing he was heading straight into a fresh killing field with the possibility of enemy combatants afoot.

With Fischer and Charles manning the caisson, the four corporals flanked them on either side in a phalanx arrangement, the scouts and the captain some half mile ahead, leading the way. There was only one road that led up and down Shephard Mountain, where the regiment was currently stationed, and the doctors had a time of wheeling the caisson down the heavily rutted and well-trotted path, turned slick and treacherous with mud from the on and off showers washing over the valley the last few days.

Charles was not familiar with this area of the highlands. He'd lived in the southeast corner of the state, in the swampy lowlands just south of Port Saint Louis. Carlyle it was called, where the land was flat, the landscape dotted with long railroad lines, fields of corn and wheat, shops and storefronts, the great meandering brown of the Mississippi, and a general feeling of land long domesticated by human hands. Every day he traveled by horse to the base of where the fertile bottoms met the rising ridge of the plateau that marked the start of the highlands out in Arcadia valley. There, Mine Lamott waited for him with its dark maw of sundered earth. He signed onto the mining work not knowing how brutal and unforgiving the conditions were, lured in by the promises of good money for honest labor.

Here though, in what he later learned was the Saint Francios highlands, the land was steeply graded and heavily wooded, with peach and slate-colored bluffs poking up occasionally from the sea of trees, showing off the ancient sedimentary layers like the layers of a wedding cake. The townships within Salem County, though Charles thought *villages* was a more apropos term, were severely isolated from one another,

15

with miles of rolling viridian and steep foothills separating one from the other. The land here was stony and inhospitable for most forms of subsistence farming, and so a good number of the locale were trappers and huntsmen, as wild and rugged as the land they sought sustenance from.

Though they hadn't crossed Poplar Springs on their way up the mountain, they had come across several villages in the region whose population mostly consisted of self-sufficient French Creole settlers whose features were worn raw and weary due to the nature of their work, which was most often comprised of trapping and mining. Lead and silver mines with French names were ubiquitous in this part of the highlands. Often, the only signs of habitation for miles in these unending sprawls of deciduous forested hills were open-air strip mines gouged out of these small mountains like gaping wounds in a soldier's side.

Charles had worked for many such French-owned mines down in the eastern part of the state, and it was the only facet of the land that was familiar to him out here. Charles wondered if Poplar Springs would be like those other isolated villages they came across, with its townspeople who were almost wholly oblivious to the war and their understanding of what was at stake. Most speaking a half-cobbled French-English and carrying about in their own exclusively insular environment where the rest of the world may as well cease to exist.

He noted that slaveholders were few and far between out here, often comprised of small families, sometimes even only one slave to a whole house, unlike the southern plantations and their massive sprawling estates manned by whole generations of colored families. Many were ambiguous to the federalist cause, many weren't sure exactly what the rebels fought for. Many were wary of the huge armies that rolled through their towns, camping on their ranches and farms and shitting in their woods and eating their food. Charles always felt like a stranger in a foreign land when the army marched through these primordial enclaves, not because of his status as an immigrant but because of the wary, vacant stares he received from ratty-clothed mountain men who lived a life completely alien in manner and routine than his own.

The road went on for some miles, nothing but dense clutches of white oak and short-leaf pine hemming them in on either side, and Charles's body was tense not only from the arduous journey but also from the walls of trees on either side of them. He knew firsthand how prolific at ambush tactics the secessionist guerrillas were, and it was ingrained in him to be wary of any forest or great patch of wood that could hide bodies. So, being surrounded by all this dense foliage made him feel like a helpless mouse crossing the open killing fields of a falcon, every tree trunk possibly hiding a bearded, bedraggled rebel irregular.

But they were not fired upon or molested in any way as the road devolved into a tract, which after some miles, devolved further into overgrown patches of sloping wild prairie before finally they began marching through wild forest.

As the corporals stopped to help Fischer and Charles pull the caisson through mud pits and dense thickets, Charles dared ask how much farther they had to go. He judged they'd gone at least seven miles, though with the ever-changing topography and constant unending walls of trees before them it was hard to gauge the exact distance.

"Mile or two yet, almost there, Dutchy," the corporal grunted as they heaved the wooden cart over another outcropping of stone and low boulders. Even Fischer, whose hearty vessel seemed immune to fatigue, was red-faced and breathing raggedly. He'd gone shirtless halfway through their journey and Charles marveled at just how muscled the hairy, pale body was.

"Don't worry, the payoff will be worth it," Fischer said through gritted teeth as they went on, their brogans thoroughly plastered with mud and leaves. Fischer was always full of cryptic statements like that, open-ended declarations that always left Charles wondering what exactly the mean German meant. Was he expecting the village to be wealthy with horses and food? No, Charles assumed Poplar Springs was just like the neighboring townships with its threadbare denizens barely scraping by off bush meat and foraging.

He means the carnage. Plenty of suffering for him to indulge in, plenty of opportunity to apply his 'medicine', Charles thought bitterly with a wave of anxious fatigue as he saw that the dense wood they were traveling through was finally starting to open up. Twilight was fast upon them, and through the graying blanket of branches and leaves, he could see the outcropping of a hut, could smell smoke, and with it an underscore of copper. He heard Fischer inhale audibly, a chef savoring the vapors of his stew, and Charles swore he could see the man swell up with invigoration before his very eyes as they came upon the decimated township of Poplar Springs.

CHAPTER 4

The clearing they came into revealed a row of houses that looked as if they'd weathered a tornado in the passing hours. Wood siding and tar paper roofs were torn ragged with shot and musket rounds, windows busted, glass everywhere. Bodies lay akimbo in the dirt walkways that led through town. Charles could see a number of blue uniforms among them. He also saw women, children, and men and women of old among the dead, as well. The slaughter spared none.

"Odd, buzzards are absent," remarked Corporal Gerald Wilcocks. That *was* odd, for it was high summer and there was a veritable smorgasbord laid out for the carrion birds, and yet not one was in sight. Charles looked skyward, and saw among the bloated blanket of clouds that provided a canvas for the overcast twilight that no turkey vultures or crows circled high above.

"Be on your guard, men!" Captain Lewis bellowed. Along with the scouts, he dismounted from his horse and withdrew his revolver. "Listen up, people of Poplar Springs! My name is Captain Arlen Lewis of the United States Federal Army. If there's any goddamn shit-assed rebels out there, know you're to soon face death if you do not turn tail and run. You heard right, we're not even gonna give you the mercy of being our prisoners. We have no mercy for murderous traitors! Any citizens who hear this summons, I request you stay in your homes until we have cleared the area. Otherwise you risk getting shot." Lewis's deep bassoon voice carried over the still, barren town with a lethal authority that allowed him to shout commands on the battlefield and still be heard over the hellish din of cannon barrages and musket volleys. Anyone hiding among the trees would've heard his statement clearly.

Despite the captain's bravado, Charles still felt a tingling in the back of his neck, half expecting a Minié-ball to find its way into the base of his skull. Fischer walked beside him and used the barrel of the Spencer to turn over a dead soldier whose face looked like it'd been clawed off by a wild animal.

"Marvelous," was all Fischer said as they both saw the long ratty hair and portions of unkempt beard that hadn't been sheared away along with the flesh. The uniform itself sported two bullet holes in the torso but no entry wounds could be seen on the man. A well-worn squirrel gun was clutched in the pearl-white hands. Clearly a rebel. Charles noted the way the nose looked as if it'd been chewed off.

Fischer knelt down and took the man's face in one large hand and stared, his eyes going wide. The look of concentration on his face was so intense, so ferocious that Charles thought maybe he knew the poor soul.

"What is it?" he finally asked just as Fischer let the head fall unceremoniously back onto the muddy ground with a plop. He stood, those shrewd eyes surveying their surroundings closely. Abandoning the caisson, Fischer went to each of the corpses, examining them studiously. Not knowing what else to do, Charles followed behind like a lost puppy, and noted that only the civilians sported gunshot wounds. A woman in a once-pretty dress had her jaw blown away by a musket ball, and her apron was peppered with buckshot. The soldiers though, those men pretending to be federalists . . . It looked like animals had got at them.

20

There was another oddity about this grim scene that Charles silently filed away: the flies. They all set upon the fallen rebel soldiers, buzzed and hovered in a miasma among them, but the civilian corpses were unbothered by the insects. In fact, upon closer inspection he saw that many of the Poplar Springs citizens had a legion of dead horseflies and mosquitos among their ranks, their little legs poking straight up in the air inches away from the bodies.

"Konnte es sein?" he heard Fischer whisper under his breath. *Could it be?*

"What? For god's sake, what is it, man? What—" Charles began, the weirdness of the situation about to drive him mad, when he heard a sound off to his left, toward the trees. His heart skipped a beat, and he felt his testicles shrink into raisins as he saw a man stumbling toward them. He was dressed as a Union soldier, his face cleanly shaven, a red armband to show he was with Phelps's Division. He had in his hand a boot knife, but held it limply at his side, the way a child might drag along their favorite doll.

He came straight for Charles, coming upon him with an awkward, stumbling locomotion, as if he were deep in the bottle, and he would've assumed the man were drunk if it weren't for the fact he could see the bloodshot sclera of the man's eyes, pupil and iris unseen as they rolled completely up into the skull.

"H . . .Help!" Charles managed to squeak out. The revolver in his hand suddenly weighed as much as a Howitzer, the hand that held it gone numb and useless. As the man drew closer, Charles heard him muttering. At first, he thought it was gibberish, until he heard snatches of words.

German words.

Destroy . . . For . . . The . . . She . . .

Since the night raid on their camp last year, Charles had been plagued by intense, hellish nightmares once a fortnight. He blinked rapidly, and was trying to tell himself to wake up, for surely this was one of those terrible nocturnal episodes. But he could

21

feel the cramps in his bowels as adrenaline shot into his system, felt the ache in his feet and lower back from the arduous journey here, the smell of gore thick and heavy in his nostrils.

No, too real to be a dream.

"HELP!" he finally managed to put volume to his cries, but not before the soldier suddenly charged him.

Charles let out a feminine squeal as he was knocked to the ground, his body falling in the blood-tinged mud, the breath pushed out of his lungs, the man heavy atop him. Yellow and crooked teeth that smelled of spoiled meat bathed Charles's face in hot waves as teeth gnashed loudly inches from his face.

"*Fischer!*" he screamed, and managed to pull his hands up from his sides and push at the thing's chest, but not before the madman's teeth scraped a layer of skin off the tip of Charle's nose, which was already a grizzled nub of scar tissue. He screamed and then promptly gagged as slobber drooled from those muttering lips and into Charles's mouth. He craned his neck up and saw that Fischer only stood frozen, a most perverse look of elation on his face. *Oh, Christ for god's fucking sake not now!* he thought wildly as he saw the pupils dilate to the size of a cannon's bore and the thin curl of a grin twisting his lips at the corner.

"Mein Gott . . ." Fischer breathed as the soldier continued to flail atop Charles, teeth clacking hard enough for splinters of enamel to fall onto Charles's face. "*Enthralled?*" Fischer almost whispered.

"*Help goddamnit!*" Charles screamed at the top of his lungs, but the soldiers were far ahead, all of them immediately seeking to plunder the houses for food and drink, leaving the bodies for the sawbones duo.

His arms began to tremble from the weight of the man. He wouldn't be able to hold the insane bastard away much longer. Charles began to recite the lord's prayer in his head, squeezing his eyes shut and whimpering like a scared babe before he heard a single thunderclap of a gunshot and felt his face misted in a hot spray.

The body atop him abruptly went limp and with this, Charles threw the man off with a cry. Hanz Fischer loomed before him, his face showing a bit of melancholy reluctance, the jubilation gone as he stuck out a hand to help Charles up. He slid around in the mud and inched away from Fischer on hands and knees.

"No! Get away from me! What in god's name is wrong with you!" he screamed, reverting to his mother tongue in his panic, his composure evaporated, the true feelings about Fischer that he'd kept locked deep down into his subconscious finally coming out in a boil of hysteria.

"Doctor Muller, what are you—" Fischer began calmly.

"Demon! You're a goddamn demon, you—"

"What in god's name is going on over here?" Captain Lewis bellowed, the big man along with two of the Corporals finally came lumbering over, their weapons drawn, things like smoked hams and bottles of whiskey bulging from shoulder satchels. Fischer's grin slowly withered to that of concern, the human gesture looked so forced Charles thought it pained the man to do so.

"Acting in self defense, sir. This man was upon my assistant in a hostile manner," Fischer said calmly as he lowered his rifle.

Corporal Wilcocks walked over to the body, where the man's short combed black hair was abruptly truncated by the hollowed-out back of his skull. Charles saw concern on the young man's onyx face.

"Sir, he was one of ours. Private Elijah Davis, I believe," he reported to Captain Lewis. Immediately guns were trained upon Fischer's person. Fischer made no move, his features unchanged as he looked into the assorted bores aimed at his chest and head.

"That was one of ours, you Dutch shit," Corporal Sanderson hissed, the hammer of his revolver cocked back.

"What's the meaning of this, Fischer?" Lewis said. His gun wasn't pointed directly at Fischer but at the ground between them, ready to swing up at a moment's notice. He then turned to Charles.

"What happened here?" the captain asked.

"He . . . He . . ." Charles began, looking at Fischer as he spoke, saw one bushy black eyebrow crawl up his forehead, a small lopsided grin on his face, silently daring Charles to speak his mind. He swallowed hard. In his mind's eye, he saw those terrible eyes dilating like a man in the throes of an opium delirium. "He . . . saved me. That man was insane, trying to . . . eat me," he gasped.

"Did I hear you right? You said private Davis was trying to . . . *eat* you? Have you two been helping yourselves to your tinctures?" Captain Lewis said, a scattering of nervous laughter sounded at this.

"Look at the bodies, sir, something was upon these rebels and I don't see animal scat around," Fischer said coolly.

"He's right, sir. All the civilians appear shot. The raiders . . . Not a single shot to them. It's like . . . the citizens just went mad and started going animal on them," Wilcocks said, continuing to examine the dead rebel Fischer had shot.

"Jesus Christ. What a goddamn mess." Captain Lewis sighed and wiped a hand down his face. "All right men, listen up. We're doing this damn thing house by house. Look for survivors first, and things that might aid the war effort second. I don't know what the hell went on down here, and I don't care to know. We got a dozen dead rebels and that's good enough for me. And you two"—he pointed at the two Dutch doctors— "you see another one of our boys upon you, I don't care if his eyes are glowing red and he's got a ten-foot cock with devil horns on it, you hold your goddamn fire and come get one of us, understand? It's treason, next time," Lewis said, his gaze deadly serious.

"Yes, sir," Fischer answered for both of them.

"All right. As you were men," Lewis said as he began to offload his first haul onto the caisson.

CHAPTER 5

The town was larger than Charles had anticipated as they moved away from the burg of houses that turned out to be only a small portion of Poplar Springs. They had a small trading post similar to what one would find on a frontier junction, not quite a general store but it was clear the place received shipments via wagon train, given the deep ruts and hitching posts spotted outside. Charles watched with distaste as the men raided the store, openly snacking on loaves of bread and breaking into the meat rack room for jerky and quartered meats.

This was raiding behavior, this is what the ill-equipped rebels did, stealing from towns and the dead. The federals were supposed to be a symbol of the civilized army, progressive in cause and forward in their way of operating. Instead, he saw men gorging themselves on the left-over dinners and private stashes of alcohol in each of the gun-blasted homes they came to. Once he even saw Sanderson hiking up the dress of a young woman who retained some regal air of beauty if not for the crimson rose blossom in the back of her head, a Fischer-like grin on his face as he prepared to do something unspeakable. That was before Lewis appeared around the corner and the corporal abruptly switched postures, instead pretending to inspect the entry wound in her skull.

It was an unfortunate blessing that they came upon no more of the living, as Charles dreaded having to euthanize any of the suffering. He was sure Fischer would've *gladly* taken on those duties, and Charles was relieved the mad bastard would be deprived of such pleasures.

They searched houses along with the soldiers, and in one he found the makings of a meal in progress, the wood-fire oven still warm, the coals still smoldering. He watched Fischer shove a whole boiled potato into his mouth and smack noisily as he turned bodies over with the same morbid fascination as a child overturning a rock to happen upon the mysterious insects dwelling beneath them.

They found similar scenes in all of the dozen or so houses that sat in the shadow of a knob of land, not quite a mountain and too grand to be called a foothill. The village seemed to be squeezed in on all sides by dense trees, as if the forest were doing its best to cover up this small human blight, except for the slope leading to the knob, where at the top Charles could see a large cave opening. He knew in this part of the region, he'd heard of vast, innumerable cave systems that ran into the earth for miles and miles, many of them even more rich with lead and copper than the hills Charles had mined. He'd heard rumor that the engineers piggybacked off those pre-existing systems to plant their mines even deeper than was ever thought possible, many times sacrificing safety for profits. He saw at the base of the small mountain the oak and pine thinned out enough that one could see a discernable trail leading to the knob. He wondered if this too were a mining village.

They continued searching houses, finding no horses but many a dead human, and a cornucopia of food. Charles saw men gnawing on plump shanks that looked like pork, tearing apart fluffy loaves of bread, and digging into huge serving bowls of soup congealed and gone cold. For being so isolated and without apparent access to livestock or agriculture, Charles wondered how they could cook such extravagant feasts. Prior to this, the most robust dinner setting he'd seen of the hill folk was squirrel stew served with wheat biscuits and boiled chicory tea.

Eventually they found a man who'd been brewing moonshine in the back of his house, several jars of the clear liquid lined his cellar.

The men helped themselves to the rotgut, with Fischer taking a jar for himself and taking a long pull off the stuff. He smacked his lips and handed the jar to Muller.

"To the motherland. To victory," he said. Charles only stared at the jar, the potent fumes strong enough he thought his nose hairs might singe.

"This isn't right, this isn't the Christian way," Charles replied, his eyes still staring at the moonshine. Back in his hometown of Hamburg, he'd developed a bit of a drinking problem. After the Prussian conflict, he'd opened up a brewery paid for by the government and became a renowned as a brewmaster. He often accompanied his breakfast, lunch, and dinner with the rich, stout beer the color of coffee, taste testing and telling himself it was for research. He badly yearned for a drink now, the horrors and strangeness of his situation in much need of a softening, dulling touch.

"Christian way? What does that mean exactly?" Fischer said with a laugh as he took another pull from the shine before rudely shoving it in Charles's hands. "The Christians I knew were more barbaric than the bearded nords that everyone thought were the devil. They make these rebels look like high cultured bourgeois with their toothless raids and long hair. The Christian way would be to rape the women, steal the children and baptize them in virginal blood, and then crucify the men all in order to appease their undead carpenter, to search out the heretics and put them in iron maidens to repent. Now drink up, Muller. We're authorized by the provost marshal himself to requisite these supplies. I toasted the motherland. You cannot leave such a declaration unfinished. I will not allow it."

Charles sighed and drank. He spluttered, coughed, half thinking he'd just taken a belt of kerosene oil instead of anything fit for human consumption. He gasped as his throat burned and his stomach churned lava, a liquid fire more intense than the strongest scotch he'd ever drank, but the effect was almost immediate, a warm fuzzy tingling bled into his appendages, the incipient anxiety that pulled his nerves taught from this macabre scene loosened ever so slightly.

Fischer laughed and clapped him hard on the back. All the while the dead moonshiner responsible for this firewater lay on the ground not even ten feet away, his body sporting several red craters. Despite the burning, despite the breath-stealing heat that followed each swallow, Charles took another drink, much to the encouragement of Fischer. Some invisible hand loosened the marionette strings that pulled his muscles taught with worry, and he let out a deep sigh.

When he had his wits about him, he took a moment to ruminate on what Fischer had just said. The man surely spoke of the crusades, that unfortunate blemish in Christian history that saw their evangelical might turned upon Muslim heretics. But he spoke as if he were *there*, as if he *lived* through the crusades. Fischer was always doing stuff like that. He was about to ask what the German meant by his words when Captain Lewis burst into the house. His look of utter confusion and pale consternation, two things one never saw on the stoic captain's face, was enough to freeze both men in their revelries.

"On me. We got a live one. And she's . . . She needs medical attention. I think," he said, ushering the two men from the shiner's house.

CHAPTER 6

The house stood out not only because of its size and elegance compared to its neighbors, but also the fact that it seemed to be the only house immune to gunfire. Not a single shingle or board was splintered or out of place. Draped windows kept them from peering into the two-story house, which seemed a mansion compared to the tar paper hovels that edged up to the dense foliage border.

"Why so perturbed, Captain? You look as if you've seen a ghost?" Fischer asked, his curiosity genuine.

"You'll see, just . . . come on," Lewis breathed.

As they came up the steps, he saw Corporal Wilcocks vomiting into a humble garden that grew dandelion, Mullein, sweet potatoes, and a few other seasonals. Charles knew the man was no greenie, and wondered what in God's name they would find in there to make these hardened men so ill at ease.

Captain Lewis stood by the doorway, holding open the thick oak door and using a handkerchief to censor his olfactory senses from the physical wave of death that erupted from the house. Charles was ahead of Fischer, and he froze as he passed the threshold into the house. His eyes watered and his mouth turned in crooked directions as disgust and nausea threatened to boil the shine burning in his gut into a volcanic geyser.

Blinking away the tears, Charles saw he was in a living room of sorts, the furnishings rather spartan for a house of such size, a few chairs here, a tea table, a wood-burning fireplace. No fixtures or ornaments adorned the wall.

A faint wavering light came from the room ahead of them, and in that direction, the smell somehow grew even stronger. Stealing himself, Charles entered what turned out to be a dining room. A large red hickory table the size of a coffin was the centerpiece, and atop it was one of the rebels. He was completely naked, the spots of grime on his skin made stark in contrast to the utter alabaster complexion of his body. His bearded face was frozen in a pained rictus of an O. His arms shot skywards, fingers twisted into desperate clawed things. He was clearly dead by the frozen nature of his body, his eyes glazed over, yet he sported no obvious signs of physical trauma.

The candlelight flickered and abruptly grew brighter, and in it, Charles saw the rest of the dining room, and for a moment felt the world tilt on its axis.

"Oh *my*," Fischer said, clearly impressed with this display of butchery.

"Sch . . . Schiesse . . ." Charles breathed. He made it a point not to speak his mother tongue around the Yankees, it made them suspicious, but in this instance abject horror caused his manners to evaporate.

Sitting at the head of the table was a woman of indeterminate age. Judging by the deep arroyos of flesh, craggy valleys of her jowls, and the thick thatch of silver atop a narrow skull, she was old, though the unflattering candlelight highlighted her features and made her appear absolutely ancient. But Charles's attention was soon torn away from the woman, who sat perfectly still in a denim blouse, for right behind her, plastered to the wall in a crucified pose was a writhing, moaning thing.

Fischer walked around the transfixed Charles, taking one of the many unlit candles sitting on the nearby kitchen counter and casually lighting it to the one that sat at the center of the table. This new light source further illuminated the inexplicable butchery on display before them.

Fischer let out a shaky sigh so reminiscent of a man on the cusp of sexual climax as he studied the glistening tendons, the flexing pink muscles, the exposed veins and arteries all undamaged.

"Absolutely incredible," Fischer marveled as Charles looked on in mute horror. What he was looking at was a perfectly skinned man, not a single patch of skin or torn flesh remained upon his still animate body. The flesh, he saw, had been tacked to the wall, a perfect outline of his red and pink and white body. Lidless eyes peered wide and desperate at Fischer as he continued to stare at the filleted man, his mouth moving, trying to form words but unable to due to having no lips. Teeth clacked together in a ghastly rictus. Charles could see the tongue sliding between the molar gaps.

Somehow, this man was still alive, and frozen to the wall via unseen means. He reminded Charles of the various cadavers he'd seen during his brief stint at the medical school before being shipped off to war, the way the skin was so neatly flayed and pinned about the body. It made no sense. The human body would've, *should've* succumbed to shock long before the final swath of flesh was removed from the body. The only evidence of shock however was the foul spillage on the floor released from the man's bowels. The smell of death was so strong it completely covered up that hot sulfurous odor of feces.

Then, as he forced himself to look toward the floor, at the ceiling, all around, he noticed not a drop of blood. Indeed, the dining room and kitchen were immaculate, and the area around the flayed man and his dead companion were free of a single drop of crimson.

Charles's lightly inebriated mind swam as he tried to formulate the logistics of this barbaric act. Unable to look at the skinless man and his pathetic twitching any longer, his eyes crawled over to the old woman. At first, he thought she might be dead too, so complete was the stillness in which she sat, eyes fixed straight ahead, arms crossed in her lap. But then she blinked, and Charles jumped at this small bodily function. That was her only sign of life, however.

"Well, fucking do something! Don't just stand there!" Lewis barked from behind him, nearly causing Charles to piss himself.

"Incredible," he heard Fischer say under his breath as he turned to the frozen woman, one doctor coming to either side of her. Charles reached out a badly trembling hand and felt for a pulse in the twig-thin arm. There was nothing, and the arm was cold to the touch. Charles blinked rapidly as he continued to feel for a pulse. No, no, that wasn't right. He'd just seen her blink for Christ's sake!

"Ma'am?" Fischer asked as he delicately touched her shoulder. His large hands moved slowly, with infinite care as they went to her slender but skin-waddled throat, where he too felt for a pulse that wasn't there. Black bushy eyebrows shot up into his greasy tangles of black hair as Charles knew he detected the absence of life that should be throbbing through the body as well. Still, Fischer continued his tender ministrations. "Madam, can you hear me?" he asked. But she remained frozen, except for one more slow eye blink. "Junge Dame?" He switched to the mother tongue, calling her a young woman. *Can you hear me, young lady?* he asked, in a voice so soft, so tender that he might've been whispering to a sleeping babe.

It was a side of Fischer so very dichotomous to his barbaric jovialness when in the medical tent that Charles had to stare in disbelief. There was not a single sign of the mad German, but rather a tender, caring paternal side that Charles would've never dared believe the man possessed.

His intake of air was sharp then as he saw the woman slowly crane her head toward Fischer. Thin, pale lips smiled, piling the flesh at the corners of her mouth. She sniffed his hand the way a dog does. Rheumy eyes lit up in recognition.

"B . . . Bruder?" The word was rasped more than spoken, a hush of leaves in a fall wind given sibilant meaning.

Fischer displayed one of his trademark ghastly grins once more, except his eyes now gleamed with tears. Charles Muller's mouth hung open, sure the shine was causing him to hear and see things.

"What . . . What did she just say?" Charles asked. But he may as well of been talking to the moon, how lost those two were in each other's eyes, like long lost lovers come to reunite at last.

The body suspended against the wall abruptly became unglued from its remaining mooring of flesh, and everyone except Fischer and the old woman leaped out of their skin with the heavy corporeal thud, breaking the molasses-thick silence that permeated the house.

CHAPTER 7

"All right men, make yourselves comfortable," Lewis said as he watched over the two Germans, who'd begun examining the old woman. Charles did his best to marshal his nerves, doing his duty as a doctor as she continued to stare longingly at Fischer, who did the same. "We're bivouacking here tonight." Lewis grimaced.

"What? You outta your fuckin mind?" Sanderson nearly screamed. He'd been peering anxiously out of one window, watching as the sun slowly crawled across the sky, close to being swallowed by the knob that presided over Poplar Springs like some unforgiving lord. He turned on Lewis, and Charles saw he was making a concentrated effort not to look in their direction, toward the sheath of flesh that remained tacked to the wall. "We can't stay here, reeks of a goddamn slaughterhouse!"

Just then, the two corporals, Halloway and Andrews, came into the house, apparently looking to see where the other men went off to. The scouts were right behind them, looking ashen as they caught whiffs of the permeating rot. One of them promptly vomited right in the doorway.

"Jesus fuckin Christ, what—"

"It's the smell of the dead, Andrews, don't act like you ain't smelt it before. Now listen up!" Lewis bellowed. His voice carried painfully loud in the big house with its many bare walls to reverberate off of. "We're bedding down here tonight. You all remember how tough it was today, so imagine trying to cut through that mess at night, in rebel territory at that."

"We can't just stay here! What if the rebels come back?" Sanderson said. He turned to Wilcocks, who'd been sitting silently in a corner of the living room, plump lips pursed in deep, disturbed concentration. Sanderson kicked the man's foot. "What say you, negro? You wanna sleep with Mr. Skinless over there?"

"What's he talking about?" one of the scouts said, making his way deeper into the house. He froze when he saw the flesh splayed on the wall, the mess of red glistening meat that lay in a heap on the floor. "Wha . . . What?" he gasped, taking two steps back. The other scout went to see for himself, and soon both men looked as if they might lose their eyes on the floorboards.

"That's . . . That's devil's work. Knew there was something off with this place. Come on Timothy," The one who wasn't Timothy said, and needing no further encouragement, the two young men, hardly old enough to graduate from drummer boy duty, promptly turned tail out the door, and a minute later the sound of horse hooves receded. Captain Lewis didn't bother to chase after them.

"Well, that's just fuckin great. Lost our goddamn scouts," Sanderson said, his plump cheeks, normally ruddy from nipping stolen booze, took on a deep scarlet. "We can't stay here captain . . . It ain't right."

"You got bigger balls than me, son, if you wanna try going through them woods in the dark," Lewis said as he went to the window, hands on the thick curtains that barred the sunlight. "We're here to make sure the goddamn rebels don't get to take another single village from us. Quantrill's men have already raided Salem up north and parts of Willow Springs. We're gonna play these goddamn mongrels at their own game.

Andrews, Halloway, go upstairs and garrison the room with the best view. Take my rifle, it's got the best shot on it. Sanderson and Wilcocks, keep looking out yonder and keep your pistols primed." He ripped open the curtains.

As he stepped out of the way to let the pinkish rays of the setting sun in, the house became filled with an unearthly caterwaul that stabbed at eardrums and made eyes squeeze shut.

Charles stared at the woman as her mouth cracked open to howl, her face now properly illuminated by the outside, and he could see just how truly pale she was. It was then he saw her teethless gums, her plump pink tongue, her quivering uvula as the throat opened up. She recoiled against the doctors, thrashed about like something possessed, her statue-like stillness gone.

"What—" Charles began, so utterly confused by this violent fit that he could only stare, covering his ears as the agonized howling became ear-piercing.

Without missing a beat, as if he knew exactly what to do, Fischer scooped the frail woman up in his arms and carried her like a betrothed bride. He ran toward the hallway off the side of the living room with incredible speed, the passageway cloaked in shadows. The whole thing happened so fast Charles could only blink stupidly at the now empty chair he remained standing by.

"There, there . . ." Fischer cooed as the screaming abruptly stopped, replaced by a whimpering mewl that was as pathetic as it was heartbreaking. Charles grabbed one of the candles and followed after, a litany of questions bubbling to his mind as he looked upon the frail woman and saw that her arms and face had taken on a bright red pallor like a severe sunburn. Her once glassy eyes were now bloodshot, the pupils nothing more than pinpricks in blue irises.

"What the devils? Severe photophobia you think?" Charles said as Fischer continued to hold her like a giant baby. Fischer slowly shook his head.

"No," That was all he was willing to say on the matter. "Come, let's find your bed chambers," he said softly, and Charles followed after, noting the bathroom off to the side and two doors which, upon checking were locked shut. The door at the end of the hall appeared to be the bedroom as Fischer walked to it, and Charles blinked, for he was sure in the wavering light of flame he saw the door open by itself, creaking on its hinges to allow the two passage.

Charles followed after, realizing he had the deep, primal urge to run, that being alone in a room with these two was akin to being locked in a cage with two lions. The thought was absurd, of course, Fischer was a perturbed individual but he was his colleague, and the old woman, well . . . She was an old woman. He knew it was his nerves from the journey and the strange shock of the skinned man on the wall.

He froze in the doorway of the bedroom, which was almost pitch black save for the meager ambient light filtering in from his candle, though Fischer seemed to find his way just fine as he went to the large bed in the center of the room.

The skinless man, how had he come like that? Was it one of the rebels, some madman who'd gone into a frenzy and decided to abhorrently butcher one of the citizens? How was he still alive? And what of the dead rebel on the table? What did he die from? And the soldiers outside, who looked as if they'd been mauled by a pack of wild bears?

Charles began to feel a headache pushing at his temples as his tired, fatigued mind tried to make sense of this situation.

Suddenly feeling exasperated and frustrated with his partner's peculiar behavior, he quickly entered the black room, and came upon Fischer as he was tucking the woman in.

"What are you not telling me?" Charles said in a hushed tone. He grabbed the man's thick shoulder—it was like grabbing a chunk of granite. Fischer slowly turned his head, looked at the hand on his shoulder, and his eyes then flitted up to Charles, his pupils reflecting the candlelight in a ghastly way. Charles abruptly took his hand off the man, suddenly getting the sense he was grabbing a coiled viper.

"You wouldn't understand. Go help the idiots guard the house," Fischer said dismissively, turning his head back to the woman.

"She called you *brother*! What is the meaning of this? And why are you so goddamned . . . *titillated* with this violence?" Charles hissed, his frustration boiling over once more. "You looked upon the man who was trying to eat me like you saw the face of god. And you two . . . Why, you look like two long lost lovers reunited. What the hell is going on here, Hans? I demand answers." He dared to use the doctor's first name.

Hans Fischer suddenly turned on Charles with a feral ferocity so monstrous that at first he didn't recognize the man. He put a hand out to Charles, and though the man did not touch him physically, Charles suddenly felt the air squeezed from his lungs, the atmosphere of the room taking on the pressure of the most abyssal depths of the ocean.

"You will have your answers soon enough, but I command you leave me alone with this woman. She is worth more than the entire goddamn Union army. She is worth more than all these cattle fodder combined. Now leave us!" Fischer roared, and at that moment Charles' vision pulsed gray at the edges as he swore he heard both Fischer's bellow with his ears and a resonating roar inside of his head. He felt his feet lift off the ground as he hurled through the air, the candle flying from his hands to wink out somewhere in another universe as he skidded on his back into the hallway, the door slamming shut on his way out.

CHAPTER 8

Charles cracked an eyelid open, his head pounding as if from an all-day hefeweizen binge. Wilcocks was looking at him over a sputtering candle, his face grave with concern.

"Doctor, are you all right?" he asked.

Charles could only stare, his mind muddled as he tried to recall where he was, and what had happened to him. He looked upon the long, dark hallway in confusion.

"What . . ." he began before he recalled the monstrous, almost wolfish face of Fischer in the candlelight, a ghastly snarl that made even his most rapturous moments on the operating table look almost cherubic in comparison. He looked toward the bedroom door. It remained shut.

"You're bleeding, sir," Wilcocks said softly, and handed Charles a rag. He took it, dabbed at the wet moistness around his nostrils, and saw they came away wet with blood. "You have any idea what became of Doctor Fischer? We've tried to hail him through the door, but he won't respond."

"He's gone mad," Charles said as he carefully sat upright, squeezing his eyes shut for a moment as he thought his brain might crack open from his skull like a chickling from her egg.

"Sir?" Wilcocks asked.

"Doctor, there you are. I need your help. We're going to clear out this house, and hopefully clear out this stench," Captain Lewis said from the end of the hallway, walking toward him. "We've opened up all the windows but still it smells like a goddamn charnel house in here. Christ you look like shit. Nipping off the rot gut like the rest of them?" Lewis asked as he crudely hauled Charles to his feet. He clenched his jaws and stuck his sandpapery tongue to the roof of his mouth, biting back the hot vomit in his throat. He swallowed thickly as he followed the captain back into the living room.

"I ain't touching that bastard," Sanderson said as they came upon the heap of exposed muscle and bone.

"You won't have to, Corporal, the doctor here is made of sturdier stuff than you. Come on, Muller," Lewis said, handing Sanderson his candle.

The body was still limber, rigor mortis had yet set in. Charles went deep down and dissociated himself from the scene, a unique numbing act he'd learned early on during the first bloody days of battlefield triage, when blood and screams flowed in equal measure. The tendons and muscles were cool and gummy to the touch, and as they hauled the body out the front door, Charles saw they'd disposed of the naked rebel. His body remained frozen in that clawing gesture as he was discarded out in the middle of the dirt path.

Charles suddenly had a morbid epiphany as they deposited the skinless man next to the rebel, and quickly went back inside for the brown leather satchel containing various tools used by both he and Fischer. He asked Wilcocks to accompany him with a candle as night had fully washed over the township, the sky above starless and dark

41

as a low cloud deck occluded the cosmos from them. Charles was going to ask how long he'd been out but decided against it.

"What're you doing, Dutchy?" Sanderson asked, coming out into the dirt path with them.

"Seeing something," Charles said as he took out a scalpel and knelt down next to the naked rebel. He turned the stiff body over, looking at the buttocks and thighs, where blood usually pooled in huge purple blotches upon death. There was no such bloating or discoloration he could see. He then allowed the poor soul to rest on his back once more, and looked closely at the neck, where, upon further prodding, he noticed two small puncture marks along the jugular. Not noticing them before, Charles had Wilcocks shine the flame close to the two wounds, which looked like nothing more than twin pricks from a needle. Noting this, he traced a line around and into the man's jugular with the scalpel. Blood should still seep slightly from one of the main arteries if the blood hadn't pooled yet.

None came, however, and as Charles stuck two fingers into the neatly sliced gash and gazed upon the man's sundered trachea, he saw the flesh was totally clean, bare of any crimson.

"What the hell," he said under his breath. He then took the scalpel and made an incision at the base of the sternum all the way down past the navel.

"Jesus, man, I know he's a rebel but you gotta cut him up like that?" Sanderson said, nausea in his voice. Wilcocks moved the candle toward the incision and watched as Charles examined the multicolored organs, the seams of flesh where he'd cut. No blood seeped from the wounds or flooded the various cavities of the man's body.

"What is it, Doctor?" Wilcocks asked.

"Completely exsanguinated. Like the man with no flesh. No blood at all," Charles marveled. He abruptly looked up from the body and gazed out into the stygian darkness. Like the woman's bedroom, it was pitch black outside, no lights burned in any of the houses, the small five-foot radius of light cast by the candle seemed to have a hard, solid edge to it, as if the world beyond this small burg simply ceased to exist. A sense of profound isolation gripped the doctor. Again, Charles felt the tingling in his neck when they'd first entered Poplar Springs, that feeling of predatory eyes upon him, and he was painfully aware of the miles of dense wood that surrounded them, where all manner of men and monster could hide. "Let us go inside," he said, and forced himself not to run as he made his way back into the house.

#

"Well, hell. We've aired the place out, got rid of the bodies. Still smells like the goddamn medical tent in here," Lewis said as he took off his captain's hat and scratched at the thinning thatch of red hair on his scalp in befuddlement.

"See if she has a cellar. She might have some cinnamon or chicory we could boil, cover it up," Wilcocks said.

"Good one, negro. You learn that one from your slave master? What was his name, Rutger? He teach you how to clean up the smell of dead negros when they—"

Wilcocks, who was usually extremely well composed and a fine shot, closed the gap between him and Sanderson in a blink. They all heard the click of the Colt's hammer as Wilcocks raised the gun to the rotund corporal's head.

"I've had quite enough of your words, Sanderson. Speak them again and I'll blast them out of your mouth," Wilcocks said, his voice low and full of venom, the Colt's barrel unwavering, his eyes fixed firmly on its target. Sanderson let out a whistle.

"Goddamn, you speak good for a ni—"

"Enough!" Lewis barked and got between them. Charles watched helplessly as the captain shoved the two away, his headache and the stench making it hard to think. "Sanderson, go look around for a cellar entrance. Old women always have preserves of some sort. Wilcocks, keep that goddamned pistol aimed outside. Charles, come with me. Fischer's joining us whether he wants to or not."

#

The men all attended to their own errands, and Charles did his best to help put his body weight against the door as Captain Lewis rammed it with all his strength. The door appeared the same as the others in the house, with the exception of the front door; they all appeared thin and somewhat warped. These fragile barriers, which looked at least fifty years old, should've shattered under their duress. The thin wooden barrier rattled in its frame and shook violently, and yet somehow it withstood Lewis's blows and their combined body weight. It made no sense.

"Christ, Fischer! Get your ass out here! Do it now or I'll shoot this door down, so help me god!" Lewis roared, and Charles wished desperately the man would stop yelling. Fischer and the woman were both silent.

Now in a rage, Lewis went to the nearest of the other doors and kicked it, hard, and this time, though it appeared identical to the bedroom door, the wood split and crumpled like balsa in its frame. Lewis snarled as he tore the old thing off its hinges, and looked in, grabbing his candle from Charles, who continued to lean heavily against the door, a blank look on his face.

"The hell?" Lewis said as he looked into the room.

Charles snapped out of his fugue and went to the captain's side. He stared at the piles of shoes and clothes that filled the room. Men's brogans, women's slippers and lace-ups, children's shirts and pajamas. It wouldn't have been an odd sight if it weren't for the fact the woman appeared to live alone, no evidence whatsoever that she was an elderly matriarch but rather a lonely widow. That, and the clothes were all in a giant pile, no order or sense of ownership marked the clothes, but rather it seemed this room had been a haphazard repository for the items, tossed in without care.

"Sir!" Sanderson called from down the hallway. His voice was no longer blustery but had a high-pitched squeaky quality to it. Lewis sighed and went down the hallway, Charles following. They met Corporal Sanderson in the living room, the gin blossoms on his face replaced by a curdled milk pallor. "I . . . I think I figured out where the stench was coming from. You oughta see this," he said, and Charles saw the gloved hands were visibly shaking.

The prospect of coming upon even more horrors made Charles want to lie down on the floor and resume the coma Wilcocks had stirred him from. *No more, please*, his tired mind begged as they followed Sanderson into a small alcove off the kitchen, where a door was recessed into the wall, as if intentionally built to stay out of sight. Lewis opened the door, and Charles peered over his shoulder and saw dusty steps that led down into an obsidian void. The mephitic wave of rot, which had dissipated only slightly with the men's efforts to purify the air, hit them afresh as it blossomed from the stairs like a hot breath exhaled from a leviathan's mouth. A leviathan whose diet was only the most rancid, fly-blown carrion.

"Sir!" It was Halloway. He'd come bolting down the stairs, and when Charles turned, he saw the man resembled Sanderson, his face pulled taught with worry. A thick book was held in his hands, and Charles blinked at the peculiar binding, and the partly visible title, the language he thought he recognized. "You need to look at this sir, I—"

"Good Christ, one thing at a time you hysterical children!" Lewis shouted, his normal commanding baritone taking on the slightest tremor as the evidence that this was no mere woman, and this unassuming house was the receptacle to some great and terrible practice mounted. He descended, and against his better judgement, Charles followed.

CHAPTER 9

"Dear sweet Jesus," Lewis breathed. "Sweet mother Mary and . . ." his voice trailed off.

Charles was at a loss for words. Descending the stairs, he'd apparently made his way down to the first floor of Hell, where the devil's butcher shop was on display. The bodies were suspended via large meat hooks through the Achille's tendons. There were six of them, two men and four women, their naked bodies all suspended upside down, fingertips barely touching the stone floor. Their necks had been neatly cut, large buckets placed beneath their heads to collect the drippings.

What was even worse than this though were the cuts of meat hanging, curing in a corner of the basement. Despite their butchered and quartered state, Charles recognized human thighs and calves immediately. He thought of the extravagant meals these strange townsfolk had been in the middle of preparing when the soldiers came. The hunks of what they thought were smoked hams and beef stew. His stomach somersaulted and this time Charles did throw up, the moonshine combined with the stomach acid to leave a scorching comet trail of heat from esophagus to throat. Lewis joined him, the man having taken part in the pillaging and eating of those succulent mystery meats, probably putting together the puzzle pieces the same as Charles.

For several minutes, there was only the sounds of human voiding in that dark, fetid basement, before finally both men got themselves under control.

Charles approached, nose tucked into his shirt, gladly smelling his own body odor over the intense waves of coppery rot as he peered into the buckets, nudging one with his foot. The dark substance within jiggled more than splashed, and he judged by the partial coagulation the blood had been sitting here for a week or so. He looked upon the stone walls, finally noticing the messages scribbled there.

"The hell is that? German?" Lewis breathed, peering at the words, which had clearly been written in blood.

"No . . . Romani, I think," Charles said, though he did see snatches of German below this.

Destroy For Her. This was written in Romani.

She Is Us. This was written in German. But not modern German. Charles barely recognized the old, Proto-Germanic script, whose roots derived from early iron-age Scandinavia. He'd been taught it at Sunday school along with snatches of Latin. The sight of this archaic iteration of his mother tongue, scribbled in dried blood in this strange, isolated mountain hut halfway across the world . . . Charles felt a vertiginous wave assail him, and he had to lean against the wall and close his eyes before he passed out. When he opened them again, Lewis was looking at him expectantly.

Charles read the passage aloud. Lewis looked at him confused.

"What the hell does it mean?" Lewis asked, his bushy brows crushed together.

"I have no idea," Charles said. It sounded like some nonsense spewed from a febrile maddened mind. One that knew tongues of old. The captain sighed.

"Romani? Christ, they got dutchman and French mongrels out here, now you're telling me they got gypsies sacked away in the hills? What is the meaning of this? And of this . . . *butchery*? Cannibalism? Christ." Lewis huffed. Charles could hear the exhausted anxiety in the captain's voice.

He thought back to the Union soldier who spoke similar mutterings before Fischer opened his skull. He thought of the naked rebel and his skinless friend. He thought of those two small nicks in the neck. He thought of the book that was in Halloway's hand. He thought of the shared camaraderie between Fischer and this strange woman, whose house was full of dead bodies in various states of butchered preparation. He thought of the stories his nan told him and his brother during bonfires to celebrate the autumnal equinox. Stories of ghosts and ghouls, of old folktales gleaned from her time as a shepherd in the high mountains to the east, before traveling to Germany to settle down. Gears slowly turned in his head, and epiphanies began to rise like mountain formations out of the magma of his mind.

He had no sane answer for Lewis, who took one last glance at this strange scene of butchery and faced the stairs.

"I've seen enough," he said, his voice tight as the doctor knew the man was struggling to control his gorge.

Gladly, Charles followed him back upstairs, whereupon the corporals sat, talking amongst themselves, except for Gerald Wilcocks, who continued his blank-eyed vigil from the window.

"You are not to eat of any more food we find! Unless it's bread or potatoes," Lewis called throughout the house. It seemed Sanderson had already spread the news though, judging by the pale-stricken faces and fresh piles of vomit on the floor, half-digested bits of man flesh now only an inconsequential horror among these mounting depravities.

"That woman is a witch I tell you. Look here, Captain. All sorts of funny scribblings and diagrams. Devil worship! Just like them crazy wenches up in New England they had to hang for cursing the town!"—Halloway was babbling now, holding out the thick book. Andrews stood in the corner, clutching his rifle and looking around wildly like a cornered animal— "I won't stay in a witch's house, Captain. Let the rebels hang me, I don't care."

"You leave this house and go prancing off into the night, I'll make sure you're formerly charged with desertion. If the bushwhackers don't catch you, I'll make sure your faces and rank are known among all the Union officers and you'll be hanged anyway," Lewis said, shoving the outcast book aside. "It's none of our concern what hogwash went on in this house. Come sunrise, we burn this place down and head back."

"And what of the woman? Fischer seems to take fond of her," Wilcocks said distantly from the window. His voice seemed to be the only one not trembling.

"I don't know. I'll think on it. Christ, I need sleep," Lewis said, unscrewing the lid from a half-depleted jar of moonshine. "I'll make a decision come sunrise." Halloway and Andrews were already headed out the door, however, threats of desertion unheeded. "Cowards!" Lewis shouted at their backs.

"Cowards we may be, but fools we're not!" Halloway said from over his shoulder as the night swallowed them. Halloway had tossed the book into Charles's hands as he left. He stared down at the tome, which was heavy, the cover felt oddly textured and leathery.

Lewis slammed the door shut behind him, and then presumed to drink from the jar. He handed it off to Sanderson, who likewise supped from the fire water. Charles gratefully took the jar and let his insides be burned once more as Lewis cleared his throat.

"All right. We'll take shifts until the sun comes up. Wilcocks, you're on guard for the next two hours. Sanderson, you'll relieve him. We'll take shifts until the first rays of dawn. Wake me if you see signs of life out there," Lewis said, and collapsed heavily into one of the wooden chairs surrounding the table.

Charles offered the black man some moonshine, but Wilcocks waved it away. It seemed Charles had a thing or two to learn from his comrade about dissociating from a traumatic situation. The man seemed miles away.

#

The captain snored heavily from the kitchen. The outline of human flesh on the wall began to brown at the edges and peel away from the wall like old wallpaper. Sanderson was slumped in a corner, the moonshine jar nearly empty as it sat between him and Charles, who'd been paging through the book. Fischer and the old woman had yet to make an appearance.

"Betcha know was goin on here dontcha, Dutchy?" Sanderson slurred from his corner. Charles, who was hoping the shine would force him to sleep at some point, looked up from the book.

"Huh?" he asked, not sure if he heard the man correctly.

"I seen way she looked at fish. Heard her speakin' that gibberish to 'em. Bet you're all in cahoots on this. Fuckin' dutchies. Can't trust ya," Sanderson went on, raising his Colt in Charles's general direction, but the barrel kept pointing down like a divining rod over a fresh well-spring. He promptly belched and let his head thunk against the wall he'd been laying against, the pistol falling at his side. He was soon asleep.

Charles, who still felt mild pangs of anxiety coursing through his drunkenness, reached for the jar, eager to erase the many complex drawings and sigils he came upon in the book from his mind. He knew it was ancient, the pages made of brittle papyrus, the outdated Proto-Germanic script written in a fine, precise hand. Charles was too drunk and tired to recall the few words his grandmother had taught him, the few biblical phrases he'd had to learn as a child, and didn't think it mattered anyway. He didn't know what was in the tome, though he had guessed it was a grimoire of some sort given the occult illustrations he saw, along with diagrams showing certain sacrificial rituals and the correct order in which they should be done.

Finally, he felt the weight of the alcohol push his lids down, and as he finally felt himself drift off to sleep, he tried to make sense of all the clues afforded them. He assumed the blood collection was for the arcane rituals described in the book. From what he could decipher, the word blood came up ad nauseam, the book's text spoke of blood as if it were the catalyst for all occult esoterica one wished to practice.

He thought of Fischer and the woman, how they seemed to know each other. He thought of Fischer's bizarre sayings, the way he spoke of ancient conflicts and worldly events as if he'd seen and endured them firsthand. He thought of the battle that had gone on here before they arrived. The brutal animal savagery afflicted upon the dressed-up rebels. The woman, that sole survivor. Who called the madman Fischer her *brother*.

Charles's alcohol-slowed mental gears turned sluggishly. He tried to make sense of it all, but instead found the winking void of oblivion growing larger, and gladly jumped into it, finally finding some thready form of sleep.

CHAPTER 10

The creaking groan of the bedroom door awakened him. His brain was still soaked from the moonshine, Charles stared in dumbfounded awe as he saw Fischer emerge from the shadows. Only one candle remained burning, barely illuminating the living room and casting long, wavering shadows on the wall as it sat, almost melted down to its base between himself and the snoring Sanderson.

Like a specter, Fischer floated to Charles. Moonshine or not, the smooth, gliding motion in which Fischer moved was unmistakable, his passage down the hallway as silent as a feline's stalk. The man glided like something weightless and ephemeral toward him.

There came a sharp breath from the corner, and Charles turned his head, which felt to weigh as much as a cannon ball, the room blurring with the motion. He could only see the huge whites of Wilcock's eyes from the corner of the room by the window, just beyond the reach of candlelight, the night so completely dark that not even the usual ambient lighting from outside was present. Charles saw the barrel of the Colt extend into the radius of firelight, pointed at Fischer.

"Stop right there," Wilcocks said. Fischer raised his hand, fingers splayed out in that peculiar way as when he'd launched Charles from the bedroom without touching him. "You owe us an . . . explanation—" Wilcock's voice suddenly became strained with effort. The space between Fischer's veiny hand and Wilcock's revolver seemed to shimmer like a heat mirage. Charles heard Wilcocks give a surprised grunt as the gun barrel abruptly pointed down. As Charles's eyes adjusted to the gloom, he thought he saw the corporal's body trembling with effort as he struggled to raise the gun, grunting exhalations marking what sounded like a herculean effort.

Fischer then abruptly squeezed his outstretched hand into a fist. He did it sharply, yanking his hand up as he did so. Charles heard the unmistakable sounds of bones breaking, a sharp, pained gasp from Wilcocks, who abruptly went silent thereafter, sliding to the floor, head tilted at an impossible angle. Sanderson and Lewis snored in unison, oblivious to the frightening spectacle unfolding before them.

"You . . . You demon, you—" Charles rasped, trying to rouse the others, but Fischer's hand shot toward him. With his other, he pantomimed zipping his lips shut, and with this Charles felt an invisible hand pushing against his mouth, crushing his lips together as his protestations were muffled. Fischer went to him, and with the ease of a mother carrying a babe, he threw the helpless Charles over his shoulder, and proceeded back down the dark hallway, the house growing colder the closer they got to the bedroom.

Abject terror paralyzed Charles, a crushing hopelessness filling him as the comforting glow of the candle receded. Then total blackness as the door closed quietly on Fischer's heels.

Blind, his mind reeling from the paranormal display of power and the vicious hangover that squeezed his poor skull in an invisible vice, Charles began to thrash wildly, outright panic seizing him.

"There, there, that won't do," Fischer said in that same soft voice that he'd only used on the old woman. "Stop struggling, Muller," he softly but firmly said, and Charles felt a heavy somnambulant wave consume him, his limbs each taking on the weight of a fully burdened pack mule. He stilled as Charles felt himself be lowered into the soft bed. It felt as if he were floating on a cloud, and god, despite his panic the urge to fall back asleep was thickly upon him. How long it had been since he'd slept in an actual bed, and not a floor or a canvas cot?

"Are you . . . sure he's the one?" a small voice the timbre of a rusted hinge called out very close to his left ear.

"Oh yes. He's from the motherland. Can't you smell his purity?" Fischer asked from the dark. There was a dull *whoomph* as the room was suddenly filled with an orange glow. Fischer stood at the foot of the bed, a candelabra fully ablaze in one hand.

Charles turned and looked at the old woman lying beside him. He saw she was grinning again, the corners of her mouth smeared with blood. He blinked, for in the candlelight he saw she was at least a decade younger in appearance. Her eyes were no longer rheumy, her many creases and crinkles had reduced in number. No longer an ancient specimen but a woman on the healthy cusp of her golden years, the hair no longer straw-limp and white but voluminous and silver.

She was beautiful, Charles realized. A powerful commanding sense of primal feminine beauty radiated off her, especially as she raised herself to a sitting position and threw her shoulders back straight, her long hair spilling over them, and he thought it absurd he should be attuned to this while still feeling so terrified.

"Marvelous, isn't she?" Fischer said, his tone reverent, and Charles turned to look at him. Saw the neat red gash on Fischer's wrist that he hadn't noticed before. He came closer, sat on the edge of the bed. "You don't know how lucky you are, Charles.

54

A gift is about to be bestowed upon you that men have waged wars over to obtain and mass genocide committed to keep its existence a secret."

"What . . . What are you?" Charles rasped, finding the invisible lock on his lips gone. Fischer's eyes shot up in wonder.

"We have been called many things by many different men. None quite accurate," he said with a gentle laugh. "You see, me and Ida here, we're . . . hunters. Of a special sort. Her bloodline was old when these hills were young. And I . . . Well. Let's just say I am a product of the hubris of man."

"I . . . I don't understand," Charles breathed. He felt his cheek caressed by a soft palm. The woman named Ida raised his head up slightly, lowering hers in counterpoint.

"We're guardians of the night. We're the shepherds of the herd. We maintain balance in a world where human cattle are allowed to roam free. Fischer is of a different breed than me. His kind was made rather than born. But he is kin to me all the same. We make sure death doesn't go to waste," the woman said, her voice still creaky and wavering, but also soft and hypnotizing, the thick eastern European lilt giving her words a lovely cadence. Charles felt her hair brush his lips and chin as she lowered herself further, and he thought for a sickening but exhilarating instant she might kiss him.

His eyes crawled to the left, and saw her thin lips opening. He saw the pink gums, but also a glint of fine pointed enamel.

"Ahh, see. Told you, all you needed was an aperitif. No tiger can truly be defanged. Declawed, yes, but never defanged," Fischer said to the woman with hushed awe as Charles gasped at the contact of those lips against his neck. Felt his flesh tighten and pucker with goosebumps. He shivered. Felt a warm tongue graze the flesh there. Charles's eyelids fluttered at the obscenely sensual contact as the skin there began to tingle with numbness.

"Why . . . Why are you doing this?" he whispered as he felt the faintest pricking sensation. Knew that mouth was closed around his carotid artery. A cold dread flooded him at the thought of ending up like the exsanguinated rebel, his body cleanly robbed of all its precious life fluids. For he began to understand now what he was in the presence of.

"I told you, my dear Charles, it is a gift we're giving you. You shall live to see empires fall and rise from the ashes. You shall see the world reshape itself a hundred times over as the industrious maggots that clothe themselves and pretend to not be animals find further advancement in their cute little industries. You shall learn to revel in their conflicts, such as this one," Fischer said as Charles felt the woman begin to suck.

"You see, this war has been good to me, for I am of a different breed than Ida, though our lineage all branches from the same tree. My appetite is more of the . . . ephemeral nature. There is an aura that surrounds man when he is in his deepest throes of suffering, a nourishing cloud that I drink in like the finest wine. Not since the crusades I told you of have I seen such large scale destruction and agony. It has been so long since I've been able to gorge until I am lightheaded with excess. My powers are once again at their peak, thanks to the largesse of human cruelty. I am strong enough that I can afford to shed my façade. But I had been waiting so long, adorning my sheep's skin and baying like a lamb. Waiting to find another of my kind, for we used to be legion, but now are scattered across the globe like grains of sand in a high wind. Pure providence brought me to Ida. I recognized her regal blood as soon as I smelled it. I saw how dire her situation was, and knew immediate intervention was required. Together, we will do *wonderful* things."

Ida continued to suck, her audible gulp growing more desperate in its rhythm, and Charles began to feel a profound lightheadedness as he knew he was being drained.

Fischer slowly made his way over to the other side of the bed, and gently pulled at the woman.

"I know you're ravenous dear, but that is enough. He must live, remember? You have no thrall to speak of. The numbers must be replenished," Fischer said tenderly.

With a gasp, Charles felt a distant pain as the fangs withdrew, and when he craned his neck to the left, a monumental effort that used up the last of his strength, he beheld the angel before him: Athena reincarnate, a visage so beatific that Charles felt tears well in his eyes at the sight of her. Radiant blue eyes the color of pure sapphire stared into him. Charles felt a magnetic pull in that gaze, the eyes seeming to hone in on his very soul, and caress it. Luscious blonde hair spilled from a head whose skin was plump and free of a single crease, the locks falling in golden cascades from her.

"You are mine now, Charles Hersch Muller. It will take some time for the bond to solidify, the gift must take root firmly in your hearty vessel before you understand fully the depth of this connection. You will not forsake me like the others, with their foul, inbred blood. You will not turn greedy. You will serve me in all ways, and you shall prosper for it," Ida said in German, her voice no longer quavering or frail but smooth and silky, a salve to the panic and fear that paralyzed him as effectively as the spell Fischer had placed upon him.

"Wha . . .What?" Charles asked, dulled into a nearly torpid stupor, the words flowing like honey from now plump and full lips made no sense to him.

"You see, this whole village was enthralled to her. I understood that the minute we saw the turned Union guardsman. But she made the mistake of trying to turn these inbred hill folks and their rotten lineage," Fischer said with a laugh. "They did not behave as typical thrall do. More like a pack of civilized hyenas they, feeding when it suited them, only giving Ida here the meagerest of scraps. She sought refuge in this isolation, but instead found desolation. This amazing woman is far older than even I, and thus when the thirst is upon her, she must act quick, or the years will come slamming upon her with haste." He placed an affectionate hand on Ida's blanketed leg, patting it. "It's a good thing we came when we did, her thrall slaughtered, with only the diseased and malnourished blood of a few rebels to sustain her," Fischer said, shaking his head in sympathy. He went to Ida, gazing upon her with that reverential stare. He looked like a man dying of thirst staring upon a hidden oasis in the desert from which he'd been cursed to roam.

"I was indeed on the verge of death. But thanks to you two, I may begin the next chapter of my life," Ida said, and got up from the bed. "With me, Fischer. We must leave to see if he takes to it as you've promised. I cannot afford to babysit mongrels anymore. If he takes true to the thrall , he shall find us." The door opened unbidden once more.

Standing before them was Lewis, a rifle in his hands.

"'In god's name is this?" he slurred, looking dumbfounded at the renewed Ida. Bloodshot eyes went to her, and then Fischer, finally settling on Charles.

"Run, Captain. Run. Ru—" Charles began to yell, slowly gathering his voice. But instead, Lewis raised the rifle, pointing it at Ida.

"What kind of devilish hogwash is—" the captain began.

Ida waved her hand out as if to ward off a bee, and with this simple flicking motion came a great ripping sound, curtains torn from their rods, flesh torn from bone. In a flurry of motion, Charles watched as both flesh and clothes simply parted from the captain's body, and he stood there, arms still poised to aim the rifle no longer in his fleshless hands. His mouth, now all teeth and gums, cracked open, and a croaking gasp escaped from it.

Charles watched in sickened horror as the individual tendons and muscles moved and flexed as the man sank to the exposed cartilage of his knees. He began to tremble, his bulging lidless eyes gazing up at Ida in an unreadable gaze, the fascia and connective tissue of his face trembling and squiggling as he struggled to process the all-encompassing agony. Charles understood fully now the fate of the men they'd found hours before. It was worse than he ever could have imagined.

"This is a gift for you, Fischer. Let us feed, *together*," Ida said as she fell upon the red, glistening body of Lewis. Charles watched as she opened her mouth wide and bit into the fat, exposed purple tube of the carotid. Lewis continued to make those gasping, mewling croaks, lidless eyes forever staring in mute shock, and Fischer watched, that look of pure, orgasmic jubilation on his face, eyes dilated to the bore of howitzers as the skinless captain began to twitch and moan.

Before Charles lost consciousness, he understood then they were both gorging. One on suffering, the other on blood.

CHAPTER 11

When Charles awoke, he could only let out a squeaky croak so similar to his captain's poor cries as that devil woman proceeded to drain him of all life. Every muscle in his body felt as wound-taught as piano wire. There was an inferno blazing within him, a fever so profoundly hot he thought his skin was on fire. He was in the huge, plush bed, and he could see the faint rays of sunlight that pushed through the small gaps in the thick curtains that covered every window of the room. Faint though they were, even these minute rays made Charles's squint and his eyes water.

Slowly, agonizingly, he forced himself to a sitting position, feeling his joints and vertebrae grind together as if powdered glass took the place of cartilage. The sheets were soaking wet to the touch, his clothes clung to him like a second skin as his whole body was oiled in a thick fever sweat. He shivered violently despite his inner blaze, his nerve endings screaming with sensation as he managed to get to his feet, the world cold and solid beneath his feet.

My god, what did they do to me? he thought miserably as he made his way over to the door. Charles was alone in the room, no sign of Fischer, Ida, or Lewis, though a dark stain was present on the floorboards in front of the door, and with a nauseating wave he remembered how Lewis had died.

He pulled open the door, and saw the discarded Captain's uniform and the limp rags of flesh intermingled within it. He could see early morning light pouring in from the window where a dead Wilcocks sat, manning his vigil even in death. He heard loud snoring, and also a deep thudding. He thought it was his pulse pounding in his ears like the brigade of drummer boys setting the cadence to an impending battle.

"Suh . . . Sanderson?" he called out, his voice now resembled Ida's prior to her . . . *transformation*, and he held his own throat in disgusted awe at his reduced state. He tried to make his way down the hall, but the light-filled room ahead repulsed him, the light blinding, burning, barbaric in its visceral illumination of all things. "Sanderson?" he called out again, forcing his aching throat to go above a rasping whisper. The snores were truncated by a smacking of lips and a fart, before they resumed once more. "Oh, goddamnit," he hissed, and went to the room across the hall where the pile of clothes and shoes lay.

He stood before the pile, realizing these were the belongings of the victims Ida must've claimed. He tried not to think about her haunting words to him last night, tried not to think about the illness flooding his body now, the one surely caused by her bite. He took one of the brogans from the pile and walked back down the hall, wincing as he neared the living room. He tossed the boot, aiming for the outstretched leg of Sanderson.

This time, the snores stopped completely as Charles got lucky and managed to hit the drunken corporal with this throw.

"Huh? Wha?" Sanderson said, this voice thick with residual drunkenness and sleep.

"Sanderson!" Charles called out.

"The fuck?" Sanderson said, and with a belch this time he slowly got to his feet, stumbling as he righted himself. He took notice of the dead Wilcocks first, going to the man. "Hey, hey negro, get up. Supposed to be on watch," he said, kicking Wilcock's in the foot. When Wilcock's didn't stir, he knelt down, saw the opened glazed-over eyes were unblinking, noticing the head canted at an unnatural angle from a broken neck. "Oh shit. Oh fuck . . ." he said, backing away from it.

"Over here!" Charles hissed. Sanderson whirled around, bloodshot eyes wide and blinking. "Dutchy? The fuck you doing in the shadows? Where is everyone?" he asked, and as he drew closer, the pounding in Charles's temples grew louder, more insistent.

"Dead. Fischer . . . Him and the woman . . . They're . . . Monsters . . ." Charles rasped, his throat suddenly very dry, he shivered despite his inner inferno. "They did something to me. Made me ill. Please. Some water," he said, his tongue a moldy sock in his mouth.

Sanderson only stared at the haggard German. Charles could see suspicion clouding the rotund visage.

"I fucking knew it. Told the captain ya can't trust you fuckin' yellowbellied dutchmen," he sneered. "How do I know you ain't done nothing—"

"*Please*, Sanderson, some water. I beg you," Charles rasped. Sanderson studied him for a long time. Charles could sense the boozed soaked gears in his head slowly turning.

"Why don't you come out here and get it then? Why you slinking off in the shadows? You—"

"I told you, I am very ill. The woman . . . she did something to me." Charles barely spoke above a tremulous whisper, his patience close to breaking. He suddenly felt a black wave of rage flow over him, and thought of wrapping his hands around that thick, pudgy throat. The thudding pulse in his head grew louder, a timpani section mimicking the thudding beat of the heart. He imagined feeling that thundering pulse in his hands as he choked the life from Sanderson, that piggish oaf. He then imagined how much blood such a corporal form could hold.

His thirst was almost maddening now at this thought. *Oh no, Oh Jesus Christ No . . .* Charles thought as he realized what this correlation meant. *No! Just need water. You're feverish, delirious. You're just a very sick old boy*, he tried to tell himself. Sanderson was in the middle of pulling the canteen from his hip when he froze. Charles somehow heard it over the drumming in his head. Voices from outside. Several dozen.

Sanderson took a step back and cautiously peered at the window. He immediately shot to the ground, getting on his belly as the voices came closer.

"Goddamn rebels!" he said under his breath. "Whole mess of 'em. Stay there, Dutchy, I'm coming to you."

"Oh god . . . No . . ." Charles said as he sunk to his knees. This was the last thing they needed. He knew if they were found there would be no imprisonment. Retribution killings were the rebel's doctrine in this part of the country.

It took Sanderson an agonizing amount of time to get to Charles, his bulk noisily dragging across the floorboards as he crawled beneath the windows.

They both flinched when they heard a gunshot followed by a loud stupid whoop, and then guffawing laughter. As Charles listened, the laughter abruptly stopped as he heard a single voice call out. The voice was very close, as if just on the other side of the wall, and then he closed his eyes in resignation as he remembered the two corpses they'd dragged outside. The exsanguinated rebel whom Charles had vivisected among them.

The assorted sounds he heard outside weren't so merry anymore as shouts and curses drifted to them through the walls. Sanderson finally came to him, his eyes wide with fear, the canteen forgotten about. Charles ripped it from the big man's waist sash and quickly unscrewed the cap. Musty water made warm by the man's body heat coated his throat, but Charles didn't even care. He gulped until the container was dry. He smacked his lips.

This seemed to only reignite his thirst, which was absurd. He felt his stomach begin to cramp and convulse, and he clenched his jaw and squeezed his eyes shut to fight back the heaving gorge in his throat. He knew he needed water, needed hydration. He was incredibly sick, yet his body seemed to want to reject that which it needed most. Perhaps when these soldiers passed, he could search out some pine needles and ragweed to steep in the moonshine, create some sort of medicinal brew to help fight the fever.

But no, he did not want poultices or nostrums or medicine. The pounding was almost unbearable now, seeming to speed up with his dread. He heard Sanderson swallow, and with an icy dread that cut through the fever heat, Charles realized something.

"What should we do, Dutchy?" Sanderson whispered.

"I . . ." Charles said, unable to formulate words as he looked at Sanderson's flabby goiter of a neck. The pounding transformed into war drums at full climax. The thunderous percussive pulse slammed into his head, because the pounding wasn't *coming* from his head.

He watched the pulse in Sanderson's forehead veins. Realized the pounding in his head synced perfectly with the veins that visibly throbbed in Sanderson's temple.

Charles felt his jaw clench reflexively, felt them want to open wide, invisible wires wanting to pull his mandibles apart, but he kept them clenched shut, or tried to. He found he couldn't snap his teeth together the way he used to, he felt a pain digging into his gums as he did so this time.

"The fuck's the matter with you? I—"

Charles couldn't stop it. The throbbing pulse was in his very cells now, his entire existence pulsated with the man's heartbeat, his whole body attuned to it. He salivated profusely now, drool spooling from his lips like a starving dog. Sanderson began to back away, but Charles was quick. Quicker than he'd ever been in his entire life.

The corporal did not have time to scream, for inch-long canines from both the top and bottom rows of Charles's teeth closed around all that supple flesh, ripping out trachea and voice box with one savage twist of the head.

Charles put his mouth to the wound and drank. He could not stop the gulping reflex of his throat like he couldn't stop himself from biting the man. Horror briefly filled him as he realized what hot, viscous fluid he was rapidly consuming, but the horror was quickly usurped by a full body tingling that exploded into something that transcended the most powerful orgasm he'd ever experienced. His eyelids fluttered and his whole body shuddered, not with fever but with pleasure, with exultant bliss. He couldn't help but moan around the bloody rags of flesh his lips locked onto, sounding like a lover buried between the thighs of their betrothed.

He heard the men coming into the house, but didn't pay them any mind as the door was kicked in. Heard the startled cries and howls of disgust. Heard the cocking of many priming mechanisms. Many, *many* pulsing throbs filled his mind now. A polyrhythmic chorus of vitality surged in his ears.

He turned only when he was sure the last drop of blood had been excised from Corporal Sanderson's body. He faced the skinny, ragged men before him, staring down the barrels of muskets and pistols. This bothered him none at all as he lunged into their gunfire, barely feeling the lead meteors that pierced his body and tore through clothes and flesh. He hissed in pain only when he leapt into the doorway leading outside, whisps of smoke coming off his body as the light kissed his torn flesh. He retreated into the house, a whirling dervish of gnashing teeth.

Men gurgled and gasped as he caromed off them like a ricocheting Minié ball, seeking the dark shelter of the basement below. Only one man was left standing amidst the slaughtered brethren, and Charles could hear him flee the house, his pulse and gibbering cries going with him.

Soon all was quiet. When he was sure the survivors were gone, Charles slunk from the stairs and, like a puma dragging its prey back to its den, began the process of dragging the men one by one down the stairs, careful to avoid the light that spilled in from the front doorway.

There, in the dark, he feasted. Despite the several gallons of blood he consumed, he never felt full, never felt sated, nor bloated. It seemed his body used the nutrient-rich blood up as soon as it entered him, and with each soul he consumed, he felt more powerful, more vital than at any point in his life. He felt so swollen with energy he might burst from his skin and erupt like a lightning bolt.

But he didn't. Instead, he slunk to the head of the stairs, and sat on his haunches like a wolf, waiting, as still as the corpses that hung from their butcher's hooks down below, his eyes wide and dilated, the darkness before him no longer darkness but a gray monochrome of perfect visibility. Like a statue he sat like that for hours, waiting. Waiting for the pulse to return. Waiting for the sun to go down. No rational thought to his mind, only the thirst, his mind consumed by the primal needs of his new body.

When finally night was upon the blighted village of Poplar Springs, Charles Muller emerged from the house. He loped on all fours like a feral animal, the human part of his mind temporarily giving way to a deep primal impulse, and he raised his head, trying to hone in on the tidal pull that surged within his veins. An intense magnetism that pulled at the very iron in his blood, invisible hooks that yanked him to the north. He tried to resist it, but it was like sand dunes trying to stand tall in the face of the tide.

It must be obeyed.

He looked ahead, where the protruding knob loomed over him, occluding the stars behind it, knowing an endless, welcoming blackness awaited him within the caves. Not only did the darkness beckon him. So did she. He thought of the blonde hair and blue eyes, the soft silky voice.

He bounded off in that direction at the thought of her. She was his goddess. She was his new object of worship. She was his *salvation*.

She is us.

ACT II: THE SOLDIER

September, 1863—Wilson's Creek, Missouri

 CHAPTER 1

Even through the thudding of hooves, Tobias could feel the Union iron sink into the earth beneath his horse's feet, could see from the corners of his eyes as the unholy thunder tore apart ground and men alike.

"HOLD MEN!" he screams, but even his thunderous voice is lost to the hellish din of war. His horse whinnied and nearly bucked him off as a cannon ball broke through the row of mismatched colors and was a foot away from striking him and his horse. Christ, he needed someone to flank that cannon battery, but his men were scattering now. His regiment was comprised of bushwhackers and irregulars, unused to the tidy ranks and synchronized commands of traditional warfare, their training mostly consisting of a two-week crash course in guerilla tactics. It was like trying to scoop up sand with a fork.

"HOLD!" he screamed, knowing at any moment the Union would end their artillery barrage and send waves of privates and corporals surging up over the hill, and then his men could strike back, their shotguns and hunting rifles finally being put to good use. But the reign of lead and thunder shocked these farmers and trappers and non-military men into a frenzy, they did not understand the prospect of sitting tight and waiting for the enemy to come to them.

"Colonel Dixon!" came a voice from the terrible ether of gun smoke and morning mist. Dixon whirled, and saw Lieutenant Kurtz coming toward him, his eyes wide with fear, the man barely in control of his own horse. "They're decimating our leftward flank! We stay here any longer we'll be slaughtered outright! What do we—" His words were cut off cleanly as his lower jaw exploded. Dixon could feel bits of the man's teeth hit his face as the musket ball removed the few pieces of crooked enamel the Lieutenant had left and the jaw that went with them.

Just as he caught sight of Kurtz's tongue flapping stupidly out of a sundered jaw, he turned, heard the high-pitched whine of small arms fire splitting the air around him, accompanied by the blat of a bugle chorus as the order to charge was given. Finally, they were charging toward them, the sea of blue rising up over the hill like a cresting wave, their repeating rifles firing off multitudes of shots before having to stop and reload.

This was what Tobias had been waiting for. His forward advance was armed with bayonets, buck knifes, and scatterguns. The rebel advantage was in the dirty up-close fighting of tooth and claw, of the primal warfare that the west point Federals thought was below them. His plan was to lie low at the sloping hill that bordered Wilson's Creek, hoping to catch Brigadier General Lyon's advance off guard. But they must've caught wind of the ambush, for as the sky bled from cobalt to peach and purple hues with the rising sun, the beautiful summer morning was shattered by the thunderclaps of a howitzer volley.

Some men gathered their wits and fought bravely. Dixon watched with melancholy pride as those men, underfed and poorly armed, charged into the undulating mass of blue uniforms and glinting army steel, bayonets finding and sundering Yankee flesh, scatterguns peppering two or three men at a time with their buckshot blasts. But these were solitary charges, the majority of his men disorganized and clueless as they were cut down, like scared chicks trying to flee the hen house from which the fox has found its way into.

He did not want to call the retreat. There was another division of Price's men to the west of here who were in charge of overtaking the two Union-held farms that encompassed the creek. The plan was to ensnare the mass of entrenched union troops on all sides, trap them into a firing box that would render their artillery batteries useless. If Dixon's four companies disbanded now, the whole attack would have been for nothing. Yet he knew if he continued to stand his ground, his men would be so much fertilizer for the surrounding fields and forest.

Goddamnit! he thought wildly as he rode among the rear flanks, felt his colonel's forage cap be shot off his head, felt himself walking between raindrops it seemed as he rode past barrages of enemy fire, the ground around him erupting with hundreds of Miniéball impacts. He sought out the officers of the rear guard, giving each one he passed the signal for a fighting retreat. It seemed to take a whole millennia for his own buglers to blow their call, but finally they did, his men looking back with hope as the order to retreat was finally given.

They needed no further incentive, many had already turned to flee across the shallow creek and toward the thick stand of white oak and birch, hoping to seek refuge among the dense miles of forest that led away from Springfield and its heavily entrenched union presence.

Dixon stayed until he was sure every company under his command, or what was left of them anyway, saw to the retreat. He saw the Federal bastards rolling up their many barrel napoleon guns over the crest of the hill just as the last ranks of rebels scattered into the trees, and Colonel Tobias Dixon took that as his sign to run with his men.

Splinters showered him. The cracking groan of falling trees added to the cacophony of gunfire around him as the Union soldiers followed their retreat. Their devilish artillery cut down the foliage and tore men in half as they ran as fast as their malnourished bodies would take them. They could not outrun a ten-pound cannon ball however; the lead behemoths caromed off the ground and tore through six men at a time. Tobias was grateful he still had his mount, though she began to froth blood as he rode her hard through the forest. The ground here was treacherous with gopher holes, mud patches, and leaf litter covering those potential hazards, but he had no time to proceed carefully.

Just when he thought god was on his side, Tobias felt his piebald lurch hard to the left, let out a whinnying cry, and then he was flying over the head of the downed horse. At the last minute, Tobias tucked his limbs in and rolled his body as he hit the ground to keep from landing at an angle that would see to his neck snapping. He scrambled for his fallen pistols, and dove for a copse of trees. He put his back to a thick birch tree, revolvers held out, jaw set. The famed rebel colonel stood his ground, ready to go out in a blaze of glory.

He knew the Federals wanted his scalp, and probably to string and quarter him as well. One of the few soldiers in this conflict who was around to fight the British in the War of 1812, the old colonel possessed a tactical cunning that few on either side possessed. He understood hit-and-run tactics better than no other, and led some of the most notorious bands of guerilla fighters in the war. Fighting with lightning-fast speed, they charged in from forested ambushes and got up close, startling Union men into paralysis. Dixon learned quickly how to exploit the Union's better-equipped soldiers and minimize the vulnerabilities of his own men by getting up close. The rule was simple: don't fire a shot until you can see the whites of their eyes and yellow of their teeth.

Despite this, Price had strict orders handed out that today's battle would be fought in an organized, concise manner. Dixon had the sinking sensation that in a full-on assault, the Union would tear his men to pieces, and he had just been proven right. But Price staunchly refused to allow the hit-and-run tactics and autonomous divisions to work independently as they had before, claiming too much disorganization would ruin the assault.

Dixon knew the real reason though. Political posturing. The Missouri State Guard had a reputation for being dirty, unfair fighters. Men who only knew the brutal savagery of up-close ambushes and lightning raids. Price had a point to prove, that his rebel army could go head-to-head with the Federals. And he'd just been proven wrong, a whole ocean's worth of rebel blood spilled. All for a proverbial cock measuring contest among generals.

And now here he was, sure the blue bastards would be upon him at any moment, feral with bloodlust, eager to take down the colonel who'd been harassing and embarrassing Union supply lines and patrols for two years now.

But the men did not come. They knew the thick woods were the rebels' home advantage, and probably the regiment in charge of taking the farms was keeping them busy. As Dixon finally allowed himself a full breath of relief that he would live to fight another day, he felt an immense pang of guilt as he knew he left those men to fight the blue horde on their own.

No, it was either stay and die or retreat and regroup, he told himself as he took stock of his injuries and his inventory. His saber was gone, stuck in the horse's ribs on the fall. The horse itself thrashed wildly, letting out pitiful naying cries as its lamed foreleg flopped uselessly, the exposed bone protruding through flesh and striking earth as it struggled to stand. Dixon wanted to shoot the poor beast, put it out of its misery. But he couldn't even do that; they were on a strict munitions rationing ever since the Federals cut off their supply line from the little Dixie region in northern Missouri.

He left the poor horse to die of its own means, and proceeded to run through the woods, feeling humiliated at his position, a colonel without horse or hat. He felt like an imposter, a man in a fancy coat whose stripes meant nothing. But he could not let his men see this dissolution of resolve. He was almost mythic in his fame among the rebels for how much the Union hated him. When his division, the 1st Arkansas Irregulars, had absorbed the ragged remnants of the 5th Missouri State Guard, these new men swooned over him like some smitten lover when they realized whose direct command they were under. It was through the heroic (though heavily embellished) acts from men like Dixon who kept these tired, starving men going.

"Sir! You made it!" came a familiar voice. First Lieutenant Daryl Lacroix came riding up alongside him, his heavily whiskered face bright with relief and ruddy with exertion. "I saw you stay back there to guard the retreat. Thought the bastards got you. Shoulda known better. You without horse?"

"Aye. Took a spill back yonder," he said, his rough voice hoarse from shouting commands for the last half hour.

"Want mine? I—" Lieutenant Lacroix was already getting off his horse, but Dixon put up a hand to stop him.

"No, no. Ride on, soldier. Continue with the rendezvous. We'll take stock at Haverson's Mill," Dixon said, not wanting the further humiliation of riding in on a lower-rank's horse. They'd simply have to steal more later on. Horse thieving was one of his stronger suits. Leading men into real battle apparently was not. Lacroix gave him a puzzled look, but was obviously glad he didn't have to relinquish his mount.

"Suit yourself, Colonel. We'll be waitin' for ya with whiskey and slops," Lacroix said, popping off a salute and riding on, leaving Dixon to lick his wounds, which comprised mostly of an eviscerated ego.

CHAPTER 2

Haverson's Mill was a sad little amalgamation of wood and stone, long abandoned by the family that built it, it was the designated rallying point for Dixon's men. Situated along Wilson's Creek, it was the closest secure clearing they could find to the theatre of battle. Now, tired and wary of the Union's growing presence around them, Dixon gazed upon the thick wall of trees they'd escaped through and doubted they would truly be safe here.

He'd been sitting at the edge of a high burning pyre, the men kept the fires big in camp so they could see well in case of an ambush, when Second Lieutenant Arthur Lacroix approached him.

"Sir," Arthur said, saluting his colonel. Sweat poured down Dixon's face as he drank hot whiskey and honey and stared up at Lieutenant Daryl's twin brother. For a second, he couldn't tell who he was looking at, both men sported patchwork beards, a protruding Cro-Magnon brow line, barrel chests, and hazel eyes. Dixon had to look at the stripes on the man's shoulders to realize he was speaking to Arthur, who was a rank below Daryl, a fact the colonel knew brought ire from the younger Lacroix.

"Lieutenant, what do you have for me?" Dixon breathed, wiping sweat out of his eyes with his sleeve, which resulted in only smearing around the dried mud that coated his uniform onto his face. The night itself was already muggy with humid heat, and the huge fire made the immediate vicinity a sauna. But Dixon took to sweating and making himself almost delirious with heat. He preferred the heat over the never-ending hordes of mosquitos and horseflies, drawn to the area by the festering corpses past the tree line. Besides, this sweat was clarifying. The whiskey heated him up from the inside, the fire from the outside, and like the Osage he'd observed ranting in their sweat lodges (before Dixon helped the state militia purge them from these lands), their bellies full of the psychoactive truffles that grew in the hills, he was cleansing his body, clearing his mind. He listened, expecting more bad news.

"We've taken the farms, sir," Arthur said, but he was not smiling at this report of victory. He sweated too, but from the exertion of riding like his life depended on it. He was part of the scout team, and scouts only ran hard when there were enemies afoot.

"Good. You don't sound too thrilled about it though," Dixon said, his voice tired.

"Well, sir, we've got reports that Lyon's men are rallyin' for another full-on assault come morning. The Federals we drove out today are currently en route to meet up with a full regiment of Sigel's men in Carthage. They're mighty pissed we took their farms, and I reckon they aim to take it back. Come morning this whole county is gonna be as blue as the ocean," Arthur informed.

Dixon nodded slowly and finished his drink in one long pull. He longed for the somnambulant embrace of a deep drunk, but he sweated it out as fast as he put it in, and like the munitions, like the food, like the fucking *horses*, the booze was in scant supply.

"Thank you for the field report, Lieutenant. Anything else?" he asked.

For a moment, the big man didn't respond, only looking at his muddy brogans forlornly.

"What is it, Lacroix?" Dixon sighed.

"Well, sir, it's just that, uhm, well, you know, I've been pulling my weight a lot recently. "Between scoutin' and huntin', I just, well, you know Daryl got his promotion after—"

"Not now, son. You pester me about a god damn promotion again, and I'll *demote* you back down to private. Understood?" Dixon said, turning the full heat of his fierce gaze upon the Lacroix twin. Dixon was told his handsome features could quickly turn animal when his blood was up. The fiery red hair, bushy eyebrows, and piercing blue eyes could take on a hard, ferocious edge when he put his mind to it. He put his mind to it now, hoping to not hear another word from the dimwitted Lacroix on the matter.

"Ye . . . Yessir," Arthur Lacroix replied, and began to walk away.

"I didn't dismiss you, Lieutenant." Lacroix froze and turned back to face him, his face tight with confusion. "Help me gather these sorry ass rags for men, the plan has changed, need to rally," Dixon said.

He was too tired and his voice too raw to try and conduct some rousing speech for his men. But he must, for he saw how clueless they acted without clear direction. Of the brigade he'd initially been in command of prior to the Wilson's Creek engagement, he now had at most two divisions of soldiers left, the hundred or so men mostly unfamiliar faces to him, only a handful of which had any sort of senior rank. This included captain Lance Marshall, ordinance sergeant Bruce Mayfield (though his rank was useless as they no longer had armaments for which to provide ordinance for), and Major Curtis Robertson, who was the second highest in command aside from Dixon. He sought the competent man out, looking for his trademark long greasy black horsetail and dark, bushy chin curtain of a beard.

79

He found Robertson squatting beside a cooking fire, his coal-black beard speckled with grease drippings from a stringy leg of rabbit he'd been gnawing on. Dixon's stomach grumbled at the sight and smell of fresh meat. But at this moment the men were in charge of their own meals aside from the rationed out portion of hard tack and salted pork they were allotted for breakfast. Dixon didn't believe in dressing down subordinates to get what he wanted. He would hunt for food himself, if he had the energy and time for it, that was.

Robertson didn't stand at the colonel's approach, though the men around him did. Unlike the Union, which strictly forbade informal fraternization among ranks, Dixon allowed the senior ranking men some leeway when addressing him, unless, of course, they did something out of line. But the curt nod that the major gave him was good enough. The man had been on the front lines since the very start, one of the few original remnants from Dixon's guerilla war party. He and Dixon were well met and well known to the point where Dixon was there when Robertson's two fingers, now healed over nubs, had been shot off during a skirmish along the White River. Those were good days, back when they still had a patriotic fire in their balls and were able to effectively harass the few Missouri State Militia bands that scarcely patrolled the isolated foothills in this corner of the state. They had made out like bandits, then.

But as the major met his gaze, Dixon saw the war had worn this man down too. Streaks of gray now shot through the once raven-black hair, and eyes that used to hold a fiery shine to them, that look of ornery vitality that told you this was a man who enjoyed the fight, was dimmed to a tired gaze.

"Colonel," he said simply, continuing to scrape off every last strand of gristle from the bone he was holding with his teeth.

"Major, let us palaver away from the others. I need to talk strategy with you," Dixon said. The major nodded, threw his bone in the fire, and stood. Like the rest of them, Roberston had lost weight, though this was a man who had scant weight to lose.

His major's jacket hung limply about his skeletal frame like a child in his daddy's work shirt, and Dixon thought somberly that they'd need to find some real food sources soon. A starving army was a losing one.

Together they walked away from the main gathering, toward the mill itself, its big useless wheel now forever unmoving as the creek it sought power from was bone dry.

"Our scouts tell me we won the battle here today, and that the Federals are mighty red-assed about it. Apparently that Dutch shithead Sigel is planning on taking the sorry sumbitches we whooped today into his regiment. Gonna come back here tomorrow with at least two regiments, drive us out. I reckon Price's men will try to stay and fight."

"And what do you reckon we do?" Robertson asked, taking out a plug of tobacco and began to chew noisily. It was what he did when he had to use his noggin for tactical matters.

"You think we got another fight left in us?" Dixon asked. The question was semi-rhetorical, but he wanted to hear Robertson's opinion on the matter to further validate his own.

"Nosir, I don't think we do. I think Price is out of his mind to try and fight them boys on Federal terms. We was giving them a whoopin' the way we was doing it before. Sneak up on 'em, take ten good men and ride right up on 'em. Raise hell, get in close, let the blood fly, and then ride out before they even know what happened. This shit like what happened today? May as well bend over and hoped they greased their hog legs up before sticking it in. If I'm to speak frankly, sir."

Dixon smiled, and hoped he didn't lose Robertson. The man never bullshitted, and his knowledge of the region was invaluable. Dixon was an Arkansas native, his lands were the Boston Mountains to the south. But Robertson was born in Pemiscot County and worked the French-owned lead mines in Rolla up north before it became a Union town. During the early days of the conflict, back when they were a simple raiding band snuffing out the meager Federal presence in the state, Robertson had guided them through the steep, confusing grades of the Saint Francois Mountains to the northeast, and led the men to the creeks and rivers with the best populations of fish. Dixon would need the man's expertise on the land now more than ever as he spoke.

"I agree wholeheartedly, Major. I think we ought to go back to the way things were. Independent raiding parties hitting supply lines and disrupting their foundation. Let Lee's Corps in the south fight the big conventional engagements. They have cannons and repeaters and full bellies. We don't have the resources for that hogwash."

Robertson nodded in agreement, looking toward the stringy men by their individual cooking fires, occasionally the faint screams from someone getting a ball dug out of them floated up to them. They lost their sawbones today as well, and now they had some asshole sergeant named Red Finkley who practiced animal husbandry and veterinary medicine hacking off limbs and digging into men to the best of his ability. Christ, it was a sorry state of affairs.

"I can lead your men out of here, sir, but our options are limited. The southeast corner is mostly Union held, Cape Girardeau is blue now, as is everything to the north of it. Sigel's men are coming up from the south, a whole goddamn mess of 'em it sounds like. We can go toward the heart of the state. We passed through some of the high country on the way over here. Lot of little bergs and towns tucked away into the hills, folks so isolated they don't even know there's a war going on. We can hide away up yonder, lick our wounds, find some food and horses. Make ourselves a fighting force again."

"That sounds mighty fine to me, Major," Dixon said. The idea of tucking away into the many hills and hollers and taking some time to rest and resupply helped quell some of the lingering anxiety that boiled in his gut like rotten stew.

"Going won't be easy though. The land gets pretty rugged north of here. It'll be worth it, I think. There's a few villages in the Courtois hills that I know are loyal to the secessionists. They'll open their doors to us, help in any way they can. And if the Union does somehow follow us all the way there, lots of caves to tuck down into, lay low till we're ready to hit back. Bout a week's walk or two days ride, though some parts I reckon you couldn't even get a horse through."

Dixon pondered on this for a moment. The idea of walking even more made his old bones hurt, but sanctuary was what these men needed, even if they had to cross through Hell to get to it. He put a hand on Robertson's shoulder.

"All right then. I'm trusting you on this one, old son. Stick close to me when it comes time to head out. We lose you, we'll be wondering ducks," Dixon said, and took a moment to compose himself. He saw Arthur had done his job of corralling the men toward the open field where a bare caisson sat, the last of their supplies burned through with the Wilson Creek battle. He made his way over, felt a legion of tired eyes upon him as he clambered atop the caisson, so as to have a judicial-like position over his men as he spoke, commanding their attention.

"All right y'all, listen up!" Dixon bellowed, his whiskey and honey concoction coating his throat just enough to allow him to rasp out his words. The men stopped in their scattered conversations and turned expectantly toward him. "I've received word that the Federal boys are mighty sore about losing their farm today." He expected a jovial quip from one of the men, a *damn right!* Or *we whooped 'em sure as hell!* But they were silent, another sign of their growing disillusionment. Dixon continued, "It seems that German mutt Sigel has it in his mind to take this farm back. Seems they'll be amassing here tomorrow with a whole horde of blue boys, ready to mulch us into the ground. Price seems to have forgotten how we were winning this war in the first place. He wants us to fight like Federals. You all saw how well that went over today at Wilson's Creek," Dixon said, letting the assorted grumbles and nods of agreement pass before continuing.

He was aware this very speech could be considered inciting a mutiny and treasonable, but he didn't care, and he was sure his men didn't either. If Price wanted them to fight like Federals, he damn well better make sure they were *armed* like Federals.

"But I don't intend on sitting here in neat little rows and watching these good southern men get turned into cannon fodder. Unlike the Federal generals who sit atop their horses in their clean uniforms and spy on the battle from the safety of their camps, I care about what happens to my men. So here's what we're gonna do—" He spent the next five minutes laying out a basic retreat strategy, advising all the men to spend the next two hours getting what rest they could. They'd leave an hour before sunup, as to not give the Federals a chance to sneak up on them with their britches down around their ankles.

The general reaction was ambiguous, but he didn't hear any outright protests or complaints, and that was good enough for Dixon.

"Load up your rifles and say your prayers before turning in tonight. The journey ahead won't be easy, but it's time we go back to our roots. I promise you by Saturday you'll have a roof over your head and hot food in your bellies," he said, hoping Robertson would help him fulfill this promise. He saw the pathetic, tired desperation in their faces, saw the multitude of sunken eyes and hollow cheeks turning up to him when he said that. If he didn't deliver, he was sure the men would see past the veneer of a mythologized immortal rebel hellraiser and see him for what he really was: a tired, raw-boned fool just trying to stay alive, same as them.

CHAPTER 3

The dark ate at their torches like a ravenous thing whose diet was light. The ground sucked at their boots with equal fervor; the very earth seemed intent to swallow these men whole as they pushed through the steep foothills, tired, sore muscles flexing and cramping for every foothold.

Dixon was in front, Robertson ahead by a few paces as he continued sure-footed and confident through the mired ground. They'd been on the march for some four hours, the sun finally coming through, everything painted soft in its bruised light, revealing endless vistas of rolling green, pockmarked by the occasional peach-colored karst outcropping or bluff. The only solace Dixon took in this hellish journey was that he was sure the union would not dare come after them, or even know where to look, in these dense, rugged highlands. They left no trace of their encampment at the mill or their retreat, and the march so far had only taken them through rough and steep foothills that showed no evidence that modern man had been there. He half expected to come upon an isolated band of Shawnee or Osage, somehow squirreling away in the hills to escape the emancipation.

They came upon no humans whatsoever. Lots of squirrels and coons though, which men took fire at when they could and strapped to their belts as they walked. Not even a sign of a wagon trail or footpath. Just a few game trails, and trees. So many goddamn trees.

Dixon thought to himself that he could settle down in a place like this once the war was over. A place far away from any and all people. He'd had a wife once, a beautiful blonde belle of a woman who saw something in his mangy, rough-around-the-edges hide. They'd always planned to stake out a claim somewhere in the Boston Mountains, which this section of the highlands reminded him of quite a bit. But now the wife was gone, disowning him after begging Tobias not to go off into that fool's war, not to go and get himself killed. She warned if he did, she wouldn't be around to see if he survived.

Now, he had no interest in finding another bird to roost with. He was too old for all that. The bluffs and outcroppings weren't as majestic here, nor the forest as varied as his home dirt, but still. It was quiet save for the many footfalls and grumbles of his men. The sense of solitude was so strong here that his army's presence almost felt like a violation to the natural order of this land. He could see himself living out his days here, alone, in a cabin made by his hand, turning into one of those funny hermit hill folk with a four-foot beard and a coonskin hat. Some kind of tracking mutt by his side, bluetick or a beagle maybe. Something mangy but loyal.

They stopped at a shallow stream sometime around noon judging by the high merciless sun. They all filled their canteens, drank their fill, and then dunked their sweaty long hair and beards into the cool, clear water, seeking respite from the hot humidity of the day.

They went on, covering more identical ground, Dixon judged some twelve miles or so, before nightfall came and he ordered his men to bivouac in a shallow valley between two of the larger knobs. The ground was too uneven to use their canvas shelters, so some of the men, the more country raised of these rednecks and hillbillies alike, demonstrated some backwoods ingenuity and built lean-twos and other rudimentary shelters for themselves, while the less fortunate slept out in the open. Before this though, the smells of squirrel and racoons cooking over spit fires filled the night air, and Dixon gratefully ate from a passed around bowl of squirrel stew, which was nothing more than broth, stringy squirrel meat, boiled cattail chutes and wild onions.

Dixon slept like the dead that night, they all did, the utter exhaustion of the past few days catching up with them. So thoroughly asleep was he that the screams he'd heard for some time pierced his dreams and mixed with them like molasses in water. He'd been dreaming of chasing a child through the woods, this child was his daughter that he'd never seen before but knew existed. A letter from Lucille, his ex-wife, had confirmed that. He chased and chased her, only catching fleeting glimpses of the young girl and her red hair, taken ginger like her daddy, as she bound giggling and skipping through the forest. The screams came to him high and distant, and his pursuit of his daughter hastened even more as he felt the need to protect her from the source of those spine-freezing caterwauls.

What finally kicked him over from comatose to awake was the loud bark of a scattergun. He shot awake, scrambling for his pistols, disoriented by the blobs of shifting firelight and the chaos of several bodies moving through the dark. Then he heard the unmistakable roar of a bear and understood immediately what was happening.

Tobias Dixon almost forgot bears were a part of the land here, so used to traversing well-worn farmland and country roads to the southeast was he, where man had a firm foothold of the earth there. He tried to see through the shifting bodies of shadow and man, and in the flash of someone's musket he saw the huge, heaving dark shape as it stood up on hindlegs to its full height. He then heard the grunts of men, followed by the distinct sound of bayonets piercing flesh, the symphony concluding with a low, thunderous gurgling moan from the bear, before the ground shook as it fell onto its back. *Must've been drawn by the cookin'*, Dixon had time to think.

Triumphant cries from the men, but underneath Dixon heard someone moaning. He shoved passed men until he came upon the black bear, its thick coal-colored coat marred with buckshot and glistening in places from stab wounds. Next to him was the disemboweled body of one of his men. He yanked a torch from one of the stupefied soldiers and knelt down next to the squirming, moaning private. His guts rainbow-colored and glistening in the torch light. Leaf litter and dirt stuck to his exposed intestines, that strange smell of half-digested food, just before it turns completely into shit, wafted up at Dixon.

"What's your name, son?" he asked in a tender voice as soldiers crowded around to look at their fallen brother.

"P . . . p . . . Private . . . Joshua . . . Wuh . . . Wuh . . . Wicker . . .sir," the man stuttered out, shivering now. Dixon knew that shiver was from the reaper tickling his spine, not from the cool night air.

"Private Wicker. You're a good man, Private Wicker," Dixon said. The horse doctor, Red, was there, staring down stupidly at all those insides that were now outsides.

"Am I . . . Am I . . . going to die?" Wicker asked as Red knelt down to examine the damage. Not only had the bear swiped the poor bastard's guts out with one claw, he'd managed to chew on the young man's face a bit, and Dixon could see the yellowed molars of the boy's jaw clattering together through his cheek as he shivered. It was obvious there was nothing that could be done, and Red had whispered so in his ear.

"Don't think of it as dying, son. You're simply going up to the pearly gates before the rest of us. You got any kin I should relay a message to?" Dixon asked, gently taking one of his revolvers out and setting it beside the dying man. His bedside manner left something to be desired, but he was a colonel, not a doctor, damnit. Still, he did his best to comfort the poor soul. killed by a beast during a battle between men. What a damn shame.

"My . . . My muh . . . Mother . . . She . . ." Wicker began, and then let out one violent spasm, a deep sigh, and then stopped abruptly. His eyes, which had been looking into the colonels' with a desperate need, glazed over. Dixon let out a sigh of relief. He'd had to put down one of his own before, and it always fouled his guts doing so, like they were nothing more than a lamed horse past its prime. It was a blessing the man died of shock instead.

Tobias looked at the bear, and saw another blessing present itself before this tragedy.

"All right, y'all carve this bear up right quick! Get a big fire going. We gonna eat what we can before he spoils," he said, the tragedy that just befell him already being overpowered by the thought of biting into a full, juicy steak of bear meat.

While the meat cooked, he helped two other men give Private Josiah Wicker a proper Christian burial, digging him a shallow grave and then lining it with heavy stones from the hillside to keep the critters off him for a good while.

Every scrap of meat was cleaned and cooked off the bear, the eighty-five or so men left over from the battle each getting about a pound and a half each. No one talked for a long while, the sounds of mastication and sizzling fat, punctuated by the occasional burst of gas from one end or the other, were the only sounds in the hills for some time.

Dixon was almost drunk with fullness, it'd been so long since he'd had a truly full stomach. For a minute, he thought he might throw up. But he forced his gullet down, not daring to relinquish any of the nourishing meat he so badly needed, and soon a heavy, corporeal somnambulance overtook him, the heavy meal pushing him back down to the ground. He ordered his men to take rest for an hour, let the food settle in their stomachs, and then they would head out again, try to make good time before the sun came out from behind the mountains to cook them alive again.

He didn't intend on falling asleep again, didn't think he could, but the next hour winked by in a dark stupor as First Lieutenant Lacroix was gently nudging his boot, waking him up, telling him it was time to go.

CHAPTER 4

Revitalized from their meal and sleep, the men marched a good pace now as the land slowly steadied. Eventually, they descended into the wide gorge of a river valley, the pine studded banks of the Big Piney River waited for them. Though he recognized the river, Dixon had no idea what county they were in. He did know the Piney was located in the lower central quadrant of the state, and they followed the river north. He did some quick mental calculating, and guessed they would be heading toward the Francois Mountain range if they continued on their present path. Robertson could fill in the blanks from there.

"We'll follow this downa ways. If memory serves correct, there'll be a sandbar we can cross over on, and head east. After that, it gets swampy for a bit," Robertson informed the colonel as they followed the river south. It ran clear and deep, and Dixon could see schools of bass and other sunfish darting through the water. How he wished he could stop this march, shirk off his sweat and mud-encrusted uniform, and just float in those serene, cool waters.

Several miles downstream they came to the rocky sandbar, whereupon they crossed and Robertson plunged headlong into a thick stand of trees, the men following after like hunters trailing their coon dogs. They saw evidence of hill folk in the region, traps and old fire pits were found at odd intervals as the land turned hilly again, but still no people. It wasn't long though before they descended into a large bowl-shaped valley, where the land turned mushy as they came upon huge swathes of moss-covered water. Dixon marveled at how quickly the land could change out here as he took in the thick cypress trees with their large-fanned roots poking up from the primordial pool here and there. He noted the thick, messy webs from orb weaver and black widow spiders that clouded the branches and scintillated in the sunlight, promising headaches for any men trying to cross.

The stultifying journey turned downright miserable for a while as they crossed through the swamp in the late morning, the sky ahead clear and open for the sun to do its terrible job of cooking their necks raw and boiling them alive inside their tattered uniforms. The micro-climate of the swampy bottoms added an unbearable humidity to the heat that made breathing hard and the sweat cling to skin instead of evaporating. The mosquitos were thick enough to occlude one's vision as they crossed through the muddy water, the relentless hordes of them going into ears and eyes, their incessant whining drone enough to drive even the most stoic among them mad. Then came a screaming commotion followed by a splash of water as one of the men accidentally stumbled upon a nest of copperheads. Dixon saw the man flinging the tan hourglass-printed vipers off him, and felt his genitals hoist themselves to safety deep inside his body as three or four of the serpents disappeared under the water, heading toward him it seemed.

First Sergeant Joshua Lawrence got bit six times before he managed to whack away the vipers with the butt of his gun, and managed to walk another fifty feet before he collapsed into the foul water. Dixon waded his way over and saw the man's face was the color of ash, his leg swelled up enough to pull his pants leg taught. Violent spasms rocked him to the point the men couldn't keep hold of him.

"Copperhead bite's a bad way to go," Red, the useless sergeant-turned-doctor informed him as he stood over the convulsing man. "With the amount he got bit, it'd be like getting boiled alive from the inside. Blood thickens up and your heart just sorta chokes on its own supply."

Dixon ended the man's suffering with a pistol to the temple, and they trudged on, their once elated mood from a full belly now fouled by the hostile land they tried to cross. The land itself felt inimical to the men's journey as its protean shifting from one challenging gauntlet to another hindered their progress in new and dreadful ways.

"We better see civilization soon, Major, I don't know how much longer my men will put up with this," Dixon said to Robertson as they came near the sloping bank of another foothill, and out of the swamp.

"It gets better for a stretch before we get into the knobs and hills again. No more swamp though, I can promise you that," Robertson said as their boots sucked and slurped their way through the foul mud.

CHAPTER 5

Slowly, they headed north, and rose back up into the highlands, these more dramatic than the rolling hills near Springfield. More hills, more sloping karst, but now, they could see holes opening up into the ground and steep bluffs, cave mouths big enough for men five abreast to cross into. The ground here was more rocky than anything, huge swathes of brick-colored boulders and rocks marking the top of each small mountain. The solid ground made the going easier, but Dixon was wary of such barren earth. During their hell-march across the state, they'd relied upon elderberries, wild onions, artichoke roots, and other wild plants to fill their stomachs until they came upon meat, but no such earthen bounty grew here.

Soon they came upon the shore of another river, this one wider and deeper, crystal clear and with a swift current, its creek bed and banks comprised almost wholly of peach-colored rock.

"Meramec River. Good place to stop, chain pickerel, bass, and bluegill run thick here. Should be a village about ten miles upstream. Poplar Springs."

"Friendly?" Dixon said as he ordered his men to stop along the banks.

"I know they ain't a fan of Federals," Robertson said flatly as Dixon watched the man scanning the stream, where silver flashes from darting fish could be seen.

"That don't exactly answer my question, Major," Dixon said, gripping Robertson's shoulder, feeling like he was grabbing a bag of bones. He made Robertson look into his eyes. "What are my men walking into there?"

"Poplar springs is one of them places kind of . . . what's the word, *insulated*, from the war. An itty-bitty little trading post town with exactly one slave-owning family. They were supposed to be neutral territory, they wouldn't fire upon you, but you weren't expected to make yourself too comfortable there. Not many soldiers have passed through there, on account of the people being a tad uhm . . . odd."

"Odd?" Dixon raised a red eyebrow. "What the hell is that supposed to mean?"

"They just have a funny way about themselves is all. Talk funny, act funny, like they're in a dream state at all times. This old Dutch woman lives there and seems to run the place. Not hostile. Least they weren't supposed to be. But . . . well . . ." Robertson took the moment to plug his lip. He'd ran out of tobacco a few miles back and took to stuffing his jaw with ragweed as a substitute.

"Get on with it." Dixon tried to restrain his impatience.

"There was a battalion that went through there bout a month ago. Ornery herd of seasoned fellers called the Mountain Grove Bushwhackers. They raided and hell-raised pretty much anything in sight, didn't matter if you were secesh or not. They'd been warned to leave places like Poplar Springs alone, on account of us needin' to build local support in the smaller places, build up reliable routes we could send supplies along. They didn't listen though. They heard one of the best shiners in the state was holed up in Poplar and they wanted to taste his work for themselves. Back when I was in the Arkansas Irregulars, I heard they was headed that way." Robertson said, toeing a rock with his boot. "No one's seen 'em since."

Dixon shook his head, unsure of how to take this news. The bit about the moonshiner had him intrigued, for he'd run out of whiskey on the day of the Wilson's Creek fiasco, and he was hankering for a drink. It was the only way he could sleep peacefully at night without those heart-rending dreams. And what was a colonel without his spirits? But the missing battalion was something to furrow brows about. Though if they were as reckless as Robertson claimed they could've met their end any number of ways. Plus, that was only a handful of poorly disciplined men. Dixon had a *full division* . . . of poorly disciplined men.

Strength in numbers, he tried to tell himself.

"All right, then. We'll be on our guard. We won't stay too long, just have a looksee and get a reading on the folks there. If it smells fishy, we just keep going till we get to the next township. You made me promise these people refuge, Robertson. Don't you go making a fool out of me. I'll have your balls for it, Indian style," Dixon said, his voice turning serious at the end there.

"I won't, Colonel," Robertson said as one of the men whooped with joy. Someone had managed to make a rough throwing net out of a hemp fruit net and a few of the ball shaped rocks along the shoreline and pull in a few spotted bass. Dixon's stomach rumbled at the sight. He almost drooled as he imagined the smell of fish frying in a pan.

#

They'd followed the bank until they saw a shallow berm and a dirt path that led up to a covered bridge allowing passage over the Meramec. This road meandered through the hills at a gentle slope, and Dixon's men were grateful to be walking upon solid, level ground. Yet as they walked, and still had not come upon a single person, Dixon began to feel that little invisible fishhook of tension that hooked into his testicles and anus and every other sphincter on his body and pull taught.

He saw deep wagon ruts. The ground was tamped down hard by the passage of an untold number of hooves and feet. Yet no one, not even an errant trade cart, was seen on the ten-mile hike to Poplar Springs. It was the middle of the day, and isolated or not, a trading post should have *some* sort of traffic, especially at this time of day.

A wooden signpost reading POPLAR SPRINGS: EST. 1825 sat along the side of the road, and Dixon saw the first row of shotgun shacks tucked up against the tree line marking the official boundary of the village. He could see a little way down the bend in the road, and saw the rest of the village tucked into a steep bowl-shaped hillside at the base of a humble mountain. His eyes fell upon a tall knobby outcropping of tan rock that marked its peak, the way it cast a shadow over the town.

Dixon ordered his men to stop along the road, and borrowed Lieutenant Lacroix's mount, adorning one of the first officer sabers and one of the cleaner muskets to strap to his back. He intended to go in with Major Robertson, and hoped by horseback and with clean weapons they would add some legitimacy to their ranks as colonel and major.

"You sure you oughtta go in there alone, sir?" Arthur Lacroix asked, volunteering to scout ahead.

"Yes. If that band of hellraisers tore through this town, I want the residents to know we won't treat them like that. Try to convince them we're a dignified bunch and that we will conduct ourselves as such while seeking shelter in their town, however temporary," Dixon said. Doubt flooded his mind then as he looked at his men, mud-spattered, a nebulous aroma of body odor and mustiness about their ranks, wild animal pelts tied off on their persons. He doubted any village of civilized repute would pause at barring these wild men from their homes and farms.

He and Major Robertson rode side by side into Poplar Springs, mustering as much dignity as they could, their eyes scanning the many little homes and fallow vegetable patches for signs of human life. Of *any* life.

"Hello people of Poplar Springs! I am Colonel Tobias Dixon of the First Arkansas Irregulars—" Robertson shot him a glance as the colonel called out, but kept silent. These people didn't need to know the mighty FAI were all but dissolved. "We're here to seek a temporary refuge among your home and hearth. We do not seek to steal or cause undue stress upon your families. We're simply passing through, hoping to bed down for the night! Your cooperation will be noted and passed along to the secessionist generals, and you will be rewarded justly for your war efforts!" Complete silence was the town's reply.

They went past the trading post, its wooden porch dusty from lack of use, any sign of footprints long blown away by the wind. More homes and a few farmhouses. Many torn apart by gunfire. It was obvious a small battle had been waged here. No animals. No men. No women or children.

When Dixon came upon the first group of dead rebels, he did not pause to see their condition, his nerves as taught as viola strings from the uncanny ride into town. He immediately turned tail and spurred his horse into a fast gallop, keeping his head low and spurring the horse to gallop in a zig zag manner, making himself a hard target, sure the lack of people and the dead rebels meant he was walking right into an ambush. He expected the pop of small arms fire and the angry buzz of lead wasps to engulf him at any moment. Robertson was hot on his heels.

"Colonel, wait!" Robertson breathed.

But the colonel did not wait. He came upon his men in a comet trail of dust, both he and his horse breathing hard.

"New plan!" he called out to his men.

Diplomacy was no longer the order of the day.

CHAPTER 6

Dixon had to give credit to his men as they crept through the houses and woods, avoiding the wide-open dirt road. For being a big band of unwashed hillbillies who smelled from a mile away and couldn't make ranks to save their lives, they could move awfully quiet when they wanted to.

Like the plague they swept upon the town in a quiet wave, men going through backyards, crawling through wooden fences and meandering through the dense tree line that hemmed the town in on all sides, eyes wide and white in grimy, gaunt faces. Soon they were approaching what passed for a town square, and were coming upon the large, almost plantation style house that sat at odds amongst the leaning shotgun shacks and other signs of hill-poverty.

Dixon made sure Robertson was on him like a shadow, this goddamn bag of bones got them into this mess, and he was going to make sure the major got them out of it.

"I'm telling you, them bodies was old. Least a month. This place is deser—"

"Keep your yap shut!" Dixon hissed, both their voices harsh whispers as Dixon peaked out over the edge of a warped wooden siding, where he gazed upon the heaps of men in brown rebel threads, their arms frozen up, fingers arced like claws, as if they'd been buried by the very air around them and were trying to claw their way out. He also spotted blue uniforms on the street as well. No flies harassed their corpses.

The wind kicked up slightly and a board fell from one of the more sorry-looking specimens of shelter with a loud crash. Someone yelled, and suddenly the air, molasses thick with silence, exploded into a chorus of hellfire. Wood splinters went flying, the few intact windows in evidence exploded in glinting shards.

"HOLD YOUR FIRE!" Dixon yelled at the top of his lungs. The men nearest him heard the command and reluctantly stopped, having to reload their squirrel guns and shotguns anyway, but those in the tree lines and behind the houses across the road continued their fire. "HOLD YOUR FIRE, GODDAMNIT!" he roared when there was a lull in the volley, and the men all looked around confused, as if they weren't sure what had just happened, as if some spell had just been cast over them. Dixon sighed and looked out, saw that a few of the more dilapidated houses had collapsed in the onslaught of shot and Miniéball, and the derelict trading post was now peppered with holes.

The town as a whole had not reacted at all to this hair-trigger fusillade, no screams from the wounded, no shifting shapes in square busted-out window frames as men shifted to get a better shot. He looked at his own men, those that he could see anyway, and saw they were all whole and without hole, no insides on the outside. They were unharmed. Then he stared closely at the nearest of the dead men. The hand reaching out toward the sky was the color of moldy bread, the eyes shrunken, deflated olives in their sockets.

Robertson was right. Those boys were more than just a foot in the grave. They were now well acquainted with the reaper.

Dixon took a deep breath, said a quick prayer, and holstered the pistol he had in his hand. He then stepped out from the sorry assortment of wood that someone had called a home, and strolled out into the open, hands raised high, his eyes watering from the sharp tang of fresh gun smoke.

Men watched in stunned awe as he strolled boldly into the center of the road junction, where anyone within a hundred feet would have a million different angles to pop him from. He stood like that for what felt like a millennium, the fishhooks of tension that sunk into him earlier now pulled tight enough that he felt like he was going to explode from the inside. Glaciers rolled off hills and melted into oceans by the time everyone released their collective breath as they all waited to see who would fire upon the colonel. No one did.

#

They went house by house, looking for people hiding under beds and in closets, along with food and other sundries to replenish their supplies. But aside from a few jarred preserves and some old potatoes gone wild with tubers, there were nothing but more corpses, many looked as if they'd been fallen upon by wild animals.

They did come upon the moonshiner's house, and this time Dixon *did* use his seniority to decide how the remaining remnants would be sorted out. He could see shelves lining the walls where many jars had been once before, but those were mostly empty now, as was the huge metal still that sat out back of the house. Fifteen jars remained, and when Dixon popped the lid on one, he felt a warm tingle in his spine as the astringent aroma of the shine burned his nose hairs and cleared his sinuses. He took a sip, relished the clean, pure burn. *Oh yeah, this feller knew what he was doing all right*, he thought as the sip turned into a gulp, and immediately his stomach was ablaze with the purest hellfire he'd ever ingested.

He kept three for himself, and let the men divvy up the rest. Judging by the potency it wouldn't take much to get them drunk.

The only house they didn't search was the big one. A fierce smell emanated from the ornate white walls and strong frame, and none of the men dared go near it. The fact a good majority of the corpses were piled outside its step also lent the structure an ominous air. Dixon ordered his men to steer clear of the bodies in case they harbored disease, and as the sun set, crawling behind the looming knob like a child hiding behind a potato sack, he ordered the men to build a huge pyre in the center of town. If anyone with a sneak to their step tried to come upon his men, they would have few shadows to hide in.

Night fell, the stars lay atop them in vivid winking cascades, and the fire roared. Dixon told his men to bed down in the houses nearest the square, no outliers, in case men and things with ill intent lurked in the surrounding forest. The bear incident had him wary of things both feral and war-bent. The men made quick work of the shine, while Dixon savored one of the jars, taking small but frequent sips, keeping the fire stoked in his throat and belly, wanting to match his internal temperature to the roaring blaze a few feet ahead. Purifying sweat screamed from his pores.

He thought of how desolate this land was, this town blighted by some unseen force, a pervading sense of isolation and growing odds cut through the pleasant drunk haze he'd been culminating. He was manning a rogue division now, probably wanted by Mccullough or Price for desertion, and wanted by the union for being a southern devil. He had no allies now outside of the men he commanded, the men who saw him as some biblical hero, who couldn't see past his stoic façade.

He drank more, wanting oblivion, but instead found the face of his ex-wife, looking at him with pity and sorrow, telling him to leave this fool's war behind and come home.

She would never understand what it was like, being in the bush, fighting for your life. How men could grow to hate and love the small glimpses into their feral sides such circumstances brought. Dixon was a man made for war, even if he was growing increasingly disillusioned for the cause he fought for. He accepted that as he slumped back against the empty caisson they found by the big house that smelled like death. His men hooted and hollered and a few scuffles broke out and were quickly resolved, but they were far away, counties away, unimportant. He could feel his body liquifying and his consciousness draining out between his toes as the drunk took him somewhere deep and dark.

A place meant only for him.

CHAPTER 7

He awoke to a throbbing head and a sour gut, and groaned as he extricated himself from the wagon wheel he'd passed out against, his neck and upper back feeling like they'd been used as an anvil for some maniacal blacksmith to pound his iron against. A heavy mist hung about Poplar Springs like an ethereal quilt, coating what he could see in a glistening dew. From the fog, he could hear the sounds of retching and shitting and groaning, and felt like he could do an equal measure of all three.

Slowly, Dixon got to his feet, his head lolling to the left as it felt over--ladened with a gallon of blood, and leaned against the caisson as he dug his manhood out of his britches and let loose with a dark, almost tea-colored stream of urine. As he dribbled onto the grass, he looked around, saw men sprawled on the ground around him. He didn't know which ones lived and which ones were among the dead.

He looked toward the tree line, had half a mind to stumble into the bushes and look for something to eat, something to soak up the last bit of shine that was slowly burning a hole in his stomach. Then remembered the barren, rocky earth and the hardy oak and short-leaf pine that grew from it, fruitless trees upon a ground with no sustenance to find.

They needed to leave this place, needed to head on to a town that had living people and not dead bodies. That had horses and fresh food and some sense of commerce. The thought of trying to corral his drunken men up into some semblance of an army sounded monumental though, and he took a few minutes to breathe deep and try to control his gorge as sloshy waves of nausea lapped at the back of his throat.

He lost that battle though, and his head throbbed hard enough he thought he felt his skull crack as a great, hot acidic geyser erupted from his mouth. The force of the ejection was so great he passed out again, nearly falling in his own piss and vomitus.

When he awoke again, it was to First Lieutenant Daryl Lacroix's huge form hulking over him.

"Sir . . . Colonel, you alive?" he asked, gently shaking him.

"Humn . . . huh?" Dixon gasped, blinking back tears as the soft misty morning was gone, and another bright hot day forced itself upon him. His tongue was a dried-out slug in his mouth, he tasted bile and copper and thought for a terrible moment he'd upheave again. But then he swallowed thickly and took a deep breath, realizing how late he'd slept. He shot to his feet, backpedaling and bumping into the caisson as the world abruptly canted sideways with the sudden motion.

"Lieutenant," was all he could think to say for a moment. It took him a minute for the events of yesterday to replay in his mind, coming to him in stuttering, half-baked images. This place, yes, they needed to leave it. He finally noticed that Daryl was looking at him with worry, his face pulled tight, obviously preparing to relay some bad bit of news. "Report," he said.

"Well sir, uhm, it seems a few of the men are missin'. Did a head count this morning, and we're short three men," Lacroix said.

"Missing?" Dixon asked. That was bad news, yes, but Lacroix looked like he was working himself up for the colonel to kick him right in his manhood, preparing himself for a fatal blow. "Who?"

"Uhm . . . Well, Corporal Daniel Wardell, Sergeant Mitchell Lambert, two privates whose names I don't recall, and . . ." Lacroix looked down at the ground.

"And?" Dixon said, thinking this wasn't that bad. He barely knew those men, probably got drunk and wandered off into the forest, got lost. They'd either catch up or be left for the federals.

"Major Robertson, sir," Lacroix said, and just as Dixon was processing that blow, the twin Lacroix came up, his face sheened with sweat, his face also tight with worry.

"We can't find 'em anywheres. Looked all over the place. Colonel, we—"

"I told him already, dumbass. Keep lookin'! It's Robertson we need," Daryl barked at his brother.

Dixon could only look at the two Neanderthal brothers in numb silence.

"Robertson is gone?" Dixon croaked. Suddenly his eyes were looking everywhere at once, taking in the bullet-ridden houses and the wall of trees that seemed to herd them into a killing box. No, they were mistaken. Robertson was just holed up in one of these houses. He had to be. Sleeping off a hangover like the rest of them. "You search the houses?"

"All of 'em, even the big one, sir. Something's wrong here, Colonel. Witchcraft or somethin' close to it went on in that house and this village. Dead bodies strung up on meat hooks. Old books with . . . some kind of devilry . . . Symbols like I seen before in the homes of mountain witches down south. I think there's madness in that house, and Robertson ain't here. We gotta go, Colonel. This is a cursed place," Arthur said.

Dixon looked over his shoulder at the big house. No, they're wrong. *He's somewhere in there, or nearby, they just didn't look hard enough, the half-drunk imbeciles*, he thought and walked toward the big house. A firm hand held him in place.

"You don't want to go in there, Colonel. I promise you. He ain't in there. He ain't nowhere around. And some of the men . . . Well, we were all pretty soused last night, but some of the men said there was a ruckus in the night. Probably just some drunken nonsense," Daryl said, holding Dixon back from the doorstep.

"They said some folks came in the night, took our men while they were sleeping. I recall hearing something late last night, I—" Arthur began.

"Men say they saw things they didn't when they're in the drink, and you were drunk enough you started going on about how you and cousin Margret . . . I can't even speak of the hogwash you uttered. We ought not waste the colonel's time with this nonsense. We was all drunk and out of sorts. We just . . . We need to leave," Daryl replied sharply.

"Well, maybe it's not nonsense," Arthur insisted. They both looked at Colonel Dixon at the same time, identical expressions of lost helplessness softening their hard features, and his head spun as he tried to differentiate brother from brother, and reality from the booze-sodden dreams he'd crawled from, and the fact he might have to lead these men in a strange land without the one person who knew how to get them through it.

#

In a daze, Dixon walked through the camp they'd made, men weakly saluting him as he walked by, the twins ahead, taking him to one of the men who spoke of such a ruckus. Arthur led him to a man he didn't recognize, must've been one of the stragglers from the state guard. He looked like so many of the other men; long brown hair, greasy face, matted brown beard, his only distinguishing feature was his youth. Dixon would be surprised if he was a day over nineteen. He was in the middle of cleaning his Colt revolver, one of the few army-issued guns Dixon saw among his men. Must've stolen it off a dead Federal. Good for him.

He stood to attention when he saw Dixon meant to have a word with him.

"Colonel Dixon sir," he said, trying to hide the quaver in that sharp muster.

"What's your name, boy?" Dixon asked.

"Private Brian Ellison, sir!" he barked.

"At ease son, this ain't Westpoint," Dixon said with a wince. Loud noises grated on his nerves like salt in an open wound. "Lieutenant Lacroix tells me you know what happened to Major Robertson?" He watched the private's eyes flit to Arthur, an unreadable communication passing between them. Ellison seemed flustered, as if he were not expecting to have his account of his events audited for any legitimacy.

"I . . . Uhm . . . Not exactly sir. I . . . I don't know what I saw, except some of our men . . . They got dragged off into the night. Thought it was a nightmare I was havin, sir. I'm still not sure if—"

"Dragged off by what? Another bear?" Dixon cut him off. Ellison swallowed, his prominent Adam's apple dancing in his throat. He shook his head.

"I . . . No sir. People . . . I think." The waver was prominent in his voice now. Dixon didn't see a rebel but a scared boy in a young man's body, far from home and way over his head.

"*People?* Federals you mean?" Dixon asked, his pulse speeding up at this, thinking *my god the balls on those bastards.* Then anger as he thought of those blue sumbitches stealing his navigator, stealing the one man he needed to get through this desolate hostile land. *The balls on those—*

"No sir. I . . . I'm telling you, it was a nightmare . . . Except I remember getting woke up by their screams. You . . . You can't wake up into a nightmare . . . Can you?" he asked, his gray eyes looking pleadingly into Dixon's as if he seriously expected an answer from the man on such an esoteric matter. Dixon grabbed him by the shoulders.

108

It was meant to be a comforting, fortifying gesture, but it turned into something desperate as he felt his fingers digging into those stringy shoulder muscles against his will, the need to know coming upon him something fierce.

"What'd they look like, son?" Dixon asked, his voice tight.

"I . . . I reckon they was naked. Not a stitch on 'em. One of 'em was big, had long shaggy black hair. Hairy all over really, like a goddamn monkey. Other one was shorter and kinda chubby. They moved quick though, like, mountain lion quick. Saw 'em run into camp and pick up one of the men like they was just a sack of potatoes. That was the only time I saw 'em, but it shocked the drunk right out of me, and I didn't sleep a lick after that. I heard a few more screams from other parts of camp a little while later. Saw pale shapes by the firelight, zipping around faster than any man could."

Dixon didn't say anything for a moment, just looked deep into those gray eyes, and he could see the marrow-deep fright in the boy. It was the look fresh faced privates got when they're in formation and just saw their brother get split in half by a howitzer shell not two feet to their right. It's the look that comes upon all men when the initial glazed-over shock has worn off and the unescapable horror has settled into their bones. This boy was telling the truth, or convinced he was. Dixon turned to the twins.

"Anyone else report anything like this going on?" Dixon asked them.

"I heard one of the privates mention something about someone screamin' bloody murder last night, but other than that, no," Arthur said.

"Just drunk men seeing what the booze wants 'em to see. The ones missing probably tied on a mean drunk and stumbled off into the woods," Daryl said, shaking his head. No one responded to this. Dixon realized they were all waiting for him. He was the colonel after all. He was expected to lead them.

Tobias Dixon looked around at his men. Then his eyes fell upon the dead soldiers, and noted the Union soldiers among the dead. Six of them to be exact.

CHAPTER 8

It was hard work, rotten work, getting those uniforms off the corpses, who were as stiff and unyielding as the branches of a green oak. They had to snap the limbs like chicken bones in order to work the jackets off, and Dixon had to coax six volunteers into slipping the musty uniforms on by offering up one of his jars of fire water for them to split. He would've volunteered himself, but his chiseled features and a description of his fiery red hair and piercing blue eyes were on enough Union WANTED broadsheets to assume any Union officer sharper than a butter knife would recognize him.

Eventually, though, he found six men, half of them were still drunk and probably wouldn't have signed up if they were in their right minds. He promised them all promotions to get them to slip into the grimy things, the stink of the long dead permanently enmeshed within the fabric.

It was an old tactic but a tried and true one. There was one road leading into Poplar Springs and one road out. He wished he'd had the mind to turn his drunken gaze skyward last night to take note of the north star, but it didn't matter anyway. They would follow the road, it was their only choice. The six 'Union soldiers' would walk the road, the strongest weapons they had among the company, those that looked military-issued, were given to these poor souls in case of a conflict. The uniforms were badly torn in some spots and had bullet holes in a few of them, so any Union boy that crossed paths would only have to look twice to see the deception, if the beards and general wildness didn't give them away first. But that was all right. The men would hesitate before firing, and that hesitation is when the men stalking alongside in the surrounding tree line would swoop in. Dixon had led several successful raids doing this very thing.

Part of him wanted to stay behind, scour the surrounding woods for signs of Robertson, but Arthur, for all his dimwittedness, was right. Poplar Springs was a town corrupted, a land blighted by some unseen scourge. He could sense it in the dirt on the streets and smell it in that musty air and hear it in the silence of the utter lack of life. Call it intuition, call it old-time hill-folk superstition, but his brain was squirting more of the fight or flight juice into his veins with every passing minute he sobered up within the town square. They would simply have to make do and head out.

They left sometime in the late afternoon, Dixon and his men keeping pace with the six imposters as they kept an easy speed about them, walking at parade rest with rifles resting against their shoulders all prim and proper like how the union taught their boys to march with.

And they marched.

And marched.

Then marched some more.

The day dragged on like some dying animal with a busted leg. It was drawing upon evening, and the unending dirt road meandered on and on. Dixon, tired, dehydrated, somewhat delirious, had half a mind to think he'd actually died last night and was now in some kind of purgatory, doomed to march on through the unending road and its unchanging landscape.

He could see, using the sloping knob that overlooked Poplar Springs as a reference, that the road meandered around the base of the wide uplift, the road itself constantly angled to the right, until a few spots where it jigged off to the left.

Just when Dixon was about to call a halt, debating taking the risk of cutting through the woods and making better time at the possibility of being lost, he heard one of the imposter soldiers give a sharp, high whistle toot, a signal that someone was coming up on them from the road. They all froze as one, the small metallic sounds of hammers being raised and balls being loaded were the only thing heard in the forest. That was the other odd thing about these woods. Dixon had not seen a single squirrel or hare or even a goddamn racoon since crossing through the swamps. Though it was high summer and the wood should be teeming with life, there was none save his men.

They waited, Dixon peering through the tree line, trying to get a better look without exposing himself. Finally, he heard it. The hysterical cries of a woman, a babe screaming, rushed footsteps.

"Oh, my gods! Oh, sweet Jesus, you all came!" the woman cried. Dixon could see her now, a harried-looking woman in her thirties or forties, dressed in only a soiled shift, a purple-faced babe clutched to her bosom. Her blonde hair had twigs and leaves in it, as if she'd been running wild through the woods recently.

"Whoa there, easy, ma'am. What's your name? And what's this all about?" one of the imposters said.

"I'm Ruthe. They took everyone. Made 'em all disappear in the night. Some of 'em came back but they're not the same, mister, they ain't the same at all!" the woman balled. "We put out three messages over the weeks hoping y'all would send some men out here. We figured this was rebel doing. Using that southern witch magic or somethin' to turn a spell on us! They cursed the whole town they did!" She was rambling now, yelling over her howling child.

"Where you from, ma'am? Can you lead us back——"

"Oh no, I ain't going back there. Night's coming. Is this all they sent? Y'all need an army to go back there. There's too many of them. There's——"

"Just point then, Jesus, woman," another man said. The woman's hysteria was clearly wearing them thin. Dixon saw a wavering finger point straight back the way she came.

"Lordell township. You better hurry. Night is their time. Night is when the death comes. I can't let them get my baby boy, my little Joseph!" she cried, and ran past the men, dirty bare feet softly patting on the dirt road as she ran, the baby's cries trailing off in the distance.

Thoroughly confused by this unexpected interlude, the deceivers looked toward the tree line, silently waiting on Dixon to give them a command.

"All right, let's double time it!" Dixon called out, no longer fearing a real Union presence in the vicinity. It was clear something was going on, something that had to do with the bizarre scene in Poplar Springs and three of his men missing. He felt on the verge of some vast terrible cliff, with only an unending abyss to be seen below.

They would deal with it though. Whatever strange blight fell upon this land, they would deal with it, they just needed food and shelter first. And he needed his firewater. Revelations came to him when he was deep in the drunk. He could deal with this. He just needed some food, and some booze.

They still kept to the trees, but the imposters were running now, no longer trying to imitate a West Point cadet. The sun was beginning to slip behind the slope of the small mountain, its peak had been lording over them all day as the road wound around it, and Dixon was growing tired of that domineering knob looming over him. He had seen enough of the Francois Range to be convinced this land was barren and blighted from foothill to foothill.

The fishhooks pulled once more as the space between the trees harbored ever-elongating shadows as the dark swallowed up the road behind them and gave the surrounding woods an impenetrable, foreboding quality.

Within a mile or two, they finally came upon Lordell township.

CHAPTER 9

Dixon thought for sure he was losing his mind as they came upon Poplar Springs. Except it wasn't Poplar Springs. It was Lordell Township. The signpost said so. Population 125. Except that wasn't right because this small homogenous burg was identical to the one he'd fled from this morning. A dirt road led in, small wooden houses hugging the shoulder, trees flanking on either side of these. The mountain lay to the left instead of the right, the back of the karst peak hollowed out by a large bowl-shaped opening that seemed to pool the gathering shadows into something beyond pitch black, a portal tucked away on the side of the ancient uplift.

Not a soul was on the road, no lights burned within the houses. The silence and the shadows were equally thick.

"Christ, another ghost town," he heard one of the Lacroix twins breathe.

Dixon held up a hand and they all stopped where the road meandered around a bend, the dark obscuring what lay beyond it. In that moment the urge to take out one of his jars and take a long pull was incredibly strong. But he had to be resolute in front of his men, who were clearly as confused and frustrated and scared as he was. The hysterical woman suddenly gave Brian Ellison's testament to last night's goings on a terrible, final validation.

Dixon took a deep breath and did what he always did when faced with a particularly stumping situation. He broke it down into small pieces, what his needs were and what needed to be addressed first.

First, they needed light. Torches, then a pyre. Once they found a good place to make camp and build the fire, they would go house by house, searching.

Fire. He needed the cleansing flame, the final effective instrument against evil in all its shapes and forms.

"Torches!" he bellowed, his voice deep and commanding, his battlefield tone, the one that cut through the fog of his men's emotions. It was all that needed to be said.

Branches were snapped off the nearest trees, then the tearing of cloth as someone ripped up random garments from the looted houses of Poplar Springs. The last of the bear tallow was smeared onto the rags, the bark from the short-leaf pine, sticky with flammable resin, was the final ingredient. A small fire was made on the outskirts of town, and the torches were lit. Dixon's stomach growled as he smelled the cooking bear fat spitting atop green branches. He prayed silently that whatever horrors might face them in town, there would at least be some food to make up for all this mess. He thought of how juicy those bear flanks were, and his mouth flooded with saliva.

He took point, the men going six abreast down the dirt road, his pistol loaded and ready to fire on anything that showed itself, his finger hugging the trigger enough that one small twitch would be enough to bring the hammer down. Dixon vowed he would dress and cook anything that showed itself so long as it wasn't on two legs and could speak.

The layout was slightly different than Poplar Springs, and there was no large manor house presiding over the claptrap houses that lined the road, but otherwise, the place was identical, right down to the wood front general store with its covered porch.

FUR TRADING HERE—DRIED MEATS—SUNDRIES

Dixon looked at the wooden banner for a long time, his stomach now feeling six sizes too big. The general store in Poplar Springs was a bust, besides a few unspoiled bags of tough venison jerky, all the preserves had been knocked to the ground and busted open and left for the ants, along with the few spirits. The pelts were the only thing undamaged.

Please let there be something in here, please—

"Sir?" It was Daryl, who caught the colonel staring up vacuously at the storefront's masthead.

"Right here. We make the fire right here," Dixon said, pointing to a spot some fifteen feet in front of the store. "Let's get the blaze going, but don't be going off into the woods now. That house, right there"—he pointed to the smallest of the nearby shacks—"tear that thing down and use it. But search inside first. We need food, Daryl," Dixon said. "And no one goes wondering off on their own!" he called over Daryl's head to the men as they gathered upon the general store. "From here on out we travel in teams of four! I don't care if you gotta shit or piss or pray to Jesus, you do it with three other men to your back!" There was scattered ascent to his command, and he turned his attention to the general store.

He so expected the doors to be locked that he almost just went on ahead with using his rifle to mash off the handles when he instinctively gave the door a pull just to see. The doors swung open easily on a scream of old hinges. The musty, earthy smell of drying furs came to him, but no rot, no tang of spoiled meat. That was good. He turned and saw the twins standing at the storefront steps like two lost puppies unsure of where to go.

"On me," he said to the brothers, and together they ventured into the store.

#

"Goddamnit!" Dixon hissed as torchlight revealed bare shelves, save for a lowly jar of peach preserves. He'd taken this and sucked the contents of the fist-sized jar down in ten seconds, the sweet nectary fruit like heavenly ambrosia, the two brothers looking on wordlessly, not daring to ask for a bite. The small taste of sustenance only served to ignite his hunger further though. He wanted meat, he wanted real fucking food. He kicked over the empty shelves in a rage as he felt his stomach gnawing on itself.

"Some kerosene, sir . . ." Arthur dared speak, both men obviously wary of the colonel after having seen that lapse in composure.

"Great, then maybe we can set this whole godforsaken town ablaze," the colonel said bitterly. He wished Robertson was here so he could throttle that skinny little neck of his. "Christ, didn't that woman say they had just been attacked? Where is everyone?" he nearly screamed.

A commotion was going on outside and they all turned toward the doors as Dixon heard a gunshot. He pushed past the brothers and went outside, pistol at the ready.

He saw the house he'd pointed to lay in a splintered heap, the men making quick work of the shack, and he saw two groups of men, each holding a man back.

"It was mine, goddamnit! Finders keepers!" someone roared.

"You ain't got claim to nothin'! There was enough to share!" one of the men being held back screamed in reply.

"The hell is going on?" Dixon interjected, stepping into the throng.

"Private shithead here thought he'd hog all the pickled eggs! Sumbitch was scarfin' 'em down by the handful and wouldn't share!" Dixon recognized the man, he was a sergeant from the state guard, his cheeks were sunken and his eyes were ablaze with rage. Dixon could smell the vinegary tang from the shattered jar that lay between them, some of the men were scooping up the dirt-covered eggs and shoving them whole into their mouths, ignoring the refuse that clung to their sticky shapes. Dixon almost had half a mind to scoop one up for himself.

"That's enough! Christ, y'all are like a couple of dogs fightin' over a hambone!" Dixon roared. His men looked at him with fatigued exhaustion. He saw doubt in their eyes, he saw their faith in him dissolving like the bear fat in their torches.

"We haven't eaten in two days, Colonel. We've marched for miles. We're hungry. And . . . And we found more bodies. Like the ones in Poplar Springs. They's fresher, but not a drop of blood to be seen though. The devil's come to this land, sir," one of the men called from the crowd. Dixon swallowed and sighed.

"I know things are rough right now. I know we're in strange country. But that don't mean we can't start acting like mongrels for Christ's sake. Get this blaze going, I want this fire big enough to be seen from Saint Louis! If there's something in these woods, they won't have the luxury of shadow. Once that's done, y'all scour the town. If you find food, split it among your squad. No fighting. If you find a stash, you tell me immediately and I'll make sure it gets distributed fairly. Hoarders will be punished," Dixon said, taking one of the jars of kerosene and smashing it against the pried-up pile of planks at his feet. "And if you find any bodies, you bring them here, and you burn them," He said as an afterthought.

Without being bid to do so, Arthur Lacroix knelt down, having taken off the bayonet from his squirrel gun and striking it to a piece of flint. The resulting sparks took to the kerosene and erupted with a *whoomph*. Dixon's face was aglow in the orange flame, and if he could've seen himself in the glow of the fire, he would've understood why his men glanced at him uneasily. In the flame, his visage was haunted, his eyes shined with madness, or something close to it. His face was even more gaunt than before, his facial bones taking on a ghastly sharp definition. He resembled a corpse more than a man.

The men scattered, keeping to loose groups of four as they spread throughout the town, the houses bleeding into the shadows at the edge of the firelight. Bigger than Poplar Springs he noted, Dixon prayed his men found food, and prayed they wouldn't rip their own throats out over what they did find.

Goddamn you Robertson. Goddamn you to hell, he thought bitterly as he finally allowed himself a sip of the shine, relishing the inferno it set ablaze inside him.

CHAPTER 10

He did not join his men in the pathetic raid. He made sure the fire burned high and bright, and made sure the blaze in his stomach burned with the same intensity. The shine burned out the hungry pit in his stomach, and for a while, he felt some semblance of peace as he heard doors kicked in, men fighting amongst themselves, the splintering of wood. He was vaguely aware of bodies being added to the pyre. Smelled the searing of flesh. Told himself the smell of that cooking meat didn't reopen the vast chasm in his stomach.

Eventually, Daryl Lacroix came to him, a single potato in his outstretched hand.

"Here, sir. The men found a potato cellar in one of the houses. Weren't enough to feed everyone, but I managed to grab one for you," he said.

Dixon only stared at the spud, its brown skin speckled with dust and grime, a few stumpy tubers beginning to sprout from the skin.

"Thanks, Lieutenant. You eaten yet?" Dixon said as he took the potato and began to gnaw on the tough thing halfheartedly, not having the energy or the patience to cook it.

"No, sir," Daryl replied, the desperation and want on his face quite obvious as he watched the colonel eat.

"Go on then, find something for yourself. Don't worry about me," Dixon said, and his eyes went back to the flames.

The sky ahead was black and impenetrable, low clouds obscuring the stars and the moon.

Dixon, his thoughts becoming untethered by the alcohol, was beginning to think there was some incipient madness about the land, contagious like a disease, perhaps something in the water that caused people to see things, for they'd been there for some hours and nothing fell upon his men.

But just as this thought took root in his mind, he heard shouts from somewhere on the other side of town. Heard a scatter of gunfire. Then a single, wavering scream that rapidly receded, as if the man whose throat it bled from was falling down the same terrible cliff Dixon stared down from in his mind's eye. He didn't want to go over there, he didn't want to find out what the source of the scream was, for he knew. If he just kept sipping the moonshine, and kept staring at the fire, he could wait for the sun, he would have his equilibrium, he would—

"Colonel, sir!"

Dixon looked up, and squinted at the anonymous man, another bearded mangy mutt, barking and waiting for commands.

"Yes?" Dixon said, his voice thick and low. Before the man could respond, there was another scream, another burst of gunfire. The reality of the situation was starting to cut through the shine buzz, and Dixon blinked as he realized that scream was one of agony, and those were multiple shots. Either his men were really starting to tear each other apart over some scraps or the things that the woman and the private spoke of had finally come to visit the haggard remnants of his division.

"Something's happening, sir. These things, they ran off with Corporal Mayson and Sergeant Briggs, sir."

Dixon only nodded at this, trying to make his tactical mind work faster, trying to make his old self, the military-trained colonel who was quick of mind and feet, who always outran Union iron, come to the surface. But the old, tired dog that just wanted to sit and rest these ancient bones and burn from the inside and out was stubborn in leaving.

It wasn't until he saw the streaking form that flowed through the tree line like a ghost, a man slung over his shoulder and flailing like a ragdoll go flying past that Dixon was shocked out of his introspective stupor. His eyes followed the specter and began to get a bead on it with his pistol, but then the thing jerked hard to the right, as if anticipating the colonel's intentions and disappeared into the woods, running toward the direction of the mountain.

Hardened instinct ripped the drunk out of him as Dixon began to look everywhere at once, saw the scatters of torches and the loose gaggles of men flowing through the dirt paths in a panicked frenzy.

"Colonel! This town is haunted, this—" a man had screamed, Dixon could see the fool hollering, trying to outrun the panicked mob behind him before he tripped over his own boots in his haste, and he was quickly trampled by filthy feet as the men began to stampede like a horde of buffalo.

"ON ME!" Dixon roared, summoning his best battle call, speaking as if trying to command his voice over the cacophony of howitzers and musket volleys. A few of the men looked in his direction, but many still ran blindly, scattering out. "ON ME GODDAMNIT!" he screamed as loud as he could, feeling something tear in his throat and knew he would not be able to yell like that again. He raised a pistol and fired it, and *this* got the men's attention. They swarmed toward the burning pyre like night bugs to lantern light.

He spotted the two brothers, stumbling doppelgangers who stood a whole foot taller than the men around them, holding in each arm what looked like clumps of hard tack.

"What the hell is going on?" Dixon asked them, his voice raw and cracking from the torn vocal cord, speech grated at his throat like a dull saw.

"They've come back!" Arthur spat. "Christ, they move so fast! Like devils!"

Daryl didn't say anything, he just looked at the ground, his face blank, as if not wanting to process the things going on around him, he smacked noisily on the hardtack, trying to stuff his face, as if relishing one last meal before being killed, his animal instincts usurping intelligence. Men were speaking over each other, snatches of conversation coming to Dixon before it all got swallowed up in a mishmash of words and syllables.

"You see that thing? It—"

"It was a man, I swear it. Naked as—"

"Was a ghost! You see how white he was? Fuckin' ghost I tell you—"

"Listen up!" Dixon tried to shout, but his voice was robbed of all baritone authority, he sounded like a squeaky post-pubescent boy. "*Listen up!*" he tried again to no avail.

Not wanting to waste ammo but not seeing any other alternative, he took his other pistol and fired it just over their heads. The whole crowd ducked as one, the conversations cut off as cleanly as a skinning knife through fish belly.

"Hu . . . Help . . . Me . . ." came a croaking voice, more pathetic than Dixon's own. He looked for the voice's owner, but the men before him all stared in awed silence. There was a squeaking cry, and then their heads all turned back, some of them parting for Dixon to see the man who'd been trampled over in the stampede. He lay on the ground, some hundred feet away, his body shaped wrong, his legs twisted up and flopping like half-baked pretzels, his whole body shook worse than a hound dog shitting peach pits. He let out a single retching cough and Dixon could see a dark spatter erupt from his mouth. He reached out a hand, the fingers jutting in all directions from being stomped on repeatedly, clawing toward the men. "P . . . Please . . . Ple—"

Dixon was about to order his men to retrieve their fallen brother when a blur of ivory erupted from the woods, streaking across the dirt road as gracefully as a puma sprinting down an elk. The trampled man let out a squawk of pain as the white form streaked by him, his body abruptly jerked to the left before Dixon saw him be dragged off in a tail of dirt and dust. Then the sound of branches breaking and leaf litter being disturbed as man and blur alike disappeared into the woods.

No one spoke as they listened to the thing crash through the forest, the sounds growing steadily fainter until the silence rushed in like a tsunami, even the crackle of the fire seemed to be muted in the collective shock of them all witnessing that terrible exhibition of predatory grace. Dixon felt as if he'd just been given an ice water enema, at odds with the shine boiling in his stomach, creating an intense fever chill that washed over his body.

For a second he didn't know what to do, this situation went so far beyond his battlefield experience that he felt his mind tripping over itself in a desperate scramble to find some sensible command to give to his men. The long rows of trees that surrounded them now felt more like the fence run to a slaughterhouse, his men the stupid cattle being herded down the line, ready to be turned into hamburger and chuck steak. Then he turned toward the store, looked at the solid walls of brick and the wood siding reinforcing it, the doors each a thick slab of oak, the intact windows. Short of a town jail this was their best bet. If they could all fit, that is.

"In the store, now!" he yelped more than yelled. He turned and ran up the steps, flinging the doors open. He was nearly bowled over as men piled in behind him. He saw immediately there would not be enough room for all of them unless they took out the shelves. The juice flowing a little quicker in his brain now. *Break it down. You need light, you need fire, you need shelter.*

He looked for the two brothers and snapped at them to help him, their two huge frames would make easy work of the wooden fixtures. It was a chaotic jumble at first, men getting in the way of other men as they tried to file in while Dixon and the brothers tried to move the shelves out, but finally the men, in their collective panic, began to understand the colonel's orders and more of them took to taking the shelves and piling them atop the fire out front.

The flames jumped, and Dixon saw with some satisfaction that they could see at least some two hundred feet in all directions now, except for the back of the store, which butted up against the tree line. He noted with an icy spike of dread that caused his manhood to recede into the safety of his body that he saw two sets of eyes glowing from the most distant part of the tree line. He'd seen eyes like that once before when he was a boy, his father taking him on a hunt up into the Boston mountains for Eastern elk. A puma had been stalking them as they stalked a shot elk whose blood trail they followed, those feline eyes like two dime-sized emerald portals in the night, only ceasing in its relentless pursuit when his father fired off a warning shot with his scattergun. Tobias Dixon knew the reflective orbs he saw in the tree line belonged to no puma though. Those eyes belonged to something whose very existence was an affront to God.

He ignored the spectral gaze of those nightmare things, focusing on reinforcing his shelter and making sure the fire burned bright. He worried about the door at the rear of the store, how there was no light back there, how it butted up right into the black depths of the forest. But it was solid wood too. For right now that had to be good enough. But as the shelves were cleared out, Dixon saw he had another problem. It was going to be an incredibly tight fit. *Like sardines in a tin,* he thought miserably.

"Come on now, pile in!" Arthur commanded. He spoke for the colonel now, and while he didn't ask Arthur to do this, Dixon was grateful for it, his projecting voice making up for the colonel's rasp. The men piled in until shoulders rubbed together, and then they piled in some more.

"We can't all fit!" someone called out. Dixon stood on his tiptoes and looked out over the sea of stinking, unwashed man flesh. He saw the throng of disheveled soldiers bleed out through the doorway, some ten men were stuck outside and clambering to get in. But there was simply, absolutely, no more room. Dixon felt a sharp wave of claustrophobia hit him and for a second he felt invisible fists ringing his lungs like wash rags. He forced himself to take a deep, ragged breath, inhaling a wave of body odor almost as pungent as what bled from the manor house in Poplar Springs.

"What do we do colonel?" asked one of the men who stood on the threshold of the double doors, he and the other men stuck outside glancing around everywhere at once, expecting one of the things to come streaking out of the night like a meteor and swoop them.

Dixon pointed to the front of the store, and both Arthur and Daryl, his defacto right-hand men now that Robertson was gone, bowled soldiers out of the way. Dixon felt like a stubborn turd being pushed out of a straining rectum as he forced his way through the soldiers until they were up front. He saw the fear plain and naked on the exposed men's faces, two of them were the fake Union soldiers, men who'd already demonstrated valor today and this pulled at Dixon's soul to ask even more of them.

He had one and a half jars of shine left, he'd been clutching them close in his Haversack since they moved into the store. He pulled out the full one, looked at the clear liquid, and felt like he was giving away one of his own children as he held it up.

"Listen up," he said, trying his hardest to sound like a commander and not a teenage boy flustered by his first pair of tits with his cracking voice. "Not everyone can fit in here, as you can see. You men need to stand guard tonight, form a picket on the porch, you—"

"No, Colonel, you don't understand, they'll get us, they'll—"

Dixon whipped his hand out and smacked the babbling young private, he didn't know his name, across the face.

"Quit your blubberin', this is war, and this is what you signed up for. Now listen"—his eyes smarting from the burning in his throat. He held out the shine—"this is payment for tonight. Tomorrow, we head out, and we keep going till we find a town sympathetic to us. A town with telegram services. I'll put a commendation in for every man who stands guard tonight, all of you eligible for promotion. All you gotta do is stay on this porch, stay by the fire, and shoot at any goddamn thing that moves," Dixon said, remembering how he'd passed out, alone, last night and the night before that, but he'd been unbothered by the monsters from the woods because he'd been right up on the blaze. "You'll be safe, just stay close and stay alert. You all got ammo for your guns?" he asked.

They all nodded, some of them showing grim resignation more than fear now, but a few looked as if they might still fill their drawers at the sound of a pin dropping.

"All right, then. You're brave men, you're good men, and I wont let anything happen to you. Don't drink this all at once now, I need you all to have your wits about you. Just enough to keep you calm, got it?" he said as he reluctantly relinquished the moonshine to the nearest of the doomed soldiers.

"Yes, sir," they mumbled more than spoke.

"All right, then. We just gotta stay put till morning. The sun comes, and we go, simple as that," he said, though as he melted back into the sea of bodies and felt the doors close behind him, he had a feeling it would be anything but.

CHAPTER 11

For a long while, an hour or two, he might've guessed, nothing happened. Many of the men attempted to organize a sleeping circle, fellers sleeping nuts to butts and sometimes butt to butt, in an attempt to get comfortable, but many were still too wired from the night's events to sleep. Once a small scuffle broke out when someone saw Daryl gnawing on his bit of hardtack he'd been saving, trying to snatch it from him.

"Come on, you big sumbitch, I ain't eat all day!" The man, a private by the looks of it, was grabbing at the bland clod of flour and butter. Arthur promptly put an end to the mess with a ham-sized fist to the young man's noggin. He dropped like a sack of bricks, and that was the end of the matter. Daryl ate his hard tack unmolested after that, sharing with his brother and the colonel.

Sometime around midnight though, if Dixon had to guess, he'd been making a small mental game of taking a sip of shine every ten minutes (each blessed swallow numbing his throat with that medicinal burn), he heard the picket make some commotion. Men stirred from half-sleep and some stood, looking out the windows of the shop.

"The hell?" one of the men grumbled, squinting.

"What is it?" Dixon croaked, his voice thick and raspy from hoarseness and shine.

"There's a woman out there, just . . . standing out there, naked as a jaybird. Lordy, she's a pretty thing," someone said, and at this, all the men that could afford a view were staring out the windows. *Christ, what now*, Dixon thought as he pushed his way through.

The windows had fogged up from the inside on account of all the sweating bodies crammed within, and Dixon had to wipe away a smear of condensation to see what his men spoke of.

First, he took notice of the fire, which he saw to his dismay had almost burned itself out, a huge glowing pile of coals was still in evidence, but only a few licks of fire squirted up from the smoldering remains of the shelves. Just beyond this, Dixon saw a pale form standing perfectly still in the red glow. Her feminine curves were obvious, a perfectly sculpted hourglass shape, pale flesh washed in a red glow, blonde hair turned golden and fiery by the coals.

For an unknowable moment, time seemed to dilate to syrup-slowness, Dixon beheld what he thought was surely an angel, the most beautiful thing he'd ever seen. Alabaster skin, bulbous breasts whose nipples were erect and seemed to point right at Dixon like accusing fingers. He saw her cleft was hairless, as was her whole body, save for the golden hair that spilled over her shoulders. His eyes finally found hers, and he saw they glowed in the firelight, it was the eyes of the puma all over again, the eyes of an apex predator, and the instant he stared into those reflecting orbs he felt a warm wave of bliss wash over his body. A deep stirring in his groin and tickling in the primal base of his brain that he hadn't felt since being a virile teenager made him want to kick this door down and take her on the spot. He had to strain against his own skin not to do just that.

She raised her arms in a sudden, fluid movement, long elegant fingers curling into a come-hither gesture.

The picket of men who'd been trusted to stand guard all moved at once. They'd stood completely still and totally transfixed this whole time, faces blank, mouths open, gossamer strands of drool spooling from their parted lips, and proceeded forward as if sleepwalking. Dixon knew far down, deep in his rational brain this wasn't right, this was wrong, this woman was not a woman but was in cahoots with the things from the woods. But he could only go on staring, a chorus of ragged breaths filled the room as he knew the men who were caught in that hypnotic glare were put in similar spells, reduced to a feral state of need, all of them like bitches in the deepest state of heat.

"What is it, Colonel?" came the high-pitched voice of Arthur. Dixon blinked and managed to pull his gaze away from the woman, he saw to his horror one of his hands had been sneaking toward the door handle, only a moment away from pulling it open.

"We gotta . . . we gotta stop them," Dixon breathed, and meant to pull open the door anyway but stopped.

The men moved in single file, a shambling sort of stumble like ducklings following their mother. Rifles and scatterguns lay discarded against the porch, as well as the shine, a quarter of the jar left by the door. Dixon banged on the door, tried to yell through it, but the men outside paid him no mind.

The woman turned then, hair swishing about like a golden corona as she presented the gawping men with a perfectly shaped, marble-colored backside that made Dixon weak at the knees. He watched as those plump, pale cheeks began to sway in a hypnotic rhythm as she sashayed away from the store, leading the men on an invisible leash into the darkness.

"STOP!" Dixon forced his crackling voice to carry, and pulled open the double doors. He grabbed the nearest rifle, an Enfield, and put it to his shoulder, sighting it. The second he drew a bead on those golden cascades of hair, he saw her turn, those eyes catching the glow of the coals, as if she knew he meant to shoot her in the back.

Dixon screamed in pain just as he fired off a shot, and dropped to his knees as it felt like someone had just pounded a railroad spike through his eye and into his brain, white flashes scored his vision and he could see the delicate veins in his eyelids for an instant before everything washed gray.

"Blind, I'm blind!" he screamed as he began to flail in a panic. He felt strong hands pull him back into the humid heat of the store.

"Give him some room!" Daryl shouted as if they could do such a thing. Dixon was hyperventilating, he needed his shine damnit, his shine!

He told Daryl, and in a moment, there was a scuffle as the big man wrestled away the jar from some thieving corporal or another, and Dixon felt the comforting glass pressed into his hands. He took a long gulp, and then another.

"What happened?" someone asked, their voice anonymous to him. Dixon blinked rapidly, and saw that slowly, by degrees, his vision was coming back to him. First they were all just featureless gray blobs, then he could make out arms and heads. Things were blurry, but he could make out individual faces if he squinted.

"Sir, are you all right?" Arthur asked, and Dixon realized the big man was holding him. He'd slumped against the Lacroix twin as he felt his knees give out from the shock of being blinded.

"Lock the doors. Barricade them. Don't look outside!" he breathed. The men were all in an uproar now, some saying they oughta go after that witch, oughta throw her in the fire. Others began to lose their minds, high hysterical laughs as they claimed to be in Hell, they'd all died on the battlefield and this was the plains of hell whose desolate hills they were walking. Various states of human distress all bled into a vague cacophony of anxiety and fear.

"Don't look out there!" Arthur said ineffectively, trying to speak for the colonel, but his voice was simply swallowed up by the tide of exclamations and frenzied conversation.

A fierce headache began to drill itself into Dixon's mind as he drank, both of his eyes feeling like someone was trying to push through his sockets and pop them from inside his skull. He managed to wedge himself into a corner of the shop, wanting only to slump down and find oblivion at the bottom of the jar. They just needed to wait until daylight, goddamnit. He willed the sun to move faster in its celestial journey around the planet.

He drank, and waited for more unnatural nightmares to make themselves real. But none did. Eventually, his men settled down. Someone barricaded both the front and back doors using the stocks of rifles through their metal handles. Some men slumped against the doors for extra measure and fell asleep that way.

Soon heavy breathing and snores flooded the air as the darkness became a complete thing, the coals from the bonfire out front dying down until Dixon, his vision already compromised, couldn't even see his hand in front of his face.

He heard something walking on the roof of the shop. Heard scratching at the walls and the doors. Then there came laughter. Men tried to look out of the windows, but it was too dark to tell what was out there, what was taunting them, playing with them. Eventually, it got to the point that Dixon didn't care anymore. He slugged his shine until he felt his head knocking back involuntarily against the wall, the headache deadened by the monumental drunk he was tying on.

Morning. Just gotta wait till . . . he thought before that final stage of darkness, the darkness within himself, swallowed the rest of him whole, and finally, blessedly, he slept.

CHAPTER 12

"Sir . . . Sir!"

Dixon at first thought they were in an earthquake. His whole body shook violently, his vision blearing until he blinked away the ghostly afterimages, until he saw one of the Lacroix twins looming over him, shaking him awake.

"What? What goddamn—" he began to shout when the big man put a hand over his mouth, then put a finger to his own lips. *Shhh.*

Dixon looked around confused, his head throbbing fiercely once again, but he welcomed the sting that the daylight searing in through the windows brought. Except . . . all of his men were still inside, rifles aimed through windows.

"It's the Federals, sir. They're outside. At least two hundred of them."

"Come on out now, we're here to help!" came a muffled voice from outside. Dixon blinked, his mind trying to process this information, but the headache, and the heat, good god it was like a Dutch oven in the small store, only made him lie there and stare up at the rafters. *Union men? What are Union men doing here?* Then it all slammed into him like an ethereal sledgehammer, yesterday's events coming to him in a whirlwind of images and memory and feeling, the clearest of them being that hysterical woman with the screaming babe.

We put out three messages over the weeks hoping y'all would send some men out here. We figured this was rebel doing. Using that southern magic to turn a spell on us!

Dixon began to laugh, he couldn't help it. The giggles bubbled up out of him and he tried to put a hand to his mouth to stifle them. Arthur, or Daryl, whichever one of the goddamn bastards it was, looked at him with something akin to horror as he saw their leader turn south in the brain.

Dixon balled his hand into a fist and cracked himself upside the noggin in a last ditch effort to keep the insanity from grabbing hold. His head rung like a church bell and his vision pulsed a deep red for a second and he thought he was going to pass out again.

"They're comin' this way!" someone hissed and at that, the colonel heard a metallic chatter of guns being loaded. He sighed, swallowed, felt his stomach bloated with a burning, nauseous soup of half-digested potato and moonshine, and put a hand out. The Lacroix twins heaved him to his feet, and if they hadn't been packed in like fish in a barrel he would've fallen over.

"Unlock the back door. Keep it open. Let me through," he slurred in a raspy voice. He fought his way to the front of the store, pulling out the shotgun that had been slid between the handles.

"We got your call! And we know you're in there! Just come on out, let us know you're okay!" the voice came again. It had a European lilt to it, of course it did.

Dixon felt no fear as he threw the doors open, blessedly cool morning air drying the sweat on his face. These men and their rows of guns meant nothing to him. They did not know what true hardship was. They thought they could kill him. He was Colonel Tobias Dixon, and Union metal could not touch him, nor could the strange beasts that lurked in these woods.

A man in a full brigadier general dress sat atop a beautiful gelding at the front of the row, a neatly primmed mustache glinted with wax off the morning sun. His expression turned from confusion to shock as he saw who emerged from the general store.

"My word, is that Colonel *Tobias Dixon*? Fire-haired devil of the traitors?" the general asked.

"Correct," Dixon yelped, and whipped out his manhood as the urge to pee came upon him suddenly and forcefully. Slowly, the men who stood behind the general began to raise their weapons as more men filed out behind Dixon. He looked around surprised as his haggard and bedraggled men began to take up arms beside him, his arc of piss streaming all over the porch as he wobbled.

"Jesus Christ. Look at this. Should've known it was a filthy traitor such as yourself responsible for this. Where are they, Colonel? What did you do with the townsfolk?" the general asked.

Still pissing, Dixon pointed a finger toward the tree line.

"Gone. They got took," he said, knowing trying to explain this absurd situation was useless. He knew how this all looked. He almost felt himself laugh again but bit his lip to stifle it as he tucked himself back into his trousers.

"'Got took' by *who?*" the general asked, taking out a shining new revolver, not a speck of dirt on it, and waved the barrel around to indicate the utter desolation of the surrounding township.

"Don't know. Somethin'," Dixon said, the words sort of just tumbling out of his mouth now as he tried to formulate a plan. He may not be scared of death, but his boys were, and he led these men into this, didn't he? He trusted that skeletal bastard Robertson and made these boys go through hell, and now they were staring down a line of Union iron.

"You have nothing to say for yourself?" The mustached general raised his hand, holding it above his head. There came a chorus of snicks and clacks as guns were loaded.

"What can I say that will stop you from cutting us down like rabid dogs?" Dixon asked, his voice gaining a bit more clarity. He looked over at the Lacroix twins, who stood on either side of him, faces squinting down their muskets, arms trembling.

"I suppose nothing. In that case, I, Brigadier General Mattias Jackson of the 4th Missouri State Militia, sentence you, Colonel Tobias Dixon, and your men, to de—"

Dixon raised his remaining pistol, the big bore flintlock that only had one shot, and fired it without pause. The gelding's broad brown chest exploded in a fan of gore, and the horse reared back, throwing the general off his mount and onto three of the men standing rank behind him. There was perhaps a two-second pause of confusion as the men looked around unsure of what to do with their leader indisposed of, and it was all the time Dixon needed to turn tail and run. He was past honor, he was past pride, he was past battlefield formalities. Self-preservation was the only thing that mattered now. He'd just bought his men a distraction, it was up to them if they had the wits to use it.

He heard his men fire off a volley before the Union men could fire off their own, and then the whole world simply exploded around Dixon as he ran through the empty store, diving out the back door and into the tree line, wood planks and windows shattering around him. He dared a look back as he began to throw himself into the trees, and saw that some of his men had the sense to retreat as well, though the ones he did see running were cut down, doing a little dancing jig with the impact of federal lead before falling to the ground.

Dixon turned, his head pounding, his vision throbbing gray with each heartbeat as he stared toward the summit of the mountain. He knew there was evil in these woods, knew something unexplainable and terrible lurked somewhere in this sylvan desolation, but he would rather take his chance with those things than face being drawn and quartered alive with Yankees cheering on his death and pissing on whatever gristle of his remained.

The hillside seemed to go on forever, the trees presenting a wooded maze that made his ascent all the more confusing and frustrating. Branches exploded and trees shook as men took aim at him, and he began to laugh at their potshots, a whole division of the army's finest bearing down on him, and they couldn't even—

He cried out then as something punched into his right calf. A hot, breathtaking wave of pain surged up his right leg as it collapsed under him, and for a horrifying moment he felt himself begin to roll back down the hill, back toward those bloodthirsty men in their clean uniforms and army issued guns. He flailed his arms out, grasping for anything to stop his descent, and found himself rolling right into a big stinking body.

"Colonel!" It was Arthur, who saw the colonel had been shot and was apparently more concerned about that then the barrage of bullets slamming into the hillside around them.

"Go on son, leave me!" Dixon croaked, though he knew in his heart none of them would do such a thing. Arthur looked at him for a split second, and he could tell the big bastard was deliberating as hard as his mildly inbred hillbilly mind could, briefly ignoring the chaos around them and looking right into the colonel's eyes. Then he vehemently shook his head as he stooped down toward the colonel. A brief swell of emotions welled up in the colonel's mind as he bore witness to the flagrant display of unquestioning loyalty. Then pain usurped the warm flair of paternal bonding he felt and agony became everything. He cried out, a high-pitched, undignified sound as Arthur picked him up and slung him over his shoulder. Dixon couldn't stop the hot geyser coming up out of his throat then, and he vomited all over the back of Arthur's mud-spattered uniform. The big man paid him no mind as he hurled them both up the mountain, the very earth seeming to come apart around them.

"Into the caves!" someone shouted, and when Dixon looked up, his vision blurred from tears of pain, he saw a few brown blobs making their way up the hill toward him.

Then Dixon was being swallowed by the mountain, rock walls closing around him as Arthur took one of the many bottleneck cave entrances honeycombed into the hillside. Before he could begin to marvel at this blessing of escape, he heard a grunt as Arthur slipped, Dixon could hear the soles of his boots sliding on the slick rock, and then they were half sliding, half tumbling down a steep stone throat . Dixon was flung about, his shot leg flailing like a half-cooked piece of pasta, and he was still sliding down that stone chute when he passed out, his brain simply shutting down from the pain, his last thought was wondering if there was ever a bottom to the goddamn thing.

CHAPTER 13

He awoke to an assortment of so many different aches and pains they all bled into one big throbbing full body pulse of agony that stole the words from his throat and turned them into gasping moans. It was dark around him, and he had to wonder if he was dead. He groaned, it was a pitiful sound, and the groan turned into a retch. But he tossed up the last of his stomach onto Lieutenant Lacroix's back, and so he simply dry heaved and spasmed, bile and drool coating his beard. The violent stomach contractions amplified that full-body throb and he prayed they would stop. He let his head, which felt like it'd taken the brunt of a howitzer shell, fall back against hard, cold stone, and when he let his eyes crawl up, he saw a narrow shaft of light coming down, realizing that was where he'd fallen from. He could hear shouts in the distance, the odd gunshot here and there.

"A . . . Arthur . . ." he called out, his voice cracking and squeaking. Water, he needed water something fierce, and about six spoonfuls of opium tincture. And a whole jar of that sweet, sweet moonshine.

"Yessir?" Arthur breathed, his breath ragged.

"Are we alive?" Dixon asked. It was a stupid question, but it was the only thing he could think of.

"I . . . I think so, sir," Arthur said. He sounded like the most tired man on earth.

"How bad off are you, son?"

"Ankle is busted up real good. I can hobble I reckon," Arthur replied, though by the sound of his voice, Dixon guessed that was the last thing that big galoot wanted to do.

They heard more gunshots, but they were closer, and reverberated strangely, the sound wave carrying in front of Dixon instead of above him. Then he heard scrabbling footsteps, the swish of feet against bare rock echoing up toward them. Dixon tried to reach for his pistols and discovered he was without a weapon. Like he could see to shoot anyway.

"You got a weapon, Lieutenant?" Dixon asked. As if to answer his question, he heard Arthur loading his musket. Christ, he'd have to give the big bastard a double promotion if they ever made it out of this alive.

"Whose there?" Arthur called out, his voice reverberating into a dissonant whine that widened the fissures forming in Dixon's skull. He looked through squinted eyes and thought he saw the wavering orb of a torch in the far distance, coming toward them.

"It's me!"a voice called out, but the cavern played hell on acoustics, the voice was warbling, echoing, unidentifiable.

"*Who?*" Arthur barked. When the torchbearer didn't respond, Arthur fired off a shot, the musket boomed in the small cavern and Dixon was sure his skull split open thoroughly now as his ears rang. He half expected to feel brains pouring out onto his chest, hoped they would, *anything* to relieve the tightening vice on his skull. He heard the Minié-ball whine off stone and slam into rock some ways down.

"It's me, you big dumb sumbitch!" Closer now, they heard the distinct whine of Daryl's voice.

"Duh . . . Daryl? That really you?" Arthur called out, as if he couldn't believe it. Dixon couldn't either. Not even the devil himself could keep these two big jug-eared brothers separated apparently.

"No, it's the holy ghost, coming to claim your dumbass. We gotta go Arthur, they're burnin' the mountain!"

"They're *what?*" Dixon called out, those words cutting through the fog of agony.

"Colonel?" Daryl said as he came upon them. Dixon looked around in the torch light, saw they were in some vast stone atrium, with two large passageways cattycorner to each other, Daryl having come out of the leftmost one.

"Crazy bastards are gonna set the whole mountain afire to burn us out! We gotta go deeper. We stay here the smoke's gonna get us," Daryl said. Dixon looked up, and already he could see whisps of smoke coming in through the small shaft above him, swirling in the weak draft that blew through the cave. *Christ almighty, they're like ticks on a horse's ass,* Dixon thought miserably. Daryl lowered the torch to Dixon, looked him up and down as if appraising a long dead animal. Dixon got a good look at his leg for the first time since falling down here, and what he saw made him want to vomit all over again. The shin bone was completely shattered, the once muscular and straight limb now had a canted, limp quality.

"Sir, you look like a dog turd baked in a coal fire, if I'm to speak frankly," Daryl said with some concern. "I thought they gunned you down back there."

"Nope. God or the devil or whoever runs this god-forsaken shit show has decided I must live on a bit longer, my suffering is not yet exquisite enough," he grunted as he shoved himself against a rock wall, trying to get up into a sitting position. Death did not sound so bad right about now, but he refused to let it be by union hands. He would live on out of sheer spite of those blue bastards. Let the abominations from the wood take him, he would rather find out what their purpose was than die by those self-righteous inquisitors.

"Can you walk, brother?" Daryl asked. Arthur shrugged.

"I can hobble," he replied. Daryl sighed and knelt down to tenderly scoop the colonel up. Despite his care, the minor jostling of the colonel's leg sent thunderbolts of pain radiating through his body, bright stars flashed across his eyes.

"We gotta take care of his leg 'fore we head out, he'll bleed—"

"We'll die of smoke before we get done jury-riggin' a splint for him. Let's get deeper and then we'll see what we can do. You're a tough sumbitch, ain't you, Colonel? You got that Dixie luck. It's in your name," Daryl cut his brother off as he began to head down the rightmost passageway, torch in one hand, Dixon over his shoulder. He saw Arthur using his musket as a crutch as he began to hobble to keep up, his face pulled tight with pain.

God bless these big dumb ox's, Dixon thought as he let himself be carried deeper into the mountain, starting to feel like the world's largest infant.

"What about them . . . them things?" Arthur huffed as he struggled to keep up, the passageway narrowing and chicaning left and right, the sense they were descending into the bowels of some great earthen leviathan overwhelming.

"What about 'em?" Daryl breathed as he did his best to walk at the best speed without jostling the colonel too much.

"What if they're down here?" Authur asked.

Daryl stopped and whirled around. Dixon's head came within inches of glancing off the stone wall.

"You wanna take our chances with a horde of pissed off Yankees, you be my goddamn guest. I don't know what them things was or where they came from. All I know is if we don't move it them sumbitches are gonna have smoked secesh butt on the menu tonight. Now shut up and move your ass!" Daryl barked.

CHAPTER 14

The torch was now only a sputtering, weak little thing that barely cast a light. They'd been walking for some thirty minutes, the tunnel they followed began to slope deeply, and the brothers had to slow to a near crawl to avoid slipping on the slick stone floor. Daryl abruptly stopped as they came to a junction of sorts.

"I see light down yonder," Daryl whispered. Dixon couldn't see, his view had been of Daryl's muddy ass and the back of his shoes for some time. The pain had dulled to a pulsing ebb, and he was aware he couldn't feel his right foot at all. He knew this was a bad sign, but he was thankful all the same for the brief respite from agony.

"Who is it?" Authur asked.

"I don't know dummy, why don't you go ask— Oh shit, they're coming this way," Daryl said. "Get that gun on him, brother!"

"It ain't loaded! Hold on!" Authur said, his voice high with panic as he attempted to load the musket in the tight, dark quarters. Dixon squeezed his eyes shut as he could hear the poor fool fumbling blindly with his gear.

"Hey, you down there! Secesh or Yankee?" Daryl called out, his words carried from his mouth like a physical, deformed thing as the narrow walls distorted his voice.

"Wh . . . What are you?" the voice called back, high-pitched and timid. Despite the aural aberration, Dixon thought the voice sounded familiar.

"I asked first, boy!" Daryl cried out.

"Oh, for crying out loud, we're *rebels*!" Dixon barked, all this shouting was playing hell on his head.

"Oh, thank Jesus," the voice said. Dixon could see Daryl's shadow backlit by a strong light source. Soon the voice's owner was upon them.

"Name and rank!" Dixon commanded, though he felt to be in no position of commanding anyone at the moment.

"Private Brian Ellison, sir!" the voice called out. Dixon blinked. *One of the first ones who saw them.*

"Turn me around, Lieutenant," Dixon said, trying to sound like a colonel, and not a scared, tired old man being carried like an invalid. With some cajoling and a few stifled grunts of pain from Dixon, Daryl unslung the colonel and held him in his arms like Dixon was his newly wedded wife. He saw Private Ellison was holding the shattered stock of a rifle, its end wrapped in burning cloth, a makeshift torch.

"You break your own gun to make that torch?" Dixon asked, genuinely perplexed.

"No sir . . . There's uhm . . . There's bodies in these caves. Lots of them. Some of them had weapons. Gunked up, couldn't fire, but at least the wood stocks were good for somethin'," he said, holding the torch out.

"Federal or secesh?" Dixon asked. Ellison swallowed.

"Both, sir. Some were pretty far gone, some were fresh. Think some were the men who got took last night," Ellison said, his voice tight now.

"I see . . ." Dixon said. Sweat dripped into his eyes, and he wiped it away. It was growing steadily hotter down here. He supposed that mountain was burning something fierce for the heat to come all the way down here. He'd also found he was struggling to breathe, and didn't know if that was from his injuries or the fire burning up the breathable air. In the silence, he could hear the whistling wheeze from Daryl and knew it was probably the latter.

"What should we do, Colonel?" Daryl asked. "I can tell the whole mountain is burning. Feels like I'm breathing air thicker than my mama's chili."

Dixon knew they had no other option but to go deeper. He figured they'd been just ahead of the super-heated vacuum that was probably spreading its way down these many chutes and tunnels. He hoped if they went deep enough, they could escape the worst of the conflagration's effects, but Ellison's macabre report made him wary of venturing deeper. He remembered the speed in which those things moved. The hypnotic glare from that angelic abomination. *Damned if you do, damned if you don't.* A thin smile spread across his lips, it wavered at the corners of his mouth, an unstable thing.

"Colonel?" Ellison asked.

"We go deeper. That way," he said, pointing down the junction toward the tunnel to their left. He had no idea where they were going, he was simply going with his gut. "We come across any bodies, we take what we can off them. I don't care if it's unchristian. We're beyond that point."

No one argued with that.

CHAPTER 15

The smell of rot hit them swiftly and suddenly. They'd been walking for some fifteen minutes when the noxious odor came, it reminded Dixon of killing fields and meat wagons.

"Christ, more of them," Private Ellison said. He'd been leading the way, his torch burning down to within a foot of his hand. They stopped for a second and looked at the two men, who appeared to have died holding each other. Judging by the state of their bodies, the yellow crepe paper skin and withered fingers, which one of the union boys had grasped around a Spencer repeater, they were at least four months old. A glob of dead maggots had found a home inside the skull of the one who'd been eating the barrel of the rifle. They'd spilled out as Daryl pushed the body over to get to the one beside it, and the bodies moved stiffly as he did so. They had a dried out look to them, not the bloated, gray rot Dixon had seen on the battlefield.

"Jesus," Arthur marveled as Ellison and Daryl made quick, shameful work of looting the bodies.

"Gun's got a few cartridges left in it, no idea if they're good though," Daryl said. They found moldy, ant-infested hardtack in one pocket, shells for the rifle in another. As they looted, Dixon looked toward the wall the gun-eater had been propped up against. He could see the chipped striations in the rock where the bullet ricocheted, but no dried brains or blood stuck to the rock, which was odd, a wound like that ought to make a hell of a mess. It was as if something had come through and licked the walls clean, and sucked the bodies dry.

"Matches," Ellison said gratefully as he extricated the booklet from a breast pocket. "Looks like this guy shot his partner and then himself."

"You gotta be real desperate to do that. Whatever they were facing was worse than death," Arthur said, the quaver in his voice making his words all the more terrible. No one commented on this stark observation.

"Take their jackets. We can burn 'em," Dixon said, knowing that having light down here was imperative to their survival. The thought of being stuck down here in the pitch black, like the black of that store they'd been holed up in, made a cold chill pass through him. Despite not having a drop of liquor today, the colonel was beginning to feel lightheaded and a bit drowsy, and he noticed the other men were no longer pouring sweat, yet it still rolled off him in wet waves. "It hot down here to anyone else?" he asked. His voice was a barely audible rasp now, and he prayed for water, half considered sucking the droplets that beaded off the cave walls.

"No, sir, in fact it feels a might agreeable down here, nice and cool," Arthur said. "I think you're taken to fever, sir."

The other two men turn and looked at him. Their expressions spoke the words no one wanted to say out loud.

"Just get it done," Dixon croaked.

The men were in the middle of wrestling the jackets off the wood-stiff bodies when Arthur spun around.

"Y'all hear that?" he asked. The other three men paused and listened. Dixon could barely hear over the dull roar of blood in his ears, but thought maybe he heard something, a slight shuffling sound. Arthur pointed toward the direction they'd come from, and Dixon squinted. His vision blurred with each thud of his slow heartbeat, but through this, and the dimming light from the private's smoldering torch, he could see a shifting mass of pale flesh coming toward them. Two glinting orbs caught the faintest illumination of the torch light. The eyes of an animal.

"Get that Spencer on him," Dixon said, his vision now blurring steadily as his pulse picked up. Christ, how he wished he'd had a weapon, almost as much as he wished for water. He hated feeling helpless, useless, staring this unknown threat down while he was as intimidating as a field mouse.

"Whose there?" Daryl called out. The shuffling thing, which was low to the ground and moved quick, paused, then let out a laugh.

"I can't stop what I've become, sir. I'm sorry," it said. It had a familiar southern lilt to the voice. It sounded human, but also insane. It came forward, and Dixon felt ice frost his spine despite the febrile heat radiating through his body.

Dixon jumped as it sounded like a bullwhip snapped right next to his ear. There was a brilliant explosion of light, just a blink, and in the barrel's flash, Dixon saw a man pale as a crappie's belly, hugging the floors on all four's in a most unnatural manner. He saw its mouth, wreathed in that coal black beard he knew so well, open. Dixon knew he was surely in the grip of a fever delirium now because the teeth he saw peeling out behind the gray worms of Robertson's lips did not belong in the realm of reality.

And then his skull was exploding in a black mist. Then everything was a disorienting negative of itself, before smearing into a dark blur. Dixon blinked rapidly trying to blink the messy after images away, and in those strobing fractals he thought he saw another shape scrabble up from behind the former Major that Ellison had shot.

"Did I get him?" Ellison gasped, his voice sounded thin and far away.

"I think—" Daryl began to say when something leapt out from that coal black void beyond the torch light, something white and glistening and hissing. Dixon, who'd been sitting off to the side of the group, was closest to it, and he'd tried to scrabble back, but his limbs each felt a thousand pounds each, the space they moved through thick like molasses, making him slow and sluggish. Then it was falling upon him, a head flashing down, teeth grinding against bone as it went straight for the wound on his leg.

The minute that hot tongue probed his exposed wound, Dixon's vision lit up with bursting black blossoms, the invisible hands back to squeeze the air from his lungs in a rasping exhalation, the pain so instant and breathtaking he couldn't even let out a crackling, pitchy scream.

"Run!" Ellison cried out.

"Ain't leavin' the colonel!" Daryl said. Somewhere in another universe entirely, Dixon felt hands seize him, felt himself being pulled through time and space. In a slow, strobing pattern of images, he saw Ellison's smoldering snub of torch hit the thing in the head. Saw the thing turn its face, and Dixon thought he might've seen that face before, one of the stragglers from the division, made monstrous. It opened its mouth in a snarl and Dixon saw bits of his own flesh caught in the thing's gums, his leg hair poking out almost comically in some spots.

Then it went back to its task, its teeth crunching through the last splinters of gristle and bone that had kept his calf tethered to his body. Dixon prayed he would pass out as he felt pulsing waves of searing hot pain shoot up his leg and into his body like acid. He tried to strike at the thing, finding anything nearby to club it with.

"SHOOT IT! SHOOT THE GODDAMN—"

"Sorry, Colonel, can't carry ya no more!" Daryl yelled as he began to pull Dixon away from the thing, who held fast to his leg. There was a ripping sound, like wet curtains being torn, and in that moment, Tobias Dixon felt the profound disconnect as his body was unburdened by that flinging mass of dead, stinging weight.

"Watch out! Drop—" Ellison was saying before his words turned into a yell. Dixon was sliding along the rocks, a few exposed nerve endings trailing from his stump catching on the stone floor as Daryl yanked him away from the thing.

"Ah, shit!" Daryl hissed and then the speed in which Dixon was hurled through space increased, his sundered leg leaving behind sparks of agony he could see with his eyes as he was sure this was his final descent into Hell. He was falling, yet again, and like before, he found himself losing consciousness before the impact.

CHAPTER 16

Tobias did not know how much time had passed before he finally came to his senses. He came too once, in total darkness, the sounds of groaning coming to him from the cobalt ether. He had enough mental wherewithal to form the idea that he had finally fallen from that great cliff in his mind, the huge outcropping that represented his sanity, and how falling into that unending void meant he'd finally lost his mind.

He assumed he was dead, and that this was it.

Blackness, a faint sense of throbbing pain. This was his forever, this was his afterlife. He acquiesced to this, then allowed himself to fall deeper into the void, finding solace in that painless abyss, going completely under this time.

When Dixon next awoke, it was to searing hot pain, to the sweaty face of Daryl holding him down, telling him it must be done. The sound of meat sizzling. And god, how *good* it smelled. Hunger and agony assailed him in equal measure, a strange sensation that made his mind reel as he realized the pain source was from his leg once more. He could see flames dancing on the walls, and they painted Daryl's visage in a ghastly light. In it, Dixon thought he saw a skeleton version of the man, his cheeks were gaunt, eyes sunken in deep like the sockets were too big for his head, his already prominent caveman brow exaggerated to an almost satirical depiction of the Cro-Magnon. Then more white-hot pain as someone was doing something to him he couldn't see. His leg was the entire world and that world was on fire, burning with the flames of hell itself. Then more darkness as his nerve endings simply erupted enough for him to pass out once more.

The third time Tobias Dixon came awake, he looked around, confused. His surroundings were tinged a dull orange. He realized he was looking at the glowing coals of a fire. He tried to move, but he felt weak, he felt hollow, he felt like a dead thing reanimated. Then there was the smell. As soon as his brain registered it, his mouth flooded with saliva, his stomach groaned like a dying animal. Tobias felt something was missing from this picture, and he soon realized through the hunger pangs that he was no longer in pain. He was sore, yes, and his right leg had a strange numbness to it, but the constant aching throb that consumed every nerve ending in his body was absent.

Now there was only a marrow-deep hunger, a ravenous feeling so intense he feared he would start chewing on damn near anything that was within his reach. It was if all those months of malnutrition and replacing food with booze had caught up to him, and his stomach demanded its debt be paid, with interest.

"Huh— " he tried to say and then coughed, a deep, phlegmy rattle, before he continued, "Hello?" he called out. The stone vault he was in made his voice distant and monstrous. He heard stirring off to his left. He slowly swiveled his head and saw a man stirring in the shadows. "Whose there?"

"Colonel?" It was Daryl, Dixon could tell from the voice and the beard as he stirred near the fire. He quickly blew on the coals, feeding them and causing them to flare up into small embers as he turned to face Dixon. "Christ, you're still alive. Thought you'd died. Really do got that Dixie luck, don't ya?" he said with an unhinged giggle.

"Where are we, Daryl?" Dixon asked, he saw there were skewers over the fire, odd white sticks, the ends of which held fat lumps of some unidentifiable meat, brown and glistening, dripping fat onto the flames, causing the fire to jump and sizzle with each drop. Tobias Dixon had never wanted anything worse in his life than one of those skewers of mystery meat.

"We're in Hell, Colonel," Daryl said as a matter of fact, the words spoken with a blunted affectation, as if he were in a trance. He saw the colonel eyeing the meat. "You hungry?" he asked.

"Gods yes. I could eat a whole horse," he said as Daryl carefully removed one of the skewers, the bare end of which had been wedged into two fist sized rocks. Dixon tried to reach a hand out but the skeletal appendage wavered and then dropped to his side. It was as if every muscle in his body had atrophied. Daryl understood and went over to him, holding the meat out for Dixon to eat.

He didn't even care that the oily juices burned his lips and tongue as he bit into the scalding hot meat. He ripped with his teeth, chewed, savoring the juices that burst between his molars as he tore the tender meat apart, swallowed, ripped some more. The meat was succulent, fall off the bone tender, the flavor rich and robust but also mildly sweet, like an angus who'd been fed a diet of wine and sugar cane weeks before slaughter. It was ambrosia. It was the best thing Tobias Dixon had ever tasted.

"Easy now, easy," Daryl said, pulling the drumstick away, Dixon managing to tear away a few more gristly strands before it was out of reach. "Been a week since you had somethin' solid. Gonna sic it all up if you don't take it easy."

Dixon made contented moaning noises as he ate, unable to stop himself as he felt the warm meat slide down his throat and into his belly, so enrapt was he in the act of mastication he at first didn't hear Daryl's words, didn't register the words *a week*.

Immediately, he felt a small spark of energy come into him, as if his body were so starved it was instantly using whatever he could swallow. A powerful cramp seized him, and he clenched his teeth together and gripped Daryl's leg as a ripping pain shot through his gut.

"Breathe deep, Colonel. Please don't throw him up. I don't think I could handle that," Daryl said, his voice was strangely flat, distant. Dixon groaned, felt a wave of nausea wash over him. He used the very last shred of his willpower to swallow his gorge and keep it down. In a minute or two, the pain passed, and the hunger was back. He reached out feebly for the meat once more, and Daryl, a pained smile on his face, offered it to him. "Eat slow now," he said.

Dixon did, taking small bites, relishing the greasy juices that exploded from the meat, the experience so sensually visceral it was almost akin to sexual congress. Even the slowest cooked and painstakingly prepared meal his wife ever cooked paled in comparison to the robust flavor and silken texture that flooded his mouth.

Please don't throw him up, I don't think I could handle that.

Dixon paused momentarily to reflect on that peculiar statement, but only briefly, his mind still too tied up in the act of consuming to really think at all.

Finally, Dixon felt a heavy, warm stone form in his stomach and he pushed the meat away. Daryl took a bite, then another, tears flowing down his face as he ate.

Dixon was about to ask him what was wrong, where he'd gotten that delicious meat from, when there was a sound from above him. A split second later he saw pieces of wood being dropped from the heavens, landing beside the fire. The colonel looked up, and saw that the small fire just barely illuminated the roof of the pit they were in, and at the very top was a circular opening slightly larger than the circumference of a wagon wheel. From this circular porthole a face looked down at him. The face was heavily bearded, long black hair falling into the hole.

The expression on this being's visage was one of such pure malice and unadulterated pleasure that Dixon couldn't speak for a second. The thing was grinning madly, its features twisted with pure joy as it watched Daryl eating away at the mostly diminished drumstick. Daryl looked up at the face then. The furry creature nodded in encouragement.

Daryl began to sob as he ate.

"What . . ." Dixon began when he saw his stump, where his leg ended in a mash of red cloth just below the knee. Whatever he was going to say died in his mouth as he stared long and hard at where his foot and shin should've been. A questing hot tongue, teeth scraping against bone. It seemed every time he'd woken up in the last week or so it was to more terrible circumstances than when he'd been awake last. Daryl set the drumstick aside, spitting out the meat like it was a glob of chaw and not the ambrosial sustenance that Dixon was still sucking from his gums and between his teeth.

"Go on, sheep. Eat it. Eat him up!" the voice cackled from above. The speaker had a low, bassoon voice, Dixon could feel it in his chest as he spoke. He noted also that this demonic gargoyle who could speak like a human had a distinctly German accent. He looked at Daryl, who stared at his meal, his primitive and rawboned face screwed up in a rictus of anguish. Tears and snot and juices from the meat glistened in his beard. It was a rough sight, but not nearly as horrifying as what peered at them from above.

"Where are the others?" Dixon asked, looking around. There was a vague lump in the corner of the cavern, just outside the glow of the fire, Dixon thought it looked like someone bundled up in a blanket, sleeping.

"Lord have mercy on my soul," Daryl said in reply, dropping the meat on the stone floor. "He made me do it. He told me to. You goddamn devil! *You made me!*" Daryl shouted up at the thing above.

"Lieutenant, where are the other men?" Dixon commanded. He found his voice no longer had that squeaky raw edge to it. Why was Daryl in such distress? It seemed whatever this thing was, for whatever odd and twisted reason, was keeping them alive, was—

"Tell him, *Lieutenant*," the thing spoke, spitting out the man's rank with sadistic sarcasm. "Tell him where the men went." He laughed. Dixon thought he'd heard Union artillery barrages that sounded more pleasant than that cackle.

"I was just . . . I was just so hungry. I was—" Daryl began and now his cries were unrestrained. It was a terrible and heartbreaking sound, seeing such a mountain of a man reduced to this.

"He was delicious though, wasn't he?" the thing cackled on like some terrible hellish loon. "Did you not eat him down to the bone, suck the rich marrow out from within?"

Please don't throw him up. I don't think I can handle that.

"Oh . . . my god . . ." Dixon breathed as the epiphany slammed into him with the force of a full charge cannon blast. Suddenly that comforting fullness in his belly roiled like a ball of snakes. "Oh, my Jesus Christ," he groaned, and slumped against the wall he was propped up on. He caught sight of the thing leering down at him, but it was no longer really looking at the two doomed men. Its eyes rolled up deep in its sockets, the corners of his sadistic grin twitched and Dixon thought he heard the thing letting out a shaky moan, the sound of imminent orgasm, of unworldly pleasure.

"Yes . . . The meat of your brother . . . Simmering in your bowels. I'm sure he would've been honored to be shat out by—"

"SHUT UP!" Daryl roared. Dixon saw him take one of the pieces of wood and hurl it up at the monster. But the portal he viewed through was small and the abominable thing had lightning quick reflexes. The wood bounced unseen off the rocks and fell on the other side of the cavern. Daryl let out a terrible cry and threw the other piece of wood just for good measure.

By then Dixon was already vomiting, but he only got out one thick pink geyser before he felt an invisible vice close around this throat. He felt some of the vomit be redirected up his nasal cavities as he began to choke, his sinuses burning with stomach acid and clogged with half-digested human flesh.

"Oh no, we don't want to waste Mr. Lacroix do we?" that clipped Germanic voice sounded from right beside him. Dixon turned his head as his hands went to his throat, saw the thing had somehow magically appeared right beside him, a hand out but not touching him. "Swallow. Do it *now*."

Dixon tried to shake his head no, felt his stomach convulsing more and was terrified his gullet would explode as the rising tide of his meal would have nowhere to go. The invisible grip only tightened at his refusal until tears streamed from his face. Convulsively he swallowed the thick, foul bolus of meat in his gullet and did his best to fight back the intense waves of revolting nausea before him, threatening to send what he'd just swallowed right back up. He kept thinking of Authur, that timid man who was always in the shadow of his brother despite being the same size, willing to do anything for the colonel to obtain promotion.

Arthur was *in* him now. Arthur simmered in his guts, slowly being broken down, his body taking nourishment from his fellow brother in arms. Soon the second lieutenant would be a runny pile of shit, he'd—

"Good," the abominable thing said as he closed his fist, and the unseen pressure was gone from Dixon's trachea. He lay on his side, gasping and holding his stomach. "They can't have you the way you are now. Nothing but bones, and so anemic that your blood is as watery as the ale they serve in this blasted land. No. You must feast. You must ripen, for *her*. But in the meantime, I shall have my fill. Now—"

Daryl was charging at the man, who was almost as tall as the lieutenant and just as wide and thick shouldered. In a blur of motion, the thing sidestepped his tackle, and Daryl went crashing into the stone wall with heavy thud.

"BASTARD!" Daryl roared as he pushed himself up. The long-haired demon put out his hand again, almost like in a salute, and a strained grunt locked up in Daryl's throat, freezing him to the spot, his body stuck in an awkward mid-stride position.

"Oh, how I hope they can be patient, let you all eat your fill. This has been so *nourishing*," the thing said. Dixon saw the terrible phallic thing that exploded from a nest of black hair at its center was huge and erect. It throbbed with wanton need as the thing glared between Dixon and Lacroix, as if their very suffering were titillating him. A most potent aphrodisiac.

"What . . . What the hell are you?" Dixon asked. The being turned to him, his eyes catching the small campfire full on.

"I am what your kind deserves," he said, boring his terrible gaze into Dixon as he hissed it. And then he was gone, leaping from the ground into the rock opening some fifteen feet above.

"Oh, how rude of me," he said from up above, and tossed a cloth covered object toward Dixon. He caught it, nearly dropping the heavy package as he reached out to catch it. "Drink up. We can't have our guests going thirsty. Plus it flavors the blood quite nicely, I'm told," the thing said, and then was gone.

Dixon pulled away the cloth sack. He saw the jar, it was three quarters full of clear liquid. He unscrewed the lid, and he couldn't stop the pained smile skinning his lips from his teeth as he drank deep. The shine burned down to his marrow. Never in his life did he so wish to find un-life, to find utter oblivion.

"Cuh . . . Cuh . . . Colonel . . ." Daryl squeaked. Dixon looked at him, saw he was still frozen in mid stride, like one of those street performers he'd seen in Saint Louis prior to the war, mimes he thought they were called. Dixon did not have the energy to get up, to assist his poor comrade. He could only stare.

"I'm sorry. I'm sorry I got us into this. I'm . . . so sorry," he repeated, and began to sob between gulps.

Soon the drunk was upon him, that blessed numbing warmth blunting the edges of his despair as he laid there, sure he was dead now. Daryl was right. They were in Hell.

He stared at the cast aside drumstick, it's charred and browned edges glistening in the fire light.

And God help him.

He started to salivate.

ACT III: THE SORCERER

November 19ᵗʰ, 1865—Saint Louis, Missouri

CHAPTER 1

The man stared up at the tavern sign. THE FLATHEAD INN it said in easy-to-read lettering, so bold not even a drunk could miss it, which he supposed was the point. Next to it was a garishly drawn depiction of a catfish with long curling whiskers, a mottled green complexion and a smile on its fishy lips, a mug of ale held jauntily in one fin. Next to the door was a handwritten broad sheet exclaiming WAR'S OVER, NO GRAY OR BLUE COATS ON PREMISES. FIGHTING WILL NOT BE TOLERATED!

Gunther held the door open for him. He looked back and saw that across the street were docks that bordered the brown swollen vein of the Mississippi River, saw the great paddle boats he knew he would soon be boarding as they began the next leg of their journey. He gave the boy a curt nod as he entered the establishment.

The tavern was deserted save for two men in a corner sipping large mugs of beer and keeping to themselves. He spotted the barkeep behind the counter, a skinny whip of a woman whose blond hair was tied back in a bun. She looked up at the two patrons as they entered, and her thin brows raised slightly at them. He was not surprised.

Even in a city such as this with its eclectic populace, his appearance tended to warrant second glances and hidden grimaces of pity.

"What'll it be?" she asked as the two ambled up to the empty bar. Though he wasn't here for a drink, he perused the selection before him anyway, curious to try the 'bourbon' he'd heard so much about back home. He pointed to the bottle labelled Buffalo Trace. "That's top shelf mister, you sure you don't want somethin—"

He placed five dollars on the oak counter, slid it toward her.

"A finger for me and for my partner here," he said, his thick accent dicing the words into sharp, staccato syllables, nodding toward Gunther.

"Herr Schmidt, thank you, but I don't—"

"You will," he said, and that was the end of the discussion.

The woman took the money and began to slide back a bill, but he put out a gnarled hand, indicating it was hers.

"Keep it. I'm paying for more than just liquor here," he said with a grin.

The blonde-haired woman eyed him closely as she poured the bourbon.

"I don't kin what you mean by that, sir, but if you're looking for a good time you ought head down to Little Missies. They got whores over yonder. I'm just a barkeep," she said as she slid the tumblers across to each of them.

"Oh no that's . . . not what I meant," he said with a crooked smile, the only kind his face would allow. He sniffed the brown liquid, it had a sharp but pleasant aroma, smokey and bold. He looked up at the space where the bottle of Buffalo Trace had been, looking at himself in the gap, where behind the bottles of liquor and spirits was a mirrored backwall, where drunken fools could stare at their own visages in reflection as they poisoned themselves.

"I don't do riddles, dutchman. Why'd you give me this money? You intend on drinking that whole bottle?" she asked, her guard up now.

He took a moment to reply. He quaffed the bourbon, letting it pool and slide around his mouth so as to get the full flavor of this revered spirit. His golden hair was tied back in a horse tail similar to the barkeep, except the sides of his head were shaven, revealing the mottled pink flesh on the left side of his face, the knub of cartilage poking out of it that was once an ear. He knew if he didn't keep it shorn in that bold Native-American style cut, his hairline would be embarrassingly lopsided.

His right eye watered up as he swallowed the drink, it burned much more than the sweet fruity schnapps the taverns back home served. He dabbed at it with a handkerchief, the single azure colored iris fixing the woman with an unreadable gaze as he dabbed at his left eye as well, though the milky orb's tear ducts had long been cauterized shut. Reflex, all that was. He took another long drink, finishing his glass and then producing the handkerchief once more to dab at the left corner of his mouth, which always dribbled a little due to the nerve damage there, the corner of his mouth on that side always a gape ever so slightly.

"I will take another drink, yes, but that shall be my last one. How about you, Gunther?" he asked the diminutive young man at his side. Like him, Gunther was blonde and blue eyed, giving away their Dutch lineage, but that was where the similarities ended. Gunther shook his head, the downy peach fuzz on his cheeks standing out as small blossoms reddened the cherubic features of his face. He let out a cough and slid the bourbon toward his mentor. "Never mind, I'll just have the boy's drink," he said with an apologetic smile.

"Would your name happen to be Ruthe Kirchdorfer?" Gunther asked after clearing his throat, cutting to the point as they saw the woman was growing impatient with their enigmatic demeanor. At hearing her name, she blinked, straightened up.

"Whose askin? You all with the bank? Cause I told them——"

"No, no, nothing like that," the man interjected. He put out a hand, a long pale pink line of scar tissue crawled across the back of it. "Adler Schmidt, and this is my protégé, Gunther Schwartz," he said with a nod.

Ruthe only stared at the outstretched hand, her eyes, blue like the dutchmen but a shade darker, flitted between them, uneasiness pulling her features taught. Adler withdrew his hand when it was obvious the woman wouldn't take it. He was told Americans loved shaking hands, that they'd shake hands with a wild bear if you'd let them, and that it was considered rude not to offer. Oh well, he tried.

"What is it you want with me? How do you know my name?" she asked. Adler turned to Gunther, cleared his throat. An unspoken signal was given, and Gunther promptly got up from the bar and headed over to where the two patrons sat, they hadn't made a single effort to conceal their stares since the two had walked in. Gunther produced more currency and held it out to the old men. There was some confused grumbling, but soon the men nodded and got up, finishing their drinks in one long pull before they headed out the door. Gunther took the CLOSED placard that hung on the back of the door and put it out front before shutting it.

"What's this? What're you doing?" Ruthe asked, and reached under the bar, pulling out a flared barrel scattergun. "I ain't—"

"We're here for information, miss, that's all," Adler said, reaching over the bar with stunning quickness, plucking the gun from her hands before she'd even had time to blink. He gently set it on the counter between them, his other hand up in a sign of placation. Gunther came back, saw the gun with alarm.

"I don't know who you think I am, mister, but I ain't—"

"I'm told you're a woman fond of the drink," Adler said as he took up Gunther's glass, sipped. "I would be too if I worked in an establishment that served up such delights," he said, relishing the bold smokiness of the whiskey, smacking his lips and dabbing them once more before continuing. "I'm told when you take to the drink, you speak of fanatical tales. Of things you saw during the war that are odd and macabre of nature. Not just the normal barbarity of war, but . . . other things. Of a certain county in the highlands west of here where strange things roam. Where things that look like men feed upon the blood of other men and act in a barbaric manner. Would you say this is true?" Adler asked, studying the woman carefully as the color slowly bleached from an otherwise beautiful face.

"Who the hell are you? And why do you wanna know about that?" she said as she reached under the bar again. Adler tensed, ready to disarm her once more if she chose to go that route, but eased when he saw her pull out an unmarked bottle filled with clear fluid. To his heightened senses, he could smell the astringent alcohol even from where he was sitting. Strong stuff that must've been. She didn't bother pouring the booze into a glass. She drank straight from the bottle, some of the color returning to her face as she took a healthy gulp.

"Call me curious is all. I'm quite a fan of regional folktales," Adler said.

"This ain't no goddamn folktale, mister. You know what they call me around here? Ravin' Ruthe. Think I'm some kind of stupid hillbilly, some dumb old broad who got slapped around a little too much before she come down out of the hills and into the city." She made to put the bottle away before abruptly changing her mind and taking one more nip before the bottle disappeared. "I ain't gonna tell you about the things that give me nightmares every night just so you can point and laugh," she said.

"I assure you, my dear"—Adler slid the gun across the bar toward her in a sign of camaraderie—"that we will do no such thing."

CHAPTER 2

"Do you think it's him, sir?" Gunther asked as he leaned over the bow of the steamboat. Adler had been silent and brooding since they boarded passage onto the *Bayou Queen*, his blue eye fixing on the pieces of driftwood that floated past them as they made their way south. Adler knew when he was in such a mood, he could unintentionally affect a rather sinister aura. Many of the milling patrons who joined him on the hurricane deck gave him a wide berth as his jarring visage was pulled into a ferocious look of rumination. Despite their hushed whispers he could hear every word they were saying, yet he paid the frightened slights no mind. He was far away, in his home village of Liepzig. There was a face in his mind's eye. A terrible, grinning face looming over him.

Do you like bacon, boy? I think we could make some very fine bacon out of you, that face said, speaking the tongue of his motherland. Then came the glow of the cauterizing iron.

He shivered briefly, a chill wholly independent of the brisk winter breeze blowing in off the river.

"Sir?" Gunther asked.

"It can be no one else. Huge of frame and stature. Raven black hair. German accent. Ungodly strength," he said as he reflected upon the woman's tale.

Ruthe had lived in a small, interconnected sect of villages at the base of what she called a "knob", which Adler later learned was a small mountain. Ruthe's village, Lordell, was the southernmost village in the county. She spoke vividly of the men who came at night, naked as jaybirds and moving with the speed of a mountain lion. She spoke of one man in particular with his raven black hair and piercing eyes. He'd come before the others, an interloper who feigned a crisis, claiming he'd been a refugee of the war and had nowhere to go. Her town had rallied to give him shelter.

And then, later that night, the others came.

She spoke of another man, shorter in stature and slightly pudgy who was particularly more animalistic than the others, who fell upon the screaming townsfolk and fed right there in the street or in the houses. *Like a goddamn starving wolf, that one*, she'd said. The bigger one, who could walk and talk like a man and seemed to be the leader of that feral pack of hominid imps, had stopped every once in a while from his abductions to leer over those who lay dead and dying in the street, seeming to take great pleasure in their agony. First it was just those two, but soon others were among their ranks. They'd done something to the townsfolk, she'd said. They'd dragged them back up the knob, and two mornings later the people she'd known her whole life came back feral and bloodthirsty.

Newly turned? Adler thought to himself as he listened on with mounting dread, thinking initially this was another Liepzig situation.

When Ruthe spoke of the blond woman of unspeakable beauty who'd lured the rest of the frightened men out of their houses like sirens haunting forlorn sailors from their ships, Adler felt the whisky in his stomach burn with a second heat. He could feel the vertebrae in his spine frost over, one by one, as Ruthe told them about the hypnotic powers this beautiful angel possessed. Powers that sounded an awful lot like the Persuasion. *An elder? No . . . Not possible. We killed them all during the last inquisition,* he thought as the woman was deep in the drink at this point, her words sliding and bumping together, her rural dialect coming out thick. Before passing out against the bar, she'd spoke of a squad of union soldiers she'd run into as she made a desperate escape from the village with her son Joseph.

Looked about as sorry as a dead coon in high summer, they did, she'd spoke of the soldiers as she concluded her harrowing story. The woman had run day and night through the hills, having no idea where she was headed, her instinctual compass only telling her to flee away from the mountain the demons had descended from. Eventually, she ended up in Van Buren, a highland township approximately two days ride by horse, to the southeast. But even then, she was not satisfied with the distance put between her and the nightmare she'd escaped from, which was how she ended up here, in a city bigger than her small hill-folk mind could possibly imagine.

Woulda kept going farther, but that river spooks me somethin' fierce. Nothin' that big should move that fast, I can't cross it, I—

That was when the woman had promptly swayed and made to fall. Adler, being who he was and how he was, had leapt over the bar and managed to grab her before she could smack her head against a corner of the serving bar, and gently laid her down in one of the booths in the back of the tavern. They left the CLOSED sign in place as they left, the woman had been invaluable in terms of information, and he wanted to leave her in a respectable manner.

"What?" Adler asked. Gunther had asked him something, but again he'd focused on a lone piece of wood that rushed by with a gentle knocking against the hull. In his mind he was on that poor piece of wood, being thrown into a current whose power far surpassed his own, helpless to the pull that surged him ever downward.

"I said, I would've thought you'd be more excited. All this time searching, and you've finally found him. The one that got away. The final aberration, to be exterminated," Gunther had said.

He could feel the boy's eyes on him, trying to read him. He knew Gunther thought of him as more than just a mentor. The atmosphere of paternal brotherhood was strong in *Die Bestellung*, The Order, as it was known now. Gunther had survived The Reckoning, and any two men who survived The Order's twisted trial had an inherent bond stronger than any blood tie, and yet, Gunther and Adler's relationship had somehow transcended even that. He refused to let the word *son* enter his mind, and yet he knew in his heart, long of age and hardened by his own unique and harrowing existence, that that was what he thought of the young man as.

"Well, that was *before* I had suspicion of an elder at work in the highlands, alongside the aberration that is Adolph Braun. That complicates things exponentially," Adler said as they crossed under a railroad bridge, a train high above thundering across the tracks.

"An elder? Do you really think—"

"Yes," Adler said, and wished he had more of that delicious bourbon, even if he knew he would have to drink several gallons of the stuff before he even felt something akin to a buzz. One of the many human pleasures he'd sacrificed when embarking upon The Reckoning.

"Should we contact The Order?" Gunther asked quietly in their home tongue. Adler grinned, the kind that saw neither side of his mouth curl up.

"No. They're spread thin as it is. We'd have to wait months for another warden to arrive, and we don't have that kind of time. It sounds to me like she, this elder, is building a thrall. If so, we must put a stop to it immediately," Adler said, not adding in that depending on how long the elder had been active in her insidious industry, they might already be embarking upon a suicide mission.

"I see," Gunther said, the slightest waver to his voice.

Adler felt immense guilt then. He was leading the inexperienced boy directly into a viper's nest. He hadn't even faced his first possession, let alone an elder-blood Strigoi.

God help us, he thought, then laughed bitterly at the thought.

Whatever god that let such abominations loose on this world could never be called upon for help. It was one of the first tenets of the order that had been drilled into their minds.

No god or man can help you with the horrors that walk this earth. You stand alone from the rest. You are the last bastion of light in a world inherited by darkness.

CHAPTER 3

The *Bayou Queen* took them all the way down to a small port town named Cape Girardeau. Adler instructed Adolph to hunt down the nearest stable and inquire about routes toward Poplar Springs, one of the townships neighboring Lordell that had also sported reports of vampiric activity. While the boy accomplished that errand, he meandered through the small, predominantly French-rooted town and inquired about a blacksmith. He was eventually directed to MARQUETTE IRONWORKS, whereupon he dazzled the rotund blacksmith who paused in mid-swing of his hammer with a few gold ingots Adler held out in offering.

"You want . . . You want to exchange gold for *silver?* Are you mad, son?" The burly old smith had said, his eyes feasting upon the gold like an island refugee toward an encroaching ship.

"It must be pure silver. No sterling *schiesse,*" Adler insisted.

"Christ, whatever caused *that* must've scrambled your thinkin' pan, but sure, I got silver," the man said, gesturing toward Adler's face before turning to point toward a worktable, upon which he spotted the bars of silver. "Mined it up near the hills in

Eminence. One of the few knobs that ain't run through with galena. Purest you'll see this side of the Mississippi," he boasted.

Adler inspected the bars, taking out a small, magnetized piece of iron which he waved over each bar. Only one of the five ingots stuck to the iron, and this he cast aside.

"Pherromagentic ore in that one, sir. You might want to refine it again," he said as he placed two gold bars on the table and put the four silver pieces in his haversack. Those alone must've weighed forty pounds, but he struggled little as he shouldered his burden. "Good day to you. Might I inquire into the nearest eatery?"

"Uhm . . . You mean restaurant?" the smith asked, still dumbfounded by the exchange that just took place. Adler nodded impatiently. He should've eaten long ago, his ferocious metabolism was already eating away at his muscle fibers, he could tell as he held the silver ingots, which should've felt weightless to him. "I reckon that'd be Dewer's Inn, up the street," the smith said, quickly falling upon the gold bars to inspect their purity as Adler made his way out into the crowded thoroughfare.

He forced himself to hunt down the boy before eating, knowing he too would need to eat soon lest he begin to fall apart from the inside. Another curse of those who've been judged by The Reckoning and saw fit to live. He found the boy, looking distressed and out of sorts as he argued with a heavily mutton-chopped stable master.

"Be gone with you, dutchie. I'll die before I lend another goddamn horse to you abolitionist—"

"There a problem here?" Adler cut off the man's tirade as he loomed over Gunther, spittle flecking the poor boy's cheeks. The stable master, rail thin with permanent gin blossoms evident on the portion of his cheeks not mired in gray fur reeled at the sight of Adler.

"Jesus Christ, and who're you? Look like you got shot at and missed and shit on and hit. You with this boy or something, you ugly sumbitch?" the man said. He was clearly not French, instead having that odd loping hill-folk accent that Ruthe spoke with.

"I am. Did you not offer this man a substantial sum for a wagon, Gunther?" Adler said, thoroughly confused by this man's belligerence. Gunther looked at him, helpless.

"I did, but he thinks—"

"Won't take no goddamn dutchman's money, won't have no German ass cheeks warming the seat of *my* wagon. Bet you were with Zigler, weren't you? Bet you set fires and raped southern women like the rest of them. No sir, I won't do no commerce with a goddamn dutchie, no sir!"

The gears clicked in Adler's mind, and he understood. He'd been so focused on finding Adolph that he'd forgotten the land he'd just entered was fresh out of a civil war. He'd heard of some folks from the motherland coming over for the mining industry and being drafted to fight when the states turned on each other. He supposed this man assigned all folk of German lineage to be that of the enemy.

"What if we bought your horses out right? Double your normal asking price," Adler said. The man was about to unleash another verbal volley when the figures struck his mind and he paused to consider. "I assure you, neither me nor my partner here had no role in your conflict. We are a thoroughly neutral party."

"Double?" the stablemaster said, and considered this. "No, I don't think—"

Adler, who was growing more impatient by the second as his stomach threatened to cannibalize its housing, put a firm hand on the man's shoulder. He hated resorting to this, using his own (albeit weak in comparison) Persuasion made him feel too much like a *strigoi*. *Use every tool at your disposal, regardless of the cost, if it gets you one step closer to vanquishing the abominations.* Tenet number two of The Order.

"Quite a deal, really. You get two dutchman out of your town, your purse grows substantially healthier," Adler cooed, his normal ragged bassoon voice pitched down even lower, to a low growl, one that, despite its low volume, could be felt resonating in the chest of its intended recipient.

The stable master's eyes glazed over, and his face went blank for just a second before he nodded.

"Suppose that'll be a fair shake. Give me my money and take your asses out of here," the stablemaster said in a monotone voice, the voice of a sleepwalker.

Immediately guilt shot through Adler as he deposited twenty dollars in the man's hand. *If you don't eradicate this pest hole with haste, these folks will have a lot more to worry about than parlor tricks of the mind*, he told himself as he and Gunther wordlessly chose two of the hardiest quarter horses from the stable and set up their mounts with haste.

"Come, we must eat," Adler said.

#

Dewer's was a modest inn that featured a specialty of fried gar and catfish and a large assortment of ails and spirits for such a small town. Gunther and Adler quickly drew the stares of the inn's patrons as they eagerly devoured plate after plate of the delicious fish, caught just off the bank here according to the woman who served them. Along with some three pounds of fish each, they also partook in several platefuls of fried Okra, delicious fried dough balls called hush puppies, and Adler, who desperately missed the rich, dark stouts they had in bounty back home, chose the next best thing, a pale, watery ale that was brewed behind the inn itself. He'd consumed at least four pitchers of the stuff alongside his enormous meal.

"Um, sirs, I don't mean to be rude, but the amount you've ordered, I need to see some money before I—"

Without a word, Adler presented her with more than enough to cover their feast, and she nodded wide-eyed at the money, which was probably the largest lump sum she'd ever seen from the humble establishment.

Once their initial ravenous appetites had been sated, Adler found the patience to speak between mouthfuls of the greasy slabs of a dense but deliciously sweet type of ground meal their waitress called cornbread. He was smitten with the stuff.

"Could've handled that yourself, boy. You got the Persuasion same as I," he said, switching to his mother tongue so as to guard their matters from prying ears. He belched loudly before washing down his tenth piece of cornbread with half a mug of the ale, which was starting to grow on him.

"I know . . . But I hate using it. I know we have these abilities to help fight the darkness, but . . . Using it on people, well, it makes me feel like one of them. Makes me feel impure," Gunther said, his lips glistening with grease as he set to work on yet another platter of catfish.

Adler nodded. Those who came out on the other end of The Reckoning had come burdened with three new extrasensory assets that were to be used only in the service of a mission. The Persuasion, a weak sort of hypnosis that allowed one to instill certain suggestions and ideas into a person's mind, a diluted parody of the insidious hypnosis their mortal enemy was equipped with. The Sight, which allowed those of The Order an augmented sense of things to come. Not visions and premonitions exactly, but rather, a tingling at the base of one's skull when events in their immediate future might soon turn harrowing. Finally, there was The Strength, which helped level the playing field against those abominations who are blessed with the physiognomies of Hell's own biology. A tool that required enormous amounts of fuel to maintain, and which Adler did his best to take reserves of as he put another dollar on the table for a wrapped bag of cornbread to go.

"I know the feeling, boy. Still, you must learn to use the tools you've been gifted. You paid an enormous price for what you have now. Hesitance in the face of the enemy is certain death. You must be ruthless in your pursuit of them," Adler said, knowing he would soon have to watch this boy perform his trial by fire woefully unprepared. He would have to see to it that they were as properly armed for war as they could be under the circumstances.

"Clean your plate and then let us be on our way. We'll need some provisions before we leave, and then we shall leave come nightfall," Adler said as he forced a final piece of the savory bread down his gullet. All eyes were on the strange duo who ate enough for ten as they left.

They stopped at a trading post to stock up on dry goods, ammunition for the small bore hunting rifle Adler carried alongside his larger, custom-rifled guns, and feed for their horses. The sun was already setting by the time they were ready for the long ride.

"To this Poplar Springs place?" Gunther asked as they took a heavily rutted dirt road northwards, the township soon sinking behind them as rolling fields and barren forests unrolled in great swaths ahead of them, the odd farmhouse dotted at odd intervals the only signs of human occupancy for miles.

"No. A side trip to Van Buren first. There's an emissary of The Order who works a smith there. It was he who arranged that meeting with the girl, Ruthe. We must make contact with him. I must update The Order, know that we have an elder in our mist, if they even believe such a tale. And arm ourselves for what lay ahead. He will have the tools we need."

"We have emissaries? Out *here*?" Gunther asked, waving incredulously at the rural desolation before them.

"Wardens are in short supply, but allies and emissaries of The Order are spread far and wide. We have them all over the world, in places far more miserable than this," Adler assured him.

CHAPTER 4

As they rode on in the dark, their eyes not needing the assurance of lamplight to see their way, Adler reflected upon his time on this earth, as he was beginning to think that time may soon come to an end. He reflected upon The Order, whose purpose he'd dedicated almost all of his three hundred years to.

An elder . . . How? How is that possible? he thought, remembering the final inquisition, which was when the dichotomy between man and strigoi had finally shifted in their favor. Before The Order had split from the Roman Catholic Church, and they'd had the resources to scour the very ends of the earth, they'd gone on crusades in the wake of the plague, which had devastated both man and vampire alike. Though immune to most human-borne illnesses, the bubonic plague, perhaps because of its transmission via rats, which a vampire will eat if hungry enough, had evolved to ravage their immune systems as efficiently as their human counterparts.

Prior to the plague, there had been infested villages all over Eastern Europe. Enclaves who housed progenitors of the original strain, who possessed not only the thirst for blood but also knowledge, and had augmented their own terrible powers via consorts with black magic. These fearsome abominations use their augmented psychic abilities and knowledge of the black arts to build an entourage, a thrall, enslaved to them via unseen biological and psychic connection, an army more loyal and fearsome than any czar or king could hope to command.

Even now, no one knows where they came from, how they came to be a blight upon this world, but with mankind facing extinction as their numbers proliferated, the single, most powerful entity at that time, the church, was desperate to fight back, sure these abhorrent creatures were the devil's work.

And so they set out to capture some of the beasts alive, an extremely difficult task that saw men die by the hundreds, but eventually, a real live strigoi had been captured, and thus the experiments had begun.

The church put their best, most educated scientists and alchemists to work, their experiments as unholy as the beasts themselves, but desperation drove them to look beyond their religious morels and the sanctity of the human body in order to create a weapon to finally use against these demons. First there was the attempts at crossbreeding. Unlucky apostates cast aside their holy vows to mate with one of the female thrall, her arms and legs bound, wooden dowels secured in her mouth to prevent biting. But almost all the seed spilled on those harrowing couplings died within a cold and lifeless womb, and what couplings yielded viable pregnancies resulted in unspeakable horrors that not even the patriarchs of The Order, who spared no details when teaching the history to new recruits, would speak of.

It wasn't until they'd mounted an all-out siege on one elder's castle, an effort that took the lives of some two thousand brave souls, that they'd managed to capture and drug an elder, having to use whole flagons of concentrated poppy tinctures to sedate it enough in order to render its powers useless. It was here that they began to see real results.

After much trial and error, the church had finally found a viable method for creating holy crusaders who could fight head-to-head with the fast, foul things.

This imprisoned elder was kept in pacified captivity for decades before an accidental discovery led alchemists to realize that silver was a potent weapon against the beings, and thus was able to keep the frightful thing in silver shackles and drug it with copious amounts of the strongest psychedelic nostrums. Able to safely draw blood, or whatever foul essence flowed through the thing's veins that imitated blood, the alchemists were able to come up with a crude sort of inoculation procedure. They began to experiment with the hardiest and strongest of the young whom the church was grooming for being cardinals of the faith. These naïve, innocent souls were injected with a diluted mixture of the thing's black blood and some of its spinal fluid. Boys of only the strongest physical and mental fortitude were chosen. Boys who exhibited almost maniacal faith and worship toward the church. Boys who might have a chance at fighting back against the small, but still potent infection coursing through their bodies. Boys like Adler.

The church soon saw results from this barbaric from of augmentation. The boys would writhe and convulse within seconds of being injected, and their bodies rippled with astounding muscle growth before abruptly atrophying again before swelling yet again with catabolic lumps of gristle. A group of archers with silver studded bolts stood ready with their crossbows, waiting to see if the boys would be able to win the war being waged in their bodies, or if they needed to be put out of their misery.

A process that would eventually be called The Reckoning.

Adler had been one of the first and most successful cases to survive The Reckoning. Chances of survival were slim. He would later learn just how slim, finding out that only one in five of the young holy warriors made it through the reckoning successfully, coming out of it a hyper-augmented hybrid with inhuman powers but with his humanity still intact, instead of an *aberration*, as they were simply called.

"Has there ever been a case of an elder collaborating with one of the aberrations?" Gunther asked as they stopped early in the morning at the small village of Piedmont, pausing to feed themselves and their horses. Adler had inquired of one of the farmers as to how far away Van Buren was and was told he had about a day's ride ahead. They weren't that far away geographically, but the country was turning more rugged and dynamic with each kilometer they crossed, and he knew they would have to go slow with their horses, as there was no real wagon road between there and Van Buren.

He found himself dreading each step his horse took toward the source of infection. Adler's stomach roiled at the thought of those things, *aberrations* were far too innocent a name for what they were, colluding with the oldest and most cunning of the strigoi lineage. Accidents of the church collaborating with the things vomited from hell itself. It was enough to make him pause in the steady inhalation of his beloved cornbread.

"No. Which is what makes this so dangerous," Adler finally said, forcing himself to continue his meal as he remembered the great ideological rift that had caused The Order to become an autonomous entity, separate from the church.

The church claimed to be an agent of peace, seeking only to eradicate the darkness that flooded this world, and yet they did not stop their twisted experiments when they learned what many of God's children had turned into. Seemingly normal in appearance, these poor, naïve servants of Christ had been transformed into the most abominable of mutants, taking sadistic pleasure in the suffering of others. It was clear they still had the thirst of their strigoi ancestors, with only the medium of sustenance changing. It was not blood these newly minted mutants survived off of, but agony. *Human* agony. It took the parishioners and cardinals a long time to figure out what exactly drove those monsters to enact the barbaric acts of cruelty they so lusted after. And, as if to further salt the wound, these bastardized mutants had all the speed, cunning and telepathic prowess of their elder counterparts. And more importantly, they could travel freely in broad daylight. The catholic church had accidentally created an apex predator. Their only weakness was that they could not spread the disease.

Despite the number of tiny coffins that to this day line the catacombs beneath the Vatican attesting to their extermination, some of the mutant children managed to escape, using their own strange forms of mind control to help them flee out into the world, running wild and full of the most twisted appetites the human race had ever seen.

Certain high cardinals and alchemists of the church who'd spearheaded this sordid operation could no longer abide by what they had done. They agreed to train what they dubbed 'Wardens', those that were successfully transitioned, but partitioned to the church to put an end to The Reckoning. But the church would not listen as reports filed in about how successful the exterminations were going. They wanted more wardens made, they wanted to turn the tide once and for all, aberrations be damned. The church considered their hands washed of the situation, citing that since the aberrations could not breed or take thrall like the elders could, they would remain isolated problems that would not threaten the greater good of mankind. In the pope's eyes, the effectiveness of the wardens in exterminating the strigoi outweighed the unholy blights that were the aberrations. Instead, the church saw them as inconvenient blemishes upon the church's façade of infallible righteousness and altruism. Things to be swept under the grand rug of Judeo-Christian influence.

Gunther was the last boy to be put through The Reckoning before the final inquisition happened and the church halted their clandestine operation. His inception into the cult of light came right at the height of the plague, before the final inquisition was ordered. Using the second wave of the black death to their advantage, the church used the full might of its holy super soldiers and bottomless wealth to hunt down the last of the weakened elders, going to every providence where strigoi activity had been reported, rooting out every last hive they could find, and burning every elder body they found. Fire, it was discovered, was the only sure way to purge the evil and destroy the vessels completely.

After the final inquisition, the church and the Order diverged. The church was confident they had rid the world of the strigoi scourge, and wanted to move on to what they deemed was the next significant threat to the church: Human heretics. The Order, however, maintained a stance of unending vigilance against those hell-spawn that reveled in the night and took succor from man's essence, and cut ties with the Vatican.

From then on, The Order's sole purpose was to hunt down the remaining aberrations who continued to reign in fear with impunity, and investigate any reports of strigoi activity, no matter how far or remote. Adler saw it was fate that had brought him to Adolph. That particular aberration was the reason he'd been orphaned and thus brought into the church in the first place. Though he no longer praised or worshipped Jesus Christ, he *did* believe some higher power had providence on this world for such fates to intertwine. One with a cruel, blackened sense of humor.

#

The morning was a bitterly cold one, the winter seeming to grow harsher the farther into the highlands they went, and the scar-flesh of his face tingled with the damp chill. After haggling with one of the Piedmont farmers for a piglet they could butcher and feast upon later, the two set out once again, their pace slow and arduous as the gentle rolling hills of pastures and farmland was replaced with bluffs, jagged knobs of stone and steeply sloping valleys bisected with large streams and rivers.

Adler hoped they could reserve some of their strength and simply ride their horses carefully up and down the troughs and peaks, but there were several times where they had to get out and carefully guide their animals through the rugged terrain. They stopped on the banks of a large stream and Adler quickly dispatched the piglet. The sight of all that arterial blood flowing from the screaming animal and splashing upon the rocks stirred something deep and instinctual inside of him. Something he quickly tamped down and replaced with the memory of that hot cauterizing iron cooking the side of his face, his own masochistic way of reminding himself he was more human than strigoi.

He let Gunther prepare the meal for him, while he went to go wade in the frigid waters of the stream. There were very few things in this world that Adler could not withstand, The Reckoning saw to it that its survivors had an incredibly high threshold for physical pain and mental struggle. But the sound of sizzling meat, of bacon spitting in a skillet, of filets broiling over a grill, was enough to make him see double and sic up whatever food he'd so ravenously gobbled. So, he went far away from the sounds of cooking pork, which sounded so much like that hot iron against his skin, and instead meandered naked through the stream, his pale body a mapwork of scars and markings.

He breathed deeply and let his eyes un-focus on the clear water that rushed past him. He detected dozens of little frantic pulses of life as the fish swam past him, he could sense their directional purpose, their hivemind disposition to go further downstream, to seek out warmer waters and bed down to spawn.

He stood statue-still for some five minutes, before, in a violent blur of motion, he struck his fist out with the precision and speed of a coiled viper, and plucked a trout from the creek. He stared at the creature for a second, marveling at the deep rainbow sheen and speckled spots of its body, before he could handle it no longer, and he bit into the thing's stomach, savoring the metallic taste that flooded his mouth. He did so out of sight of the boy, who would be perturbed by his mentor's breach of tenet.

You are a man, and you are to conduct yourself as one. This meant no killing of fellow men unless absolutely necessary. This meant no engaging in abhorrent behaviors such as wanton violence or cruelty. Most importantly, this meant fueling your body the way a civilized man does. No consumption of raw meat unless in a dire survival situation, and especially no consumption of blood for any reason, regardless of how well it fueled their always ravenous bodies. Adler suspected this was more superstition than anything. The Church feared a taste of that raw, unadulterated life would trigger some mechanism deep within their hybrids and perhaps turn them fully into the beasts they were made to slain.

Adler made quick work of the trout, mild shame overtaking him as he ate like a feral beast, pulling out intestines and gristle and savoring the various flavors that flooded his mouth. He savored the organs and sacks that burst between his teeth, and could not deny the rush of energy that flooded him as he swallowed the nutrient rich meat. The proteins and fats not rendered and destroyed by heat. It was different than eating a cooked meal, the energy immediate and pulsing. In minutes the trout had been reduced to a gristle clad skeleton, his face covered in scales and blood. He quickly dunked down into the stream to wash away evidence of his bestial lapse, and when he resurfaced, Gunther was summoning him.

"The food is ready, Herr Schmidt," Gunther said, holding up a dripping piece of bacon.

CHAPTER 5

They reached Van Buren some hours later, arriving at high noon to a bustling township bigger than Cape Girardeau but still a primitive village compared to Saint Louis. This town too had a high concentration of French in it, as evidenced by the floral names which were attached to various businesses and the many mines that dotted the squat mountains, shown by the map Adler had bought from a cartographer back in Saint Louis. They'd simply followed the stream along its bank until it gradually widened and became a river, the *Current River* the locals called it, which cut through the center of the village, a humble footbridge across its span.

Adler let his long golden hair down and parted in a way to cover the worst of his scarring. Not out of shame, but out of an abundance of caution. It was good not to draw attention to yourself in small, far away places like this, where people were often superstitious, easily perturbed by aberrant behavior, and could take quick to fanaticism. He'd heard of the witch trials that had taken place across this continent some years ago, mere women who dared to seek common knowledge above their household duties, and were accused of silly charges that saw them burned at the stake.

The irony being that those ignorant townsfolk had no idea just how cunning and dangerous a *real* witch could be. Real witches would never let themselves succumb to such an indignant death. Like the silly myths surrounding the strigoi, or vampire as the westerners called it, there was equal facetious folklore surrounding witches. All the product of simple hill folk's imagination. The reality was much more horrifying.

Gunther, with his boyhood innocence and soft, inquisitive features, was the perfect candidate for handling the more diplomatic work. So, as Adler sat with their horses by the river, Gunther inquired about the forge master, a man named Werner Jaeger. It did not take the boy long, within the hour he was back.

"Any trouble?" Adler asked as Gunther handed him the burlap sack.

"None. Apparently, he's well known throughout the county. Provided arms for the federal troops during the war. He's renowned for his craftsmanship."

"As he should be," Adler said as he peered into the sack. He could smell the sulfurous black powder and saw the individual bundles of powder sacks from within. "For one to be hired by The Order in any capacity, their work must be exceptional." He put the powder into a storage pocket on his mount, and the two proceeded to ride into town, Gunther leading, Adler behind him, a large-brimmed hat covering what his blonde hair could not.

#

Adler almost didn't recognize the forge master, for the last time he'd seen the man he was in his twenties, freshly recruited by the German branch of The Order for his exceptional designs with swords and axes. Perfectly balanced, lightweight weapons with cutting edges honed so sharply specially reinforced sheaths had to be made to house the blades without being sliced to ribbons.

"Master Schmidt, my god, you haven't aged a day," the old man said in German with a smile as he embraced Adler.

"And I see you've lived your days out quite comfortably, forge master," Adler said, patting the man's swollen gut. Werner laughed, his whole body jiggled as he did so.

"Aye, when you make the best sabers and rifles in the whole state, you can charge enough to afford Cornish game hens and fried trout every day. And you, Master Schwartz. Last I saw you, we shared a youthful glow," he said, and Adler saw the pained look in the rotund man's eyes as he took in the young warden. How odd it must be for the true born humans to watch the warden's progression through time, their own bodies growing weak with atrophy and age while The Order's disciples seemed to be immortal. They weren't, of course. Wardens aged about ten years for every hundred they lived, though the church did not know how old they could get and still survive, for even the most skilled wardens eventually saw death at the hands of a thrall horde or an elder. They *did* age though, unlike the strigoi, who, with sufficient access to blood, could live indefinitely.

Adler was the oldest living warden to date, and his age would be the milestone that saw how wardens handled their older years. So far, Adler hadn't noticed any changes.

Except for those occasional phantom stirrings for things raw and bleeding. That desire to feel the visceral surge of energy from tapping into the unadulterated vitality that flows through every living thing.

But never of the human kind. If it ever got to that, he would order Gunther to put a silver sword to his throat without hesitation.

"I'm glad you made it though. Almost certainly, the skills of a warden are needed in these hills. Something quite awful is unfolding just beyond these bluffs here," Werner said, hiking a thick thumb behind him, where in the distance a lush green wall bookended the town. "Gotten so bad that folks have burned the one bridge that leads into Poplar Springs and Lordell County. Woulda burned the woods too if the Union men hadn't seen to do that already."

190

"The army is aware of what's going on?" Adler asked. The forge master shook his head.

"No, no, nothing like that. There'd been a standoff there some months ago, platoon of Union soldiers was hunting down this Confederate colonel, a man named Dixon, they wanted him very badly. They ended up cornering him in the now-abandoned township of Lordell. There is a mountain there festooned with caves, and it was in these caves the men hid, trying to outsmart the Union army. But the bastards just said to hell with it and burned the whole mountain top!" he said with a laugh and a shake of his head. "They managed to capture some of the rebels though, and boy, the things they spoke of. Sounded like madness to those generals, I'm sure. But gossip spreads like bad gas in a high wind around here, and what I heard sounded like a textbook case of a thrall horde at work."

"Not just thrall, but elder too, unfortunately. An aberration," Adler said with a sigh.

"Gods help us," the forge master said, jovial spirit vanishing. Both men promptly spit at the ground on the sarcastic saying, to show just what they thought of the gods who most certainly won't help them at all.

"*You* can help me though. I have enough silver and gunpowder to take down hundreds of the things. I just need your expertise in putting it all together," Adler said, handing him the two sacks with the silver and the powder.

"Oh, I can do a lot more than just that. Have a special gift for you, in fact. Lovely weapons, should help level the playing field a bit. Let me get the fires going and I'll tell you of what else I learned. Something that I think you'll be most eager to know, Master Schmidt. Come now, wardens."

#

"Did some digging when I'd heard that the Union army was recruiting an awful lot of German and French among their ranks. My interest peaked when I heard of one of

191

them being a battlefield surgeon. One renowned for being particularly . . . ferocious, in his treatments," the forge master said as he stoked a large stone kiln, and then proceeded to ignite a gas fed furnace with a smelting pot within. He took one of the bars of silver from Adler and tossed it in the pot, then closed the thick iron door to let it melt. Adler knew where this was going, but was interested to hear how Adolph had come to be here in the first place.

"I think we—" Gunther began, but Adler put a hand out to shush him as the big man's face began to sweat with the heat from his work. He'd produced a diecast mold, and to Adler's surprise saw they weren't the circular orbs meant for musket rifling. No, these molds featured slim, conical cylinders. While he waited for the silver to melt, Werner took out several hollow metal casings, and began to fill them with the powder Adler had bought.

"Was able to find some of the papers and boat manifests from one of our emissaries working the docks in Boston. Turns out there was a man named Hanz Fischer who booked passage aboard *Her Queen's Majesty* and sailed across the ocean to come here, to the land of opportunity. Listed his occupation as a doctor. A *surgeon*, to be exact. Listed his origin as Liepzig, Germany. This man, who was reported to be of enormous stature and featured a mane of raven black hair had then proceeded to take a train all the way to Saint Louis, where he disappeared for parts unknown just as the nation began to eat itself alive," Werner explained as he began to use a strange ram-rod device to pack the cylinders tight with powder, his tree trunk forearms bulging with the effort.

"Any idea what happened to the division that 'Fischer' was a doctor for?" Adler asked as he watched the forge master with growing confusion. The man had used a large hook to take out the glowing red smelting pot, the silver bubbling within. As he set this on an anvil to cool, he opened up the mold case, and using the minute care of a sommelier pouring a prestigiously aged vintage for a lord, he poured the liquid metal into the diecast mold, which housed twelve of the little things. He closed the mold, set it upright, and then went to throw another silver bar in the pot and put it back in the kiln.

"Last I heard was the whole division got wiped out by Mccullough, excuse me, *Confederate General* Mccullough, at the battle for Danson Ridge. Before that though, Lyon had dispatched a small scouting group to investigate reports of a rebel raid in Poplar Springs. That was the last anyone had seen of our 'Hans Fischer'," Werner said as he opened up the diecast mold and let the cool air harden the glowing red objects. "What're the odds that a man matching your village butcher to the T and being renowned for having a monstrous disposition was last seen in a place so mired with fear by the local populace that they'd tore up every road and burned every bridge leading to it?" Werner said with a thin smile, digging out the silver cones from their mold and went about trimming away the tailings with a knife.

"Aye, the woman you put us into contact with, the one fled the village, told us of a man matching that description. I'm certain it's him," Adler said. Though he knew in his bones this was the man, further corroboration on Adolph's existence here stoked a sense of urgency in his soul. Though dread still filled him at the thought of having to face an elder and an aberration together, and whatever thrall they'd managed to build, a driving sense of vengeance now cut through the dread. A determination to see this long cat and mouse game, which spanned hundreds of years and several continents, to its end.

Even if that meant death for the most distinguished veteran of The Order.

"Sir, I must ask, what are you doing with that silver? Those do not look like musket rounds to me. I believe Master Schmidt—"

"You'll see, boy," Werner said, no one correcting him even though Gunther was probably thrice his age. The forge master proceeded to seat the silver cones into the cartridges using a mallet and several gentle taps from it. He held up the thing with pride. "Behold, gentlemen, the rimfire cartridge. Originally designed by a whip smart Swiss smith up in the alps, I borrowed his design and improved upon it. A man named Winchester has since paid me handsomely for the patent schematics for this and the guns that use it. The Americans recently proved how terribly efficient they are, unfortunately. I'm glad these things will finally be used for their intended purpose. Come, let me show you."

#

"The Colt revolver, gentlemen," Werner said, handing Adler the peculiar looking pistol with its barrel shaped loading apparatus. Adler stared in confusion before Werner promptly took it from him and pushed the barrel apparatus aside to show six of what he called cartridges, their tips lead primed instead of silver. "No more carrying your weight in flintlocks. Six shots for each gun before you have to reload," he said, grinning at the stunned awe in Adler's face.

"Six shots?" Gunther asked incredulously. "And this design of yours, it works?"

"Oh yes boy, they work. Ask any union sergeant how well they work, how many rebels they cut down with the damned things. Go on, try it, all you gotta do is pull the hammer back between each shot," he said, handing the gun back to Adler, and pointing to the far end of the back alley. There was a thick tree that grew between two buildings parallel to the back of the forge master's building. Adler took aim and fired, resisting the urge to reload, pulled the cocking hammer back instead, waited for the gun smoke to clear before he fired again.

And again.

Six rounds found their way into the tree, and as Werner promised, the gun was deathly efficient. Especially once Adler got the hang of fanning the hammer between shots.

"Incredible," Adler said, reverence in his voice.

194

"Just wait. There's more," Werner said, producing a rifle with a strange square-like attachment beneath the stock. "Going to give those monstrous bastards a run for your money, you are," he said with a savage grin.

Adler observed the weapon. The barrel was just long enough to be accurate at a hundred or so yards, but not long enough to be cumbersome, which was good. Hunting strigoi was usually up close, nasty work. The barrel was octagonal and featured a modern spiraled rifling, allowing the 'bullet' as Werner called it to spin as it rocketed from the barrel, making it go farther, faster. The stock made of pitted walnut, lightweight but incredibly sturdy. Mother of pearl sight inlays trained the eye to focus on the ivory sight bead on the barrel. There was no priming hammer that Adler could see, and confused, he watched as Werner loaded the gun by pulling back a sliding chamber. Semi-automatic, he called it. He then pulled out the square aperture attached to the bottom of the stock, revealing more of the cartridges.

"Eight shots per magazine," Werner said, demonstrating its firing mechanism as he quickly planted eight rounds into the tree. He reloaded it, handed it to Adler. It felt good in his hands, light weight and modular. Six shots with the revolver, eight with the rifle. He was starting to feel better about his chances against the unholy alliance he was tasked with exterminating. Adler could've hugged the forge master then.

CHAPTER 6

"How're we going to get across then?" Gunther asked between mouthfuls of pot roast and potatoes.

"There's a man who'll get you 'cross the river," Werner said as he refilled Adler's flagon with another cup of the strong, dark beer. The big man's talents were not only in the forging of weapons. He was a mighty fine brewer too, and had prepared a barrel of the old country style *Kräftig* just for the two men's imminent arrival, the recipe taken from a brewery back home that a man named Charles Muller had ran. Adler cherished the bold, smoky taste, and as he downed his sixth serving of the nectar, he thought he might've felt the faintest pangs of inebriation.

"A ferryman?" Adler asked, a mustache of suds speckling his upper lip.

"Aye. He won't dare go upstream more than five miles, anymore and that would put him within Poplar Springs jurisdiction, put him within sight of the cursed knob. But I think for a price . . . he can be persuaded," Werner said with a sly grin. "I know you wardens of The Order have deep pockets, and uh, a way of persuading folks."

They'd been invited into Werner's home, a spacious cottage up the street from his place of business, where he had adorned on the walls all manner of fish and animal he'd bagged over the years. Using money that'd been sent to him from The Order's regent of finance, he had prepared a hearty meal for the two tired and road-worn wardens, with instructions to provide them with everything they needed to help them succeed in their journey.

"Help yourselves," Werner said to the men, gesturing toward the large ten-gallon cooking pot he'd had levered over one of his smaller kilns repurposed for spit roasts and cooking large quantities, filled to the brim with meat and potatoes. His cooking skills weren't quite on par with his mastery of beer and weaponry, but Adler still ate the overcooked roast and mushy potatoes gratefully, moping up the remnants of each bowl with stale biscuits. "I'm not kiddin', eat till your bursting if you can. Once you step foot on the other side of that bank, you'll be in a barren wasteland. No game for miles around."

"You mean . . . No animals to hunt?" Gunther asked around a mouthful of roast. Werner shook his head, pouring himself a beer now that he had seen to his guests.

"None. Not surprising, given the remoteness of the place," Werner said, shaking his head. "Used to be some mighty fine hunting in those woods. Got this beautiful elk up on that knob," the forge master said, pointing to a large elk's head that hung above the kitchen doorway, its ten point antlers nearly stretching to the ceiling. Gunther stared at the elk and then toward Adler, obviously confused.

"When they're desperate enough, they'll drink the blood of any warm-blooded mammal within reach," Adler explained. "Lands that have been infested with a strigoi thrall for several months are often believed to be cursed by nearby locals because of the lack of wildlife. In reality, the poor animals simply can't breed faster than they can be eaten," he said to the listening Gunther.

"Especially if they got freshly turned in their ranks. Bastards feed like you wouldn't believe," Werner said, shaking his head. Adler nodded.

"When the blood thirst first comes upon them, they're more animalistic than anything. They can't talk, they can't think. The urge to feed is maddening. That's when they're the most dangerous," Adler said, sipping his brew and remembering the first time he'd come upon a fresh thrall.

Adler was a new soldier then, taken under the wing of a huge man named Baros Albescu, a Romanian who was one of the few adults to survive The Reckoning, driven from his homelands in the mountains by the scourge, and driven mad with a need for revenge. Prior to his reckoning, he'd told the church of the infestation of his home village in the Carpathian Mountains, a place named Zamesti. Baros told the listening cardinals how a strange, wraithlike thing from parts unknown had fled to the neighboring village of Ployeshti up the peak, and within weeks the village with its humble populace had been decimated, its denizens transformed into the hissing, bestial things of nightmare. It was a common story The Order had heard many times before, an elder desperate to rebuild a thrall after being hunted down by wardens.

Except this time the thrall had been wiped out by the local voivod, one of the few humans in power at the time who knew of the strigoi plague outside of the church. The desperate elder had turned almost the whole village overnight in an effort to quickly build up his numbers.

They'd come down the mountain in droves, fleeting shadows in the night that burst into homes and tore apart whatever they could find, Baros had told the listening cardinals. Baros informed them how he had to watch his wife and children be ripped to shreds, literally, while Baros and two other men, armed with torches and quick wits, managed to fling themselves down a sloping gorge and roll their way down the base of the mountain. After confessing to the cardinal, he'd gotten on his knees, begged the Vatican to allow him his own reckoning, despite the fact the trial was notoriously unsuccessful for adults. His wish was granted however, and perhaps by the vengeful rage that stoked the furnace of his heart acting as a buffer between the poisons that coursed through his veins, Baros had survived his reckoning.

They made their way up the mountain, armed with silver throwing knives and battle axes, their blades coated in a special hemorrhaging agent meant specifically for the elder. Adler was terrified, for this was his test, his first time to battle, to see if he could be worthy enough to hold the title of warden, while Baros, already a battle hardened veteran prior to The Reckoning, was sent back to reclaim his village as an experiment by the church to see if the adults who went through the harrowing trial were as effective as the children who survived it. They approached the village, their bodies clad in thick fur coats, the weather there so extreme that even the wardens, their bodies mostly impervious to such temperature extremes, had to take precautions against the freezing mountain winds.

Adler remembered how all that blood looked against the stark white of the snow. It'd ran down the mountain in a loosely defined stream, a huge crimson smear against the imposing ivory face of the mountain. The village itself was devoid of all life. Not a single intact body could be found, just frozen limbs, drained of all blood. In their blood-frenzy the freshly turned beasts had ripped apart their quarry in order to get at the hot ambrosia they so eagerly sought. There was none of the delicate, efficient bloodletting of their elders.

They'd spotted one of the thrall clinging to the cliffside at the outskirts of the village, trying to lick the frozen blood off the rocks there, its tongue torn to shreds from its desperate meal. Adler had easily dispatched that one, watching it fall some six hundred feet before it exploded against a rock out cropping below, a red corona spreading widely in all directions as its most recent feast ruptured from its splattered body.

It wasn't long before they came out of the swirling white of the snow drifts like ghosts from the ether, charging at them with crazed abandon. Adler had to make use of every augmented fast-twitch muscle he had to survive as the beasts came at him in blurs of teeth and claws. It'd been a close call that day, both Adler and Baros suffering severe bite wounds and cold exposure, the two sole survivors of the raiding party having to eat their weight in hare and mountain goat to make it back alive. The elder, who could not marshal control of his thrall-horde, was found starving and aged in a hut, a wraith of a man whose skin sagged from his bones like melting cheese.

He'd simply evaporated when the killing blow was struck, one of the easiest elder kills Adler had ever encountered. He hoped for similar circumstances heading into Poplar Springs. A greedy Elder too power-hungry to calculate the sustainability of his thrall, his horde robbing him of precious life instead of obeying the bloodline they were indentured too. Adler would gladly take on hundreds of blood-frenzied thrall than face one elder in its prime. The things they could do with their minds . . . Make you live out nightmares so vivid you weren't even aware of the many thirsty mouths biting down on your twitching body while you vividly hallucinated your worst fears. They could get inside your head, and tear apart your sanity while their thrall tore apart your body.

"Make sure you stock up before you go. I'll pack what I can for you, but I suggest fishing the Current outside of Poplar Springs. One of the few things those bastards didn't manage to ruin," Werner said. Despite his full belly, Adler's stomach grumbled at the memory of the fish. The raw meat. The blood. That immediate burst of energy. If things got desperate enough, he would have to instruct the boy to eat as he had, regardless of the breach of tenet. "You'll sleep here tonight, get your rest. You'll need it."

Werner retired early, for he was old and needed his sleep. Wardens needed sleep too, but much less than their human counterparts. A few hours a week was sufficient to keep one's mind sharp enough for battle. That being said, Adler drained the rest of the barrel of beer, hoping to find more inebriation and thus a few hours of sleep, for the anticipation of battle could be torturous. He instructed the boy to drink with him, for if Adler was nervous, he could only imagine how a warden still virgin to battle and the horrors of it must feel. Together they sat by the large hearth in Werner's foyer, wordlessly drinking beer and watching the flames, until finally Adler felt mildly swimmy in the head, the closest he would ever feel to true drunkenness. He noticed Gunther's eyes were glassy and his pupils dilated, and he grinned, envious of the boy's smaller, more youthful vessel, which still maintained some sensitivity to alcohol.

"Come on, boy, let's retire for the night."

CHAPTER 7

The ferryman was a wiry man of middle age but with corded muscles in his arms and neck, a salt and pepper beard hardly concealing the incredulous sneer on his face when presented with the two men and their intended destination.

"Listen here, you goddamn gargoyle," the man said, pointing to Adler. "I ken you're not from around here, so I'll explain it to you clearly. Up yonder way Hell has taken hold of the land. Used to be whole villages up that way, used to be a good way of life. Something evil has taken root in the hills up there. Men, women and children all dead. Things that look like men but aren't. Blighted soil up that way. I ain't going up there. You've no reason to—"

Gunther quickly approached the man, who'd been standing on his barge, moored against the swift flow of the river. The man had three boys on the barge with him, each one standing by an ore, each one sporting muscled physiognomies similar to the father. It was obvious by their muscled arms and torsos they'd had an inimical relationship to this river since they were old enough to stand and talk.

The man shied away at first, flinching and pulling his arm back, but Gunther held fast, making sure the old man met his eyes.

"Sir, I understand your reticence, but I must insist you take us where we need to go. You and your lot will be rich for this simple errand," Gunther said, speaking in a low, lilting voice, his soft boyish timbre pitching down a whole octave. It was the first time Adler had ever heard the boy use the Persuasion, and he felt a small swell of pride well up within him. The man's eyes glazed over, and, upon seeing this strange exchange, one of the boys left his station by a paddle and approached, a skinning knife in one hand.

"Hey, what're you doin' to my pa, get your—"

Adler put his hand out and waved it across the boy's face as if warding away a fly. The boy froze, the knife dropping to stick into the barges floor with a *thunk*.

"At ease, child," Adler said. He watched Gunther and the ferryman. The man's beard twitched and one eyelid spasmed as the man's ironclad constitution fought Gunther's persuasion. Some men could withstand a warden's spell, those of particular mental fortitude and stern concentration, and Adler hoped the ferryman was not of such stock. To placate his other sons, he produced a handful of quarters, flipping one to each child to show their intentions were sincere.

Finally, after a tense mental standoff, the ferryman swallowed, and Gunther put a sack in his hand. As if coming out of a dream, the ferryman looked stupidly down at the small cloth sack in his hand, opened it, his eyes fully in focus now as he saw some thirty dollars in coins within.

"What do you say, sir?" Gunther said, releasing his hold on the man. Where he'd taken hold of the burly arm, a red handprint shown against the heavily tanned flesh.

"Yeah . . . All right," the ferryman said, his voice thick with confusion. "Five miles is as far as I go, though. I'll take you to the old Poplar Springs bridge, and absolutely no further," the man said, nodding to his boys. They mustered to their corner perches, each one holding an ore as Werner, who stood off to the side, watching this exchange in bemused silence, helped the two men get their loaded down horses onto the small barge.

"Good hunting, wardens. May you come back alive and victorious," Werner said, hugging each man before seeing them off.

#

"Don't know what in god's name you think you're gonna be doing up in those hills. No one left alive up there, not even the blasted rabbits!" the ferryman yelled over the roar of the river as he and his three sons fought the river for every inch they gained, arms and shoulders bulging with strain and muscle. It was a slow, arduous journey up the surging current, which had turned from the humble stream Adler had followed to Van Buren into a large, swift-moving body of water, occasionally frothed up with rapids and other treacherous obstacles.

"We can help, you know! We can—" Gunther began but the ferryman shot him a look so hostile he froze to the spot.

"Oh no, we make our own way here. You already paid for us to retire off this damn barge. Least I can do is drop ye off at Hell's gates like you asked. We don't accept handouts, do we lads!" he barked to his sons.

"No, sir!" they said in unison as cold water splashed and spilled against the wooden flooring of the barge.

Adler had to use his own Persuasion to calm the two horses, who looked forlorn and wide-eyed as the barge bumped over rocks and listed against swirling eddies. If one of them decided to spook and rear up, the commotion would probably upset the barge and spill everyone on it.

"See to your horse, boy. That is your job until we reach the bank," Adler said sternly. Together the wardens minded their horses and watched with respect and a little awe as these raw-boned human specimens piloted their wares up such an unforgiving stream, sweat glistening on their bare shoulders and chests despite the frigid wind that blew in off the river.

An hour later, Adler caught sight of a large, blackened husk sticking up from the river, followed by another some ten feet directly in front of it. He thought for one harrowing second that the mad ferryman was going to try and shoot between the two charred towers when he realized this was the bridge the ferryman spoke of. With several great heaving strokes, the ferryman and his sons maneuvered the ferry onto the gravel bank with a crunch of wood against stone. One of the other boys quickly jumped out with a rope and moored the barge to a squat stone plug jutting out of the ground before the current could carry them back down to Van Buren.

"Better find a hole to crawl into at night. A deep, dark hole lined by fire. That's the only way they can't get to ya," the ferryman said as he steadied the swaying barge with one foot on the bank and the other tucked into a divot in the floorboards. "Night's when they come."

"I'm aware," Adler said as he gratefully stepped off the barge and produced a carrot for his horse as a reward for sticking through the nerve-wracking ordeal without spooking.

"Crazy bastards you are. If you wanted death so badly you could've just eaten a gun. We'll be on our way now. Remember, we won't come back to get you. You're on your own," the ferryman said as he untied the rope from its mooring and the river pulled at the barge. The boys were waving forlornly as the current whisked them back down the bank. Toward safety. Toward sanity.

CHAPTER 8

Adler spent the next thirty minutes trying to fish, the current swift and freezing, but still he managed to pull a few fish, trout, and spotted bass out of the water, adding what he could to the larders that bulged from the storage saddle of their already overburdened horses. Gunther, who'd purchased a fishing rod and some fly lures, tried his hand at the sport but had no luck.

"Listen, boy," Adler said as he held one squirming fish in his hands, belly up, toward his mouth. "There may come a time where we might need to breach tenet, eat unlike civilized men. I want you to try it now," he said, kicking a flopping bass toward Gunther. The boy stared with growing unease. "Go on."

"Sir? I—"

"I know it breaches tenet. But it's the purest energy source there is, son. Blood, fresh meat. There might come a time where, if we must retreat, if we find ourselves over our heads and bad with injury, we will have to resort to the way of the beast. Go on. I want to see you eat it. Get used to it. Feel that immediate burst of revitalization," he said as he bit into his trout, slime and blood and cold gristle flooding his mouth.

He let out a contented sigh as he swallowed the noxious bolus and immediately felt recharged, reinvigorated.

He watched while he ate as Gunther hesitantly picked up his bass. He swallowed, sighed, closed his eyes, and then mimicked Adler, biting into the thing's stomach, taking a bite of all those nutrient-rich organs. He began to gag, and momentarily anger flared in Adler as he thought the boy might waste such a precious resource, but with a loud gulp Gunther swallowed the meat, and then let out a shuddering breath, his eyes going wide, pupils shrinking. He stared at the bloody crescent wound in the fish's belly in disbelief, and fell upon it with more vigor this time.

"See?" Adler said as they finished their meals and washed off in the stream. He took the dying fish he'd caught and stuffed them into a random pocket on his horse and scanned the bank. He spotted an overgrown foot trail leading up the shoulder to the road that would've led to the bridge, had it still been there. Neither warden spoke of the younger's epiphany as Gunther shook with barely restrained energy, adrenaline. Adler would explain in time how not all of The Order's tenets were perfect, nor were they meant to be followed rigidly and without question. But that was a conversation for another time. Perhaps experience would teach him what Adler could not.

They found themselves on a dirt road that led in a straight line into a densely forested hillside. Beyond this, far in the distance, Adler could make out the squat plug of earth that jutted up from the land, not quite as grand as an actual mountain, but too mighty to be called a foothill. A *knob* the locals had called it. Yes, that name suited it perfectly. And upon this squat spire of stone, he saw a dark cusp in its side, a cave opening that caught the high noon sun perfectly to cast a deep shadow over the indented opening, giving the impression of a cavity in a long rotten tooth.

This desolate plug of land, with its charred and bare blackened hillside, truly looked like something Dante might've seen in his descent to Hell, a huge obsidian aberration that loomed over the land like a stain of blood in a white wedding dress.

"Come on, boy, we have quite a ride ahead of us," Adler sighed. He mounted his horse, and they rode side by side down the road. Vines and weeds that had gone brown from the winter frost speckled the road, revealing its abandoned state. As they rode, they passed other signs of ruin: a roadside trading post collapsed in on one side, broken glass tinkling in the sunlight where the windows had been blown out. A wagon that was flipped on its side like a dead animal, vines sprouting up around the busted wheels as the canvas top fluttered softly in the wind. Abandoned military armaments, cannons and rifles, speckled the edges of the tree line, which Adler imagined during the summer was so impenetrable with greenery that one had the impression of being hemmed in by viridian walls as they traveled.

With it being winter though, and the branches bare, Adler could peer some distance into the tree line that surrounded him, and he could see specks of gray occluded by brown and orange, leaf-littered corpses left to be ossified and exposed to the elements. Adler noticed they were unmolested by vulture or other animal, and knew then the work of strigoi was upon them. Those that carried the ancient taint in their blood were undesirable to even the most desperate of carrion eaters. The end result: skeletal visages that loomed at them from the ground like the rejected souls that even Hell didn't want, being pushed back up from the depths to stare in permanent, sorrowful awe at their circumstances with agape mouths and empty eye sockets. Many appeared dressed in some fashion of military uniform.

The cold must've condensed the smell of rot down to a musty trace, the frost preserving what carrion there was, for even Adler's sensitive nose barely detected the smell of death. The two paused when they came upon a three-wagon caravan blocking the road, the wagons themselves intact, with no evidence of rider or horse. He spotted the shredded canvas canopy and deep furrowed marks in the wood though and could guess what happened.

"Looks like they were fallen upon by a pack in a blood-frenzy," Gunther observed as he climbed into one of the wagons.

"Aye, looks that way," Adler said as he scoured the wagon ahead of Gunther's. Dark stains soaked into the driver's bench. He peered into the back, seeing if mayhap there was anything of value they were carrying. When he looked though, all he found were sacks of moldy flour and jars of frozen preserves.

They guided their horses around the ambushed convoy and went on, a signpost greeted them at the three-prong junction a kilometer or so ahead.

POPLAR SPRINGS – 6 MILES

LORDELL – 7.5 MILES

SULLIVAN – THIRTY MILES

YOU WILL DIE HERE.

This last was declared on a small piece of bark nailed a foot or so below the junction sign, scratched in a hasty hand. One side of Adler's face turned up in a cynical grin.

Yeah, we'll just see about that, he thought as he turned in the direction of Sullivan. He could see a vast brown wall about a mile down the straight road, and squinted. He realized he was looking at the remnants of a covered bridge whose entrance was completely blocked by a mess of thick logs and cut trees, as if a huge river had once cut through this very road and stopped up the bridge with piles of driftwood. He knew that wasn't the case, however. A desperate attempt by man to contain the blight that lived on this ground.

Of course, if the strigoi *really* wanted too, they could easily spread as relentlessly as the second wave of the plague, for there was only one blessing that kept them from driving mankind to complete extinction, and that was their extreme territorialism. But now, with an aberrant among their ranks, one who was not confined to night by their sun sickness or their strange symbolic territorial patterns, Adler wondered how the bastard worked with the elder. Their needs were different but the same, one's weakness was another's power. A terrible team they could make.

"Stay sharp," Adler said as they headed toward Poplar Springs, the only sound punctuating the breath-taking silence was the clomp of hooves against dirt.

"But it's daylight?" Gunther said, looking around at the barren desolation before them. Nothing stirred, not even birds dared fly over this hellscape.

"That matters not to the aberration. He is a day walker," Adler said as his eyes scanned the woods ahead. "He will be huge and raven-haired. He will know what we are immediately, and will probably not welcome us with open arms. *Stay sharp.*"

"Yes, Herr Schmidt."

Adler looked toward the mountain. Part of him wanted to charge right up that blackened slope, to plunge into the heart of that diseased mound of earth and rip out the infection at its heart. That was his training taking over, that need for holy vengeance, to smite all abominations with fire. But he knew they had to be smart. One old dog and a pup against a force unseen by The Order.

This was uncharted territory.

They rode on toward Poplar Springs, following the road, passing more signs of human abandonment along the way, more signs of a war given up in the face of greater horrors. Not a single living thing presented itself to them, no squirrels or hares darted through the underbrush. No deer galloped gracefully through the tree line.

A wholly dead place, this was.

CHAPTER 9

By the time they reached Poplar Springs, the sun was just above the knob, causing shadows to fall on this patch of earth even before night could fully claim the land.

They saw evidence of military skirmishes in the streets, long dead soldiers laying in yards, and on the sides of the one main road that led into town, many of the houses featured bullet holes and shattered windows. Adler wondered if this was a man versus man engagement or man versus thrall.

He soon had his answer as they made their way toward the center of town. Dressed as villagers and soldiers, he saw the dead strigoi, smelled them, their odor of decay sweeter in a sickly way compared to that of rotting men.

"These ones weren't wild . . ." Gunther said, kneeling down next to one of the near-mummified corpses, their bodies wholly unmolested by either the elements or animals. Only the trauma from musket balls, several of them it looked like. A strigoi could be killed without silver. It just took an enormous amount of firepower to do so.

"Must've been here for years, well established," Adler said, a pit growing in his stomach. Aside from the blood frenzy, a thrall-pack that had survived long enough to regain some of its human cunning was even more dangerous. This was what the Church had feared initially. That Elders would be able to raise up more than just feral imps bound to them by some psychic link. That they would regain their human intelligence, and with that learn to form tactics, perhaps even an army. These specimens possessed enough intelligence to use deception, dressing as soldiers.

"Sir . . ." Gunther said, distracted from the bodies, his gaze turned toward a huge manor house that presided over the town the way the knob presided over the land, imposing and terrible. From its white siding and intact windows oozed wavering lines of black smoke. It seeped from the bottom of the doorway and the chimney on the roof. A few whisps emanated from the windows where drafts came in.

Corruption.

"Get your gun ready, boy," Adler said, his revolver already in hand. An elder had most definitely taken refuge here. Had practiced the foulest of magic rites here. Its esoteric residue lingered in the air like nebulous poison, so thick that even the humans might be able to see traces of it. Only elders and those such as himself could see the aura that resulted from such foul habitation. Horrible things took place in that house, he knew that. But he did not smell them, not the live ones anyway.

He kicked in the door, which shattered in two as it flew off its hinges. A strong but not overwhelming smell of human decay hit him. Death that had been brought to a boil and given the chance to simmer down to something earthy. He saw evidence of suicide and barbarism within. Corpses in various states of decay, all bloodless. The leathery upholstery of human skin plastered to one wall.

"Blood magic," Gunther said, handing Adler a thick tome. He looked at the cover, in Romani script it read, COMPENDIUM OF BLOOD ESOTERICA: SPELLS, INCANTATIONS, SUMMONING RITUALS.

The book bled readily with the black aura, this grimoire had been read thoroughly, its abominable contents within heavily utilized. It made Adler nauseous to hold the damned thing, so he threw it on the floor, beside a man who was once rotund in life, but had been deflated grotesquely by death, his fatty skin spilled in loose flaps from his hollow, bloodless body like spilled, curdled milk.

They searched the house, finding evidence of blood farming in the basement. Adler stared at the withered corpses hung up by meat hooks, some falling to the ground, coming untethered from their moors by the weakening of bones and flesh. Huge buckets of a black, tarry substance he recognized as aged blood sat beneath them.

Rationing, stealth, advanced methods of butchery. Evidence that this thrall had evolved into something unseen by any warden grew as the duo proceeded upstairs. In an attic loft, they found a ritual chamber, a five-pointed pentagram burned into the ground, the eye of Horus painted in blood peered at them from a vaulted ceiling so that it may observe the unholy acts performed here. The room was so full of the corruption that Adler could barely see, his senses reeling from the concentration of miasmal residue. Never before had he seen it so concentrated in one place. This elder must've been a long practitioner of those infernal arts, using the forbidden knowledge within to augment the richness of the blood spilled within the summoning circle, getting the most from her human fodder, and perhaps learning to enhance her own powers by communication with the unspeakable things that lurk beyond the void of this world.

Gunther couldn't stand it. He ran downstairs to throw up, but only succeeded in dry heaving, his body already using up whatever food he'd put in it long ago. Adler followed him back now, his nerves alight with tension, feeling as if he were standing at the spot of a lightning strike a split moment before it happened.

"Come on. Place is empty," he said, and grabbed the boy by the shoulder, gently leading him outside. He could hear their horses whinnying out front, they were spooked. Immediately he felt the pulling at the back of his neck, the smell of change.

He saw a human form before him. "At arms!" he barked as he brought his revolver up in a flash. He froze at what the iron sights were pinned on.

Adler's nostrils flared as he took in the scent of the skinny, naked thing that shivered before them. Adler looked down at the wooden spear that had been shoved into his leg just below the knee. The crude prosthetic was not cut properly for length, however, causing the man's body to tilt to the left. His skin was nearly translucent, Adler could see fine veins and capillaries and even some vague dark shapes for organs. The man was so emaciated that his flesh clung to his ribs as tight as a drum skin, his scalp glinted in the light of the setting sun. A roadmap of scars dotted the pathetic thing's body. Not bitemarks, no. Small, surgical scars. Precise incisions. A blood sieve. Adler understood with horrible clarity then. A shuffling blood bank. Still, that did not explain the strange odor exuding from the thing, for *man* was too grandiose a term for what he was now.

A thick red beard covered his face, went down almost to his navel. Adler saw that from the thatch of red pubic hair at his center sprouted a crusted-over stub where the man's genitalia should've been.

"Oh . . . my god . . ." Gunther breathed, his pistol wavering at the sight.

"Yuh . . . Yuh . . . You . . ." the man rasped, his beard quivering with the movement of his lips. His eyes, which appeared almost comically small from their sunken sockets, rolled up into his head, revealing bloodshot sclera. His bulbous head, which sprouted a few tufts of limp red hair, began to twitch as he spoke. "She . . . She . . . Will . . . Let . . . You leave . . . here . . . Alive. Go . . . And . . . And you will live . . . Fight us . . . You will die . . ." the man said in a stilted, halting monotone.

Adler could smell that he wasn't strigoi. The fact he was standing in the sun unbothered by its rays attested to that. But he did not smell of the pure copper tang that inhabited all men either. This was something different. He was man, but . . . They'd *done* something to him. His scent was rotten. He knew this man should be dead, his traumas would've sent any normal person into shock. For them to sink their telepathic hooks into him from such a distance meant either she, whoever she was, was *very* strong, or they were close by.

"Show yourself! Too cowardly to speak in person? You had to send a proxy?" Adler called out, but the woods remained lifeless. Nothing happened. The abomination that was once a man just stood there, shivered.

"She . . . She knows what you are . . . She wants you to leave . . . leave this place."

Adler had half a mind to shoot this goddamn thing, to put it out of its obvious misery. As if reading his mind, an explosion rumbled through the abandoned valley as Gunther, unable to bear sight of this wretched thing, shot at it. He knew he was aiming for the head, they were always taught to aim for the head or the heart, but instead struck the man in the shoulder, a piece of clavicle and meat shearing off.

The man spun with the impact, fell to his knees. Blood did not spurt from his wound but instead oozed, as if the heart that pumped within did so sluggishly. With a jerking motion, Adler could almost see the invisible strings pulling the poor human to his feet. He began to walk toward the blackened summit of the knob.

"She . . . wants you to . . . leave . . ." The thing continued to rasp over and over as it began to shamble back the way it'd come.

Adler raised his rifle, took aim at the back of the thing's head, meant to put an end to this travesty, one less plaything for this cruel demon to have, when a voice spoke out from everywhere at once. Adler whirled as the familiar baritone came to him, speaking in his native tongue.

"I thought wardens were trained to never harm the sheep unless harmed by them?" Adolph Braun's voice spoke into his head. Gunther looked around wildly, his revolver trying to aim everywhere at once.

"Show yourself, you bastard!" Adler roared. He once again took aim at the poor thing shambling its way toward the knob. "Don't want me to kill your plaything? Is that it?" He said, and chambered a round into his rifle, the metallic *clack* of the gun very loud in that thick silence.

Suddenly the gun began to grow heavy in his hands, taking on the weight of a cannonball with each passing second. Adler clenched his jaw and imagined an iron cage forming itself around his brain. The barrel wavered in his hands. With a finger that felt stiff as a corpse's, he pulled the trigger, forcing all his might into the action. The rifle spoke, but he knew the shot was scrubbed, a plume of dust kicked up around the castrated man's skeletal feet. He didn't even flinch, just kept shambling toward the mountain.

"Would you be so rude as to shit in a man's lunch pale, sir? He's my dinner, you know," The voice asked sardonically. Adler squeezed his eyes shut, imagined the bars of the cage growing thicker, impregnable. He felt the psychic tethers wavering.

"Strong one you are!" Adolph said, his voice now firmly outside Adler's head, being heard with his ears and not his mind. He heard Gunther grunt as he struggled with the mental hold.

"The cage, boy!" Adler said through gritted teeth as he forced a step forward, every limb feeling as if it were pulled taught by chains. He felt his own weakening, the chains breaking with each second that went by where his mental cage fought off Adolph's insidious hooks. Christ, it was the strongest psychic pull he'd ever felt exhibited by an aberrant. He was sure the elder had some role in that.

"I was wondering when you sniveling little lapdogs would show up. I figured it was only a matter of time," Adolph said, and now Adler could pinpoint the sound of the voice, from behind him, from behind the huge manor house they'd just exited. He forced himself to turn around. He heard the sound of bacon sizzling, the sound of his mother's screams as a man masquerading as a town doctor began to dig out the fetus, a future brother or sister. The cries of his father as he was strung up and slowly slit from sack to sternum, going slow enough that his innards seeped out one rope at a time instead of falling from his cavity completely, prolonging the suffering, making the reaper of death pause just outside his door, making young Adler wait while *he* had his fun. All the while, Adler, just a boy, was forced to watch, to behold such an exorbitant display of butchery.

A black rage coursed through Adler, a rage so powerful it caused the chains to shatter. He heard Adolph grunt in surprise as Adler freed himself completely, and charged with all his speed toward the back of the house. He wheeled around the corner, and there he was. Large as ever, a huge body covered in course black hair, two red eyes peered at him from just above a huge sea of black fur, the long raven hair bleeding into the dense beard, giving the aberration an appearance of being mired in the very corruption he bathed in, of being something more feral and animal than either man or strigoi.

For a breathless moment, warden and aberrant stared at each other.

"Oh . . . I know you . . ." Adolph said as recognition flared in those crimson eyes, skull canting sideways like a curious dog. "Goodness, you've grown. I see my loving touch never went away though. Tell me, do you still hear them screaming? Do you?"

Adler fired, the repeating rifle spitting out four rounds as fast as his now-unburdened trigger finger could pull. He saw in that adrenaline-dilated battle vision as two silver meteors found their target, the first of the fusillade biting into Adolph's bicep and the other grazing part of his ear. But even as the other two rounds were leaving the barrel, the abomination was spinning and ducking, his face contorting into a rictus of pained rage as the silver no doubt burned through him.

In a flash, the aberrant was gone, sprinting around the side of the house, toward Gunther. He heard a volley of gunshots from the young warden, a yell of surprise. He hoped the boy's aim was true. Green though he was, the young warden had proven to be an excellent shot during weapons training.

Adler followed after, noticing the monster left a black blood trail in his wake. He turned the corner to see that Gunther was being dragged by his leg, Adolph pulling him along the way a child pulls a limp ragdoll by one stuffed appendage. He ran past the horses, who kicked and cried against their moorings from all the chaos. The bastard could run faster than even the strongest Appaloosa at full gallop, Adler could see that as he took off toward the knob, kicking up a trail of dust as Gunther screamed and thrashed against the no doubt ironclad grip.

"*NO!*" Adler roared, the black rage giving way to fear and shame now, that he'd let his understudy, his apprentice, no, the *son* he never had, be pulled into the viper's nest.

"Come now, warden! Enter my domain! Let us feast *together!*" Adolph bellowed from over his shoulder, zigzagging impossibly through trees like some tornado on a warpath.

Adler moved nearly as quick, running to his horse and slicing free its reigns with a quick swipe of his silver dagger. Before the horse had a chance to buck and run off, Adler was mounting him, holding a hand to the beast's neck and using a quick but intense burst of the Persuasion to keep the beast from bucking him off.

With the horse under control, he darted off toward the knob, following the acrid scent of Adolph Braun's mutant blood. The bastard was gaining distance quickly, even with Gunther in tow, but Adler was able to mark his progress, until Adolph disappeared in the growing shadows in the face of the knob. The darkness consumed him, and he and the struggling warden disappeared.

CHAPTER 10

Adler had to abandon his horse halfway to the top, the grade steepening so severely and made treacherous by loose rock that he could not safely lead the horse up it at the speed he wished to go. By the time he'd made this decision, the sun was long gone, the moon taking its place to hold dominion over this blasted land, its spectral light casting a penumbral illumination over the mist-enshrouded treetops below. He jumped off, urgency telling him to hurl himself up that goddamn mountain, but his training forced him to stay put and take inventory of everything he needed. *A warden is so fearsome and effective not because of his physical augmentation, but because of his cunning as a man as well. A warden is as effective as the sum of his parts. What is the lion without not only its fangs, but its wits?*

He reloaded both weapons, taking spare cartridges for both rifle and pistol and lining the pockets of his black duster with them. He shoved a handful of cold biscuits into his mouth, not even tasting the damn things but wolfing down what he could, needing all the energy he could get. In each boot, he tucked a perfectly balanced silver throwing blade, double-sided and wickedly sharp. As he stuffed remaining pockets with food and took great gulps from a water skin, he remembered the small glass vials which he'd brought with him all the way from across the sea.

He brought out the tiny glass container, stoppered with a cork on one end. Within sloshed a murky gray fluid that glinted in the rising moon. The tincture comprised a mixture of aminata mascaria fungi, the ground-up bell cap from a rare subspecies of night shade, and the excretions from the adrenal gland of an elder strigoi, mixed in an ethanol suspension. To humans, this mixture would induce hellish visions and violent convulsions that would most likely end in death. For a warden though, this nostrum granted them with the sight of the nocturnal beast, augmenting their already enhanced vision further, and honing their already whip-fast reflexes to that of a cobra.

Adler had only ever imbibed in the potion once before, when entering the lair of a particularly vile elder sequestered in a mired shack within a swamp. The waters surrounding the property had been infested with obsidian-glazed caimans, the ferocious reptiles under the control of an elder, one who specialized in sorcery pertaining to animal manipulation. Though it made him feel as if his very veins carried liquid fire, and for his brain to expand beyond the cramped confines of his skull, it allowed him to move with breathtaking speed and grace. For the span of a few hours, he moved like a minor god, granting him limited precognition to further augment his reflexes, showing him when the razor-toothed animals were about to strike and where their locations were in the muddy, opaque water. Not only that, but it allowed him to deal with the cunning elder with brutal efficiency.

Despite his apoplectic state, Adler knew he needed to use every tool at his disposal, and with a grimace, he popped the cork out and knocked back the noxious liquid. He almost gagged but fought it back as he felt the cold liquid slide down his throat. Before he even felt it hit his stomach with that terrible cold burning, he could already feel the poisonous potion affecting his system. The slate gray features of the night grew exceptionally vivid through his one good eye, and with his sight, every other sense amplified as well. He could hear the beating of his horse's heart. Could smell a rank corruption emanating from the very earth, and knew beneath this hollow ground laid horrors that would make Satan himself stare in admiration.

Adler proceeded forward, each step springy and light, he felt that if he jumped, he would sore off into the sky, toward the moon, and never come back down. He reached the summit in a blur of motion, time and space expanding into a foreign plane for him, he was simply a slave to the inertia that saw him to his destination. There was only the *now*, and in this now he would end the thing that walked and talked like a man, the thing that had broken something fundamental and vital in young Adler. The thing he'd been hunting all of his very long life. He would destroy everything that lurked in these many tunnels and caves, and he would rescue the closest thing he'd ever had to a son, or he would die trying.

Adler stood at the mouth of the cave entrance, where even his enhanced night vision struggled to penetrate the looming shadows as the portal to Hell opened up before him, so thick was the corruption that emanated from it. He turned, taking in the vast panorama of rolling hills stretching out to the horizon's end before him, the scintillating glimmer of the river's rapids from across the valley catching the moonlight. He took it in, savored it, for he knew this may be the last time he ever saw this strangely beautiful planet, and the many horrors that inhabit it.

Adler took a deep, burning breath, feeling every biological process in his body in a heady thrumming and pulsing of energy. Ready as he was going to be, he plunged into that onyx abyss.

CHAPTER 11

He realized it was the ectoplasmic aura of corruption mingling with the utter absence of light that made Adler squint as he traversed the stone tunnel, revolver in one hand, dagger in the other. Despite this murk, he strode boldly forward, knowing no fear now as he had the singular image of Gunther in his mind. That bastard had taken his whole family from him. Adler would not let the aberration rob him a second time.

Passageways branched off ad nauseam, this vast stone gauntlet left one with innumerable choices, but Adler didn't even stop to consider. An internal compass guided him, every cell in his body pulled toward that corrupted flesh, his soul honing in on the black, ravenous void of Adolph's existence, and he strode unquestioningly onward, going left, then right, left again, proceeding boldly forward as if he knew this labyrinthian maze like the back of his hand.

He passed several skeletal remains on his journey, some animal, most human, but he barely saw these as his eyes were fixed forward, looking for the tiniest shred of movement from the shadows, ready to fire upon anything that dared show itself. The air changed as he went even deeper, his pupil dilated to the size of his revolver's bore, twitching constantly, taking in the darkness and turning it into something gray and circular and unending. Though his left eye was a sightless piece of gristle, he could've sworn he detected phantom traces of visuals coming into the orb, as if though the potion were reactivating long-dormant ocular receptors.

One tunnel grew so narrow he had to stoop and hunch his shoulders to fit through, before abruptly opening to a large chamber whose true dimensions were unknown to him, the darkness holding the room's edges firm in an impenetrable cloak so that it looked as if he stood at the very end of the world. On the walls closest to him though were etched occult symbols, sigils of summoning and ownership, no doubt the elder's doing. Here Adler paused, nostrils flaring like a dog as he caught a scent from one of the many drafts that blew through the maze of interconnecting tunnels.

Fresh human blood. And that other smell. The one that emanated from the thrall-slave with the pegleg. Similar but different. *What the hell did they do to him?* he thought as he raised his head, nostrils flared. The scar tissue surrounding his face tingled, and the left corner of his mouth twitched.

"Come all the way to see me dead, did you? How *honorable*," Adolph spoke from the ether, really stepping on that last word. The aberrant needn't invade Adler's mind to obscure his location, the cavern acoustics made him sound omniscient, godlike. "Flattering, really, to think—"

There came the unmistakable sound of claws scrabbling against stone. Adler's left eyelid twitched as a strobing blur of a form bled out of his left field of vision.

"—that all this time, while I was scouring the east, raping and torturing and having the time of my life, enjoying this blessing the church bestowed upon me, that you were stewing—"

Adler turned his head just as his right eye corroborated with his left, registering a vague blob moving among the shadows. He raised his gun just as he caught sight of the thing lunging at him, huge bulbous head, teeth that looked more at home on the caiman whose bites he narrowly escaped all those years ago glinting with saliva.

"—tormenting yourself with fantasies of revenge—"

Adler fired, the gun's flash momentarily illuminating the cave in a brilliant phantasmagorical explosion of vision, allowing him to see with vivid clarity how the bullet punched through the roof of the thing's mouth, clipping two jagged teeth on its way in, the way the back of its head exploded outwards in a wave of shattered skull plate, dark gray brain matter and sludgy blood. That was a killing blow regardless of the hemorrhaging agent that coated the tips of each silver bullet, and the creature soared past him, dead before it'd even passed his shoulder, and fell with a thump against the wall behind him.

A thousand birds screeched in his ears and his vision was occluded by splotchy negative after images of the cavern. Adler blinked rapidly, trying to rid himself of the gun's blinding flash effects. His empty socket shot a burst of fractal color into his left field of vision, as if though some spectral eye had grown in that long desolate orbital socket. He swung his gun hand to the left just as he felt something cold and rank slam into him. Claws, which weren't actually claws at all, but simply overgrown fingernails gone long and ragged in neglect of such human notions as hygiene raked across the mottled scar tissue of his face.

Adler let out a laugh, an unhinged sound as the claws tore away his scarred hide, and he felt a deep tickling on that side of his face. Long ago he'd lost sensation in those nerve endings, so the vicious wound only felt like a peculiar, minor annoyance.

Adler was in the closest state akin to a blood frenzy a warden could get, his anger working with the twisted genes in his body, transforming him into something ferocious, something primordial, as he stabbed the thing repeatedly with his dagger. He thought he heard a yelp of surprise from the strigoi, though the roar in his ears still persisted. But no, it would not be enough to stab this beast to death. He wanted to *feel* the destruction he was causing, wanted his fingers to hook into flesh and sinew and tear and wrap around bones and shatter them like kindling for a fire.

He roared like something feral and four legged as he shoved his gun in its holster and reached out with his other hand. He left the dagger lodged between the thing's ribs and shoved it up against the stone wall. He felt teeth scrape off his skull but before the thing could take a mouthful Adler was punching his clenched fist through its sternum, it was like punching through glass, and felt the lukewarm insides, like a reptile in winter. He seized a great handful of lung tissue and pulled it out, then shot in again and pulled out some more, and again, and again, until the organs all meshed into unidentifiable viscera between his boots.

He let himself be lost to his rage. His hand was like a piston, going in and out of the thing's chest cavity, until it looked as if the creature had taken a cannon shell at point blank.

"SHOW YOURSELF, YOU COWARD!" Adler roared, but nothing except the echo of his own voice, filtered of all treble due to his tinnitus, came back to him, as if the very caverns themselves mocked his virtuous rampage. He threw the dead abomination off into the abyss, grabbing his dagger as he did so, his right arm coated with gore up to the elbow.

Adler went to the left, following that strange smell. He climbed up a ridge along the wall, and shimmied into another narrow tunnel, the ceiling so low he had to crawl on hands and knees, the stock of his repeating rifle scraping against the stone roof overhead. He thought he heard something up ahead, a mewling, a groan, sounds of resplendent agony.

Quickening his pace, Adler ignored the dull burning pain on his scalp as he felt a flap of skin pressing against his eyebrow, occasionally stopping to wipe at the blood dripping into his eye. He forced himself to pause momentarily and shove more food into his mouth, knowing he needed to be in peak physical condition for whenever that parasite finally decided to fight the mad warden.

His stomach was a roiling, discontent animal from the nostrum, but he made himself swallow a handful of raw venison flank, bought by Werner at a butcher prior to their leaving. Blood trickled down his lips as he chewed on the stringy meat, feeling a small burst of adrenaline course through him, feeling the blood coagulate on his scalp, the wound ever so slowly beginning to close itself up as his metabolism, not quite as fast as a strigoi's but close, knitted his body back together. He crawled forward, dagger in his hand, aware of the compromising position he was in. He tried to quicken his pace, wanting to be out of the claustrophobic tunnel, where the abominations could pin him from both sides if they had a mind to.

"Pl . . . Pl . . . Please . . ." He heard a faint rasp of a voice, coming from just ahead. "Let me . . . Let me die . . ." An ephemeral plea for death beckoning him. Adler's ears still rang from the gun's cave-amplified roar, so he couldn't tell just how far away this speaker was. He crawled as fast as he could now, moving at such a speed that when he reached out a bloody hand to claw himself forward once more his momentum pitched him into a vast, open chasm.

Adler could not see the bottom, and braced himself for death as he fell headfirst, having just enough time to think of the cruel irony that he should die from such a foolish blunder instead of at the hand of his mortal enemy.

CHAPTER 12

It turned out there was no fathomless subterranean cliff that Adler had plunged off of. He fell ten feet instead of a thousand, and as with the reflexes of a cat, Adler had managed to tuck and roll himself so that he took the brunt of the impact with his feet. His ankles ached with the jarring thud, but he displaced the impact of his fall by going into a kneeling roll. He rolled right into a pile of bones and cold meat.

Startled, he did his best to conclude the roll in a fighting stance, but the nebulous corruption here was so thick that he could barely see three feet in front of him, and he stumbled until he fell into a wall and backed up against it, trying to get his bearings. The smell was fully upon him now. Up close he caught something else lingering under it like the base layer of a cake. Cooked flesh. But cooked animal flesh would almost always smell good, to man and warden alike. This flesh smelled different though, its preparation giving off an aroma that both enticed and sickened. When he realized what it was, Adler forced himself to swallow a regurgitated bolus of deer meat, taking shallow breaths of the corrupted air.

Man flesh. This shallow pit reeked of cooked human, the aroma so thick, as thick as the corruption that lingered in the air, that he knew many, *many* of those tainted meals must've been prepared here. Something monstrous happened here, the impenetrable obsidian veil hanging in the air a portent to the level of depravity committed.

"Please . . ." the voice came again, breaking into a hitching sob. Blade thrust out in front of him, Adler proceeded forward, his ghostly left socket once again signaling to him, taking in information his good eye apparently could not. Directly in front of him, he could see the throbbing, pulsing outline of a man, his long atrophied ocular nerves revealing this to him via a flashing sequence of lines. Much like the rough sketch of an artist framing in his subject with quick, broad strokes, yet his right eye only took in darkness.

He took cautious steps forward, snapping bones underfoot, until finally, he was right upon the man. Adler knelt down, again his gorge revolting as he took in the brunt of this ruined thing's stench. He saw it was the poor bastard with the wooden leg. Clearly no longer under Adolph's control (or was it the elder's?), the man was helpless, lying in a heap of gristle and bone along a stone floor.

"Please . . ." he breathed, the pain and misery in his voice cut through Adler's rage, and he held up the man's head with one hand, looking at him. "Kill me. Please. *Please*," he begged, his voice no more than a quivering whisper.

Instead, Adler handed him his small water bladder and splashed some liquid into the man's foul mouth, his breath strong enough to make Adler's good eye water. He began to understand with terrible clarity what had happened here, but he wanted to know why. Surely the elder would not dare waste precious sustenance on this thing . . . unless . . .

"What happened to you? What'd they do to you?" Adler asked.

The man let out a great, retching sob, his brittle, malnourished frame shook with anguish. Adler held him now, trying to give this wretched thing some semblance of comfort.

"Please . . . Kill me . . . That's all I want . . ." he said between hitching sobs.

Adler watched then as the man reached out a trembling hand, reaching for something off to his right. His whole body shook as if trying to resist this motion.

"No . . . Please . . . I don't want . . . I don't—" The man's cries broke off with a sob as Adler watched him grasp something akin to a drumstick off a chicken. He peered into the thick cloud of blackness and saw several hunks of meat sitting in the corner next to the man, their flesh seared and brown like grilled steak, sitting on top of smoldering coals whose glow was all but smothered by the corruption. For just an instant, a sickening split second that made every nerve ending in Adler's body shoot out with alarm, he felt the faintest pang of hunger at the sight of the meat.

He dropped the man, recoiled from him as he watched the emaciated wraith begin to gnaw at the seared flesh. A few timid bites at first, and then, as if giving in to some baser need, he began to devour the meat, ripping it from the bone. Now Adler wished for the crying screech of tinnitus to return as the sounds of this abhorrent mastication and pitiful sobs bursting through mouthfuls of meat shook Adler to his core. In his heightened state though, he could hear the wet squelch of molars rending man flesh in terrible vividity. Right then, he understood who was responsible for this, and as if reading his mind, his adversary spoke from the darkness.

"We developed a rather efficient system, my dear warden. My compatriot, Charles, is a whip-smart man, you see. Served with him in the war! Meek though he is, his ideas are priceless. It was he who came up with the idea of keeping a sort of living sieve for our queen to suckle upon. A sieve whose precious nectar has been improved with this *specialized* diet," Adolph said from nowhere and everywhere, and he laughed as the man brought down the now-bare bone against the rocks with a force not of his own, his arm moving in a jerking, stiff motion.

The bone splintered in half, and Adolph could hear slurping noises coming from the darkness now as marrow was greedily extricated from within.

"Like a hog, allowed to gorge on honey, wheat and barley before the slaughter, this man serves to feed me with his delicious anguish, and in turn feeds our queen, who I must say exercises *incredible* restraint, savoring his specially flavored succor, his oh so ripened blood. Sipping on him like a fine wine, to be cherished, not gorged upon. I lure them in off the river, immigrants who are naïve to the wild frontier ways of this place, so easily they are entranced with promises of land and ore. *Gods* do I love this country. Truly a land of great opportunity." Adolph cackled.

"*Enough!*" Adler screamed, this was all too much, too much madness, too much evil. He swiveled the rifle from his back to his shoulder and took aim, his vision wavering with the need to vomit. He forced the barrel's sight to fix upon the feasting man.

"Oh no, don't you do it, don't you—" Adolph's voice was deadly serious now.

Adler fired, closing his eye against the muzzle flash. He could feel Adolph trying to pry once more, but the mixture of sacred fungi and adrenal effluvia built an impenetrable wall around his mind for the time being. Only the faintest tuggings of the demon's hooks could be felt, and he fired, his aim true. The vague purplish outline of man dissipated from his left field of vision, telling him he'd done his job, he'd given that man what little mercy there was left to give in such a depraved situation.

"Oh, now you've done it, you stupid—" He heard Adolph's voice from miles away, his ears again screeching with deafness. But Adler didn't need to hear to feel the thud of something heavy landing right behind him.

CHAPTER 13

He whirled just in time for a stone mason's brick of a fist to smash into his face. He felt teeth dislodge from gums, felt his mouth fill with blood as he was knocked off his feet. He spun in the air, but went with the spin, landing on his back and rolling backward, springing to his feet. He thrust out with his silver blade, felt the knife sink into Adolph's shoulder, but the huge man's tackle could not be stopped.

Together they slammed into a stone wall, Adler felt the wind ripped from his lungs. All the while, he kept his hold on the dagger, driving it deeper into the heavily muscled shoulder.

"Finally decided to . . . face me yourself?" he gasped as Adolph tried to crush him with his body weight. The massive body pinned him into the wall, Adolph driving his other shoulder into Adler's sternum with crushing force. He ripped the blade free just as the aberrant roared and threw him across the room. Adler fell in a heap, his rifle lost in the black corruption, his blade flying.

Just as he rolled onto his back, Adolph was upon him. The huge bastard straddled him like a lover, enormous hands seeking Adler's throat.

"Should've killed you when I had the chance, little warden. But it was simply too exquisite, feeding off your *terror*," Adolph said through clenched teeth. "But nothing could match what sort of exquisite suffering I got from that pathetic insect you just killed," he said as Adler felt his windpipe crushing, felt his trachea being mashed shut. He didn't even try to pry the man's hands apart. Adolph outreached him and was stronger than him.

Adolph was in his own frenzy now, his rage at having lost his dessert blinding him to a man's tricks, a man's cunning. Adler reached down across his body and pulled out the revolver, his head feeling like it might soon explode from the stopped-up blood that pounded at his temples. Adolph's red eyes drilled into him, becoming a blazing sun in Adler's good eye and a spectacular supernova in the other. So fixated on killing Adler was he that he didn't even notice the warden reaching for the gun, thinking the man unarmed until he felt the barrel brush against his bare sternum.

"What—" was as far as Adolph got before Adler fired. The six rounds were fired so fast they almost sounded like one continuous roar from an enraged leviathan. The cavern walls took the thunderous reports and stretched them into something monstrous.

Adler squealed in a harsh breath as he felt his already caked hand lathered in a fresh coat of gore. The iron claws around his throat had disappeared, as did the two crimson planets that bore into his soul only a moment ago. His heart threatened to burst from his chest, and he forced himself to take several deep breaths, trying to open his burning airways once more.

He managed to prop himself up on his elbows, and then slowly to a sitting position. His vision throbbed red at the edges as he tried to listen over the roar of blood and tinnitus in his ears. Before he did anything else, knowing he bought himself some time after emptying the gun into the aberrant, he reloaded. Despite his trembling fingers, he deftly took six cartridges and slammed them into the cylinder, having practiced loading the gun with Werner several times the night before until the action was performed with automatic muscle memory.

By degrees, his airway opened up, adrenaline kicking his healing properties into hyperactivity. The smell of the aberration's blood was thick now, cutting through the cannibalistic miasma like oil through water. It invigorated him, the smell of that man's insides, so long had they needed to be ventilated, so long had this monster's foul blood needed to be spilled upon the blighted earth he dared reign upon.

Adler got to his feet, his breath still whistling between his bruised windpipe, but with each breath the wheezing abated, his second sight returned as his left eye picked up a vague lump of life directly ahead. He charged through the corruption, and fell upon Adolph.

An arm swiped at him, but weakly. Adler knew with the blood-thinning agent in the bullets, only two at center mass would be enough to make the demon bleed out unless he found an immediate source of potent sustenance. But Adler had just robbed the man of his precious sieve. Only Adler's rage was present now, and that was as nourishing to the aberrant as piss from a diseased bladder. He pinned Adolph's arms down with his knees, sitting atop a chest cavity ventilated with six ragged holes which wept with pure black ichor.

"I . . . was one of the first . . ." Adolph Braun said through gurgling breaths. "Your stupid church . . . didn't know what sort of monster . . . they had created . . ." he gasped, and laughed, a laugh that turned into a gurgling wheeze. Adler could feel the man desperately trying to prod at his brain, trying to pry up any of the old traumas visited to him. Any painful memories. The smallest taste of suffering, that mental tongue trying to pry one last morsel from between the teeth of Adler's brain.

Adler holstered his gun. He flexed his hand, feeling knuckles pop and tendons stretch. Thrall slaves could be killed one or two ways: Either by complete destruction of the heart, or by the slaying of the elder in which they were enthralled too. Elders could be killed either by silver piercing the heart, or by complete decapitation, and burning the head after.

Aberrations, however, could only be killed one way, and that was by total destruction of the brain. Adler seized the long mangy locks of black hair like the reigns of a horse. Adolph sneered at him, black goo coating the corners of his mouth. He gave the demon named Adolph Braun one chance to redeem himself before he would destroy him.

"Where is the boy?" he asked. Adolph grinned.

"In Hell. A Hell of *your* doing. All your fault—"

Adler slammed the demon's skull against rock with all the force of a blacksmith bringing his hammer down upon an anvil.

"Where is he?" Adler hissed.

"Screaming in Hell, with your whole family, he—"

Adler seized the jaw of the man who'd haunted him for epochs, who invaded his dreams and robbed him of sanity. No more would this foul thing spit lecherous words and cause a single ounce of suffering.

"You will find no suffering here other than your own, demon, and yours will be, as you say, *most exquisite*," Adler gritted through his remaining teeth, and pulled. With a creaking of tendons and cracking of bones he pulled, feeling the jaw first distend and then dislocate as it became unmoored from its hinges. Adler screamed as he pulled with all his might, and with a great ripping and snapping of gristle and tendon, he pulled the lower jaw away from Adolph's face.

Adolph began to make unintelligible gurgling sounds as his tongue flopped stupidly about from its root.

Satisfied that he'd finally silenced this abomination, Adler began to pound the aberration's skull against the stone floor. The ground shook with each impact as he put all his might into the blows, Adler once again losing himself to his rage. He slammed the skull repeatedly, until he felt something give, felt bone cave in, felt spongy tissue leaking through the thick locks of hair when he put a hand behind the thing's head to investigate. Satisfied he'd cracked open the shell, he turned the head around a full one hundred and eighty degrees on Adolph's neck, feeling vertebrae pop and shatter as he did so.

By this point, Adolph was twitching violently under the man, his clever words of poison turning into stuttering, glottal noises. The back of the man's head now facing him, Adler plunged his fist into the ruptured skull, fingers sinking deep into the only organ in an aberration's body that doesn't atrophy and wither with its terrible diet. He pulled out gray bits of spongy tissue by the handful, until he felt a solid piece of gristle that must've been the brain stem. He reached into the hollowed-out gourd of a head and ripped the stem free like a stubborn weed from the ground.

He stared at the mottled pink root in his hands, stared at the very core of the monster he'd revolved his life around destroying.

I was one of the first.

The body beneath him finally stilled.

The words echoed through Adler's mind as he tried to comprehend, in his altered state, that Adolph Braun was dead. His life's purpose had resolved. He'd destroyed one of his own kind. Adolph was monstrous, yes, but he could've been just as equally virtuous. The alchemists and the scientists involved in The Reckoning had never figured out what turned the children into aberrations. Some said it was the inherent evil instilled in some people, the original sin that lies, in some form, in all men. The Reckoning brought out the true face in everyone. It was why some wardens fought with cunning and stealth, while others, like Adler, had the fires of his warden's soul forged in a deep burning need for revenge, and to defend those who could not defend themselves, and thus fought with the frantic fury of a bull.

He knew he was succumbing to the heady introspective effects of the potion, his singular need to kill Adolph Braun gone, his focus now instead going inward.

"There's still an elder to kill," he said aloud to the empty atrium. He tossed the root aside, scoured around in the darkness for his discarded weapons, and began to search the room for an accessible exit. He found one via a small tunnel about five feet up one wall. He grabbed hold and pulled himself up, eager to be gone from such a cesspit of corruption.

He walked at a crouch, eyes fixed ahead. Adolph had mentioned someone named Charles. Was that the elder? No, he mentioned a queen too. Those enthralled always thought of their den leader as some sort of matriarchal or patriarchal figure. So, who was this Charles? Surely not another aberrant. The church had listed the names and eventual condition of all the boys (and the few men) who underwent The Reckoning and Adler had never known of a Charles to be among them.

The tunnel ahead sloped upwards, and Adolph began to ascend it via the wedge method, bracing a leg on either side of the wall and shimmying up. He glanced upward and froze when he saw something far ahead, his left eye revealing a few vague squiggly lines.

"He's coming!" someone hissed.

"Release the tallow," a voice said, this one thickly accented with the flavorings of Adler's homeland.

Tallow? he thought just as he caught a whiff of something hot, something fatty. Something similar to the cooked man meat that flooded the pit he'd just crawled from.

A moment later, he sensed a molten geyser coming toward him, heard the slosh of rendered human fat sliding down the stone wall toward him.

Adler let himself drop down and scurried backward as the molten fat flowed down the walls and past him. He was grateful for the thick leather brogans he had on, he could sense the heat through them but it wasn't until he'd gotten to the very end of the tunnel that he'd felt his feet burning. He finally slipped in the muck and fell in a puddle beneath the tunnel's opening. He screamed as he rolled out of the human-rendered lava, feeling his hands and part of his forearm sear with the barbaric countermeasure.

He stared at the tunnel he'd just fallen from, saw the cloudy white goo that dripped from its opening, knowing once it cooled it would be far too slippery to have any hope of traversing.

Adler was trapped down here. He couldn't help but marvel at their ingenuity, he'd never seen a thrall horde display such intelligence before.

CHAPTER 14

It wasn't long before Adler heard them coming. He tried to listen for where they came from, his hearing somewhat restored, but the caverns ruined his sense of aural direction. He braced himself into a corner, holding his rifle.

They flowed like smoke from the many holes in the ceiling, his left eye sensing the tide of evil energy surging downwards. He immediately aimed his rifle up and began to shoot into the roof of the cavern, killing them as they fell from the ceiling tunnels. One had managed to slip past his barrage and fell upon him. Adler threw him to the ground, but not before it'd managed to take a bite out of the nape of his neck. He heard the creature retch as he slammed it to the ground, and brought his big foot down upon the thing's neck. He quickly dropped to his knees and jammed the dagger through its chest, sliding like a knife through jam as its tip pierced the atrophied heart, and just as he watched the corrupted life excised from it, he felt another fall upon his shoulders.

A hand seized his blonde hair and yanked his neck back, making as if to drink from him. Adler grinned, knowing the beast would be in for an unpleasant surprise if it did that. He shrugged the strigoi off, whipped out his revolver and fired a round point blank into the thing's chest. Two more erupted from the tallow-coated cavern, flinging rendered human fat about as they hurled themselves at Adler.

He shot one out of the air, but the other latched onto him from the front, embracing him in an evil bear hug as it tried to go for his throat. Adler roared in rage and began to headbutt the thing savagely, ignoring the pain in his head as he broke off sharp teeth with his forehead, repeatedly bashing into the thing's skull until he felt it give. Even still, the slippery bastard held on, and Adler couldn't get a proper grip to fling him off. In a last-ditch effort, he contorted his arm as far back as it would go, and wedged the gun barrel between himself and the strigoi, bracing himself for the hot heat of the compressed barrel blast.

There was a dull *whoomph* as the buried revolver shot out its round, and Adler grunted as a brief, hot fist pushed at his torso. A split second later he heard the splatter of guts slapping on stone, and the greased creature latched to him went limp. Adler flung the thing off, and then braced himself. Only eight strigoi had charged at him. Surely more would come.

He waited.

No more came. The many circular openings, like orifices waiting to excrete hell's own feces, did not produce anymore abominable spawn.

Moving fast, knowing he only had an hour or two before the nostrum worked its way out of his system, he devised a plan, and, starting with Adolph's pulpy corpse, began to stack the bodies up against the wall where some ten feet above was the tunnel he'd first fallen out of. Using the corpses as a sort of macabre stairway, he piled them until he had a four-foot mound of flesh upon which to stand. Enough for him to jump and scrabble his way up into the hole in the cavern's ceiling. From there he began to retrace his steps, going until he came to one of the many junctions he passed, and choosing an alternate route this time.

He reloaded his weapons as he walked, aware that he was now down to his last revolver load and his last rifle magazine. He forced himself to eat more of the venison meat that had gotten squished in his pocket during the conflict, feeling himself fatiguing from that immense expenditure of energy and not enough food to refuel him. In a very distant way, he sympathized with the bastards, their need for blood always hanging over them like his need for food did.

He raced down the tunnel, trusting his once useless left eye to broadcast the presence of any living things up ahead, eager to finally find the heart of this corruption.

But the tunnel seemed to never end, it continued at a gentle downward slope, stalactites hanging from the ceiling like earthen fangs.

His mind raced as he ran, sensing growing corruption ahead. A few hundred feet later, he came to it.

A solid wall of obsidian, so dense and so complete it looked as if the tunnel ended right there, the vast void of starless night beyond it. Adler steeled himself for what horrors lay beyond this portal, and plunged into that lightless barrier, his knife thrust outwards, a war cry coming from his still-aching throat.

What he'd found on the other side wasn't another cesspit of vampiric defilement, but a vivid scene from his childhood.

CHAPTER 15

He stood upon a grassy knoll, from which he could see the panorama of rolling green hills, and the small village of Liepzig, his quant little hometown of red brick colonial houses with their red gambrel roofs and chimneys, whose smoke brought with it hints of *sauerbraten* and *spätzle*.

"No . . ." he breathed, knowing this was some powerful illusion, knowing this was the elder's doing. But it was so *vivid*, so *real*. If it was magic of some sort, it was the most powerful conjuration spell he'd ever seen.

A blonde woman appeared from one of the cozy little houses, beautiful golden locks spilling from high, strong shoulders. The woman wore a blue smock-dress, which was pulled taut at the middle, enshrouding a bulging bump, a basket full of freshly baked bread tucked into her side.

"Adler, come honey! Dinner is ready!" the woman said, speaking German and sounding just like his mother, who spoke with the timbre of an angel.

"No," he breathed again, this time in a little boy's voice, though his feet were moving him forward despite his marrow deep understanding that this was a lie, this was a façade.

His not-mother smiled, and when he saw those sky-blue eyes beaming at him, he nearly wept with the beauty of it. She beckoned him with a wave of her long, elegant hand, putting an arm around him as he approached.

"Where have you been, silly boy? You've almost missed your favorite time of the day. Always hungry, my little Adler," she said as she guided him into the nearest of the gambrel-roofed houses, squeezing his shoulder.

Inside, delicious smells floored him. The sweet tang of freshly baked bread. The heavy, savory smell of a slow-cooking pork roast. His stomach roiled with hunger, and spit squirted into his mouth, though an ever-distant part of him screamed not to be fooled, that this was a trick, a lie. But that part of him was growing quieter, like a bad dream losing itself to the waking world.

The kitchen was just as he remembered it. Festooned on the walls were many canvas paintings done by his talented older sister, Muriel, who'd gone to Budapest to study at the fine arts college there. The shelves were lined with his mother's various cooking pots and baking implements. Liepzig did not have a dedicated bakery, that's how small it was, and his father refused to walk into town for things they could make themselves, and so his mother and four other women in the village who had Dutch ovens provided fresh bread for the whole town on a regular basis.

He reached for a plump loaf that peeked from the edge of the wicker basket, but his mother gently shooed his hand away.

"Now, now, sweet Addy, don't spoil your appetite. We have a guest with us today," she said, and guided him toward the large mahogany dinner table that could seat ten with enough chairs.

Sitting at the very end of the table was a man Adler didn't recognize, but could've sworn he'd seen somewhere before. He wore a starched black uniform, a color that matched the long raven hair that flowed past his ears, parted neatly in the middle, with a moussed mustache whose ends curled like candy canes. He was a huge man, even seated he was still taller than his mother. He grinned whenever he saw Adler, a wide grin that split his face into wrinkles to reveal perfectly white teeth. A smile that did not reach his eyes, whose irises were shrill pinpoints surrounded by mud-colored portals.

Part of Adler wanted to collapse with fatigue. Something was profoundly wrong here, but the smells of food were too distracting. Instead, he sat heavily at one of the chairs lining the dining room.

"This is the new town doctor. He's traveled very far to be here, Adler. Please, be on your best behavior for Mr. Braun. He's to see that our newest addition to the family arrives safely," his not-mother said, producing a steaming bowl of roast before him. Adler stared down at the glistening browned meat, mired in its own juices, surrounded by a harem of slow-baked potatoes and asparagus. He knew without even taking his first bite that the meat would be so tender, so succulent it would fall apart in his mouth as he ate it. His mother was the best cook in the whole world. He would die in defense of that statement.

She gave him a fork, and then proceeded down to the other end of the table, where the doctor was served his own heaping plate.

"Thank you, madam, this smells absolutely delicious. Please. Sit with us, you've worked so hard on your meal. You must eat, now that you're eating for two, that is," the man said, his grin somehow widening even further, until it nearly touched his ears, as the plate was put before him. His voice was pleasantly deep, it made Adler sleepy as he seemed to feel the voice in his chest.

"Oh, you're too kind, Doctor. I think I will do just that. With Warren working so much, it's nice having a man around the dinner table," she said as she made her own bowl, sitting beside Adler, who patiently waited, fork in hand, knowing he would not dare eat a single bite until his mother gave him the say so.

She said a quick prayer before digging in. Adler attacked his food, tearing apart the roast with his fork and scooping great dripping heaps of flesh into his mouth, juices dripping down his chin as he inhaled his food. He noticed the doctor did not touch his plate, only went on staring with that hideous grin, eyes fixed on Adler. He noted his mother also did not eat, instead gazing at her food, fork poised as if deciding what she should eat first, a potato or a piece of meat.

Adler didn't care. The rich, robust flavors that flooded his mouth were like pure euphoria. In minutes, his bowl was devoid of food, and he tipped the ceramic container to his mouth and loudly slurped the broth that remained. He thought the huge bowl would fill him up, but instead it only stoked his hunger.

"What's wrong? Why aren't you eating?" he asked the two adults, about to brazenly ask if he could have their share if they weren't hungry. His mother gave him a pained smile.

"Suddenly, I don't feel so hungry. This pregnancy . . . It feels different than the others," she said, holding her bulging stomach, her smile stretching into a thin line of barely concealed pain.

"Let me see, madam," the doctor said, getting up from the table and over to his mother with breathtaking quickness. He shot Addler a quizzical look.

"Go on, boy, fix yourself some more, there's plenty to go around," he said as he produced a small black doctor's bag, seemingly from out of nowhere, and began to rummage around in it. Adler was concerned, and confused, but above all else he was *hungry*, and so he went back to the kitchen, where he ladled more of that delicious roast into his mouth. He didn't even stop to bring his bowl back to the dinner table, instead setting the bowl on the counter and began to shovel more of the tender meat into his mouth.

In a flash, it was gone, and still his stomach growled for more.

He headed back toward the table to see if he could liberate the untouched bowls of ambrosia from their guest and his mother, but froze at what he saw.

His mother lay prone upon the huge wooden table, her smock hiked up around her knees. She was thrashing her head back and forth, not in pain as blood spilled from her legs, but ecstasy. She arched her back like a woman in the throes of climax as sounds of metal scraping bone and wet squelching noises came from between her legs along with that of tendons and muscle tearing, reaching their breaking point. A harried-looking Dr. Braun peered up from between them, his face speckled with blood, his arms painted in it.

"Take a guess, boy. Cunt, or cock?" he asked, his white teeth flashing in the candlelight, his jovial grin turning into something hideous, a jackal's snarl as his pack devoured a fallen water buffalo.

"Mommy? Mommy, what's happening?" Adler asked, his voice no longer the gravelly rasp of a long-worn warrior, but a child's innocent squeak. She white-knuckled the edges of the table as he watched her whole body shudder and convulse. Blood spilled over the edges of the table and dripped onto the floor now. She snapped out of her gaze and looked right into his eyes.

"Doing what needs to be done, little Adler. Getting this bastard cut out of me. This little parasite who should've died in the womb, like all of you should've. Your father's cursed seed had no right blooming in my sweet fertile soil," she rasped as Braun ripped the smock up around her body, revealing those regions a boy should never see of his mother. Her vagina was obscenely dilated as something inhuman crowned from her. Anus prolapsing further with each heaving push, a pink rose blossoming from the orifice as blood smeared feces leaked from that ruined hole.

Adler forced himself to look away, his eyes instead flitting to her bare stomach, webbed in veins and stretch marks, something rippling violently beneath the flesh.

"Your mother's sweet cunt is too tight for such a delivery. Let's open things up a bit, shall we?" Adolph produced a scalpel and stood poised over the pulsating swell of belly like a painter armed with his favorite brush, prepared to create his magnum opus. Slowly, he lowered the scalpel into the top of his mother's stomach, a small bead of blood welling up and ran down the side from the incision.

"Stop it!" Adler cried, trying to pull his mother from the doctor's murderous intentions, but she only shoved him away. With glacial slowness, Adolph drew the scalpel down, meaning to unfurl the flesh of his mother's stomach, meaning to rip out what might be his sister or brother. Slowly, just like with his father, just like—

"You want to stop it? Then be a man," his mother said, her voice no longer soft and angelic, but spiteful and hateful. She tossed Adler a dagger, and when he caught it, he saw the wickedly curved blade, the strange emblem emblazoned within the pommel. How familiar this blade seemed to him, yet he knew he'd never seen it before. His parents would never let him have such a thing.

"Eye for an eye, boy. You read the bible, yes?" Braun said as the scalpel continued to crawl a millimeter a minute down his mother's stomach. "A pound of flesh is warranted. If you want to save your little sibling's life, you must take your own. That is how this works," Braun said with infinite patience, as if explaining to some simpleton why the sun rises every day.

Adler stared down at the blade, it trembled in his hands.

"Do it, little Addy. Make your mother proud," his mother (no . . . his not-mother, right? This wasn't real, was it?) said, her once tender grin turning malicious, like the doctor's. "I should have had you scraped out when your pathetic father squirted you into my belly," she yelled, and cackled a loon's laugh.

"Go on, boy, for once in your useless life, do something *honorable*. Before I get the iron. The one you know so well," the doctor said, pausing to kiss away the drops of blood that now seeped down the sides of his mother's distended stomach, the edges bulging and moving now as the life within grew agitated. Adler saw the iron sitting on the stove, glowing red hot, its flat, glowing surface eager to sear and cauterize. The sight of it made him wet himself in terror, for a long-buried, dreadful recognition cut through his fear. He knew that iron, and was intimately acquainted with its heat, but how he knew such things was beyond him.

Adler stared at the knife. At the pommel. He'd seen that sigil before. Why did it move something so deep within him? Why did it make the edges of this terrible scene waver with darkness when he looked back up at his mother, and the doctor.

"Do it, Adler. Across the throat, just like this, honey," his mother said, looking at him from across the table, drawing a long, delicate finger across her slender throat. Adler felt himself raising the blade up, the tip tickling the side of his throat.

"Yes, that's it," Braun said, looking with feverish eyes at the boy, his grin turning into a sneer. Tears welled up in Adler's eyes as he felt the blade begin to part flesh. *Eyes*. No . . . That wasn't right. Why wasn't that right? Why shouldn't he have two eyes?

"*Do it, you pathetic little bastard!*" his mother screamed, now no longer resembling his mother, but someone else, a facsimile, an imposter. The dining room wavered at the edges again, revealing a dark, fetid space that was not his home.

Adler began to pull the knife away, but it took all his strength. Bile rose up in his throat as he felt the foul meat stuck between his teeth, knowing it wasn't pork roast, knowing his belly wasn't full of his mother's homemade cooking. Something black and heated began to rise up within him, the eternal cauldron of rage from which his soul often simmered now brought to a blazing roar. His arms trembled as he forced the knife away, feeling a thousand invisible hands push it back toward his throat.

"NO!" his mother roared as she watched him resisting, watched him move the knife away from his throat.

Adler closed his eyes, and saw wild pulsating lines in the left side of his vision. He closed his eyes against the lies. He closed his eyes against the power that tried to overtake him.

He yelled as he plunged the knife down, the high scream of a child overlaid by the deep bassoon scream of a man who'd overcome more horror than anyone alive had a right to endure, plunging that knife into his mother's sternum, putting all his weight into the blow.

CHAPTER 16

The illusion popped like a heated lance to an abscessed boil. Adler blinked, taking in the sudden darkness, the afterimage of his childhood home and the kitchen and his mother gone. He stared down at the prone form writhing below him. Slowly his vision cleared, and he saw in amazement that he was atop an altar of some sort, made of wood and bone, and atop this throne lay a blonde-haired, blue-eyed angel, so much like his mother that he had to pause and make sure this wasn't more of the elder's trickery.

But the thing curled back its plump lips, which were rapidly turning gray, and revealed inhuman teeth, tendrils of bloody saliva snapping apart as it opened its mouth in a hiss. The illusion of angelic beauty shattered like a scatter-shot through a mirror.

Realizing *this* was the elder, *this* was the source of the plague that blighted the hills, he took his silver dagger and drove it even deeper, hearing the blade scrape off her sternum. She shivered, hands pulling and beating at his coat, flailing ineffectually as he pinned her to her altar. For an instant Adler saw an ancient, decrepit thing in place of all that radiant beauty, her own façade waning as death tried to snatch away her vestiges of vanity, her illusions of grace. Her true, monstrous form overlaid with the ancient disguise she had used to lure countless humans to a fate far worse than death.

"NO!" he heard a high-pitched voice roar from behind him. Adler thrust out his hand without taking his gaze off the elder, anticipating the charging creature. The hand closed around a flabby throat, the flesh cool.

His head finally turned, and Adler glared at what he'd ensnared. The man must've been rotund in life, for his flesh drooped from his body the way thoroughly milked udders do. Those who turn strigoi can never sate the appetite they had in real life, their bodies simply burning up the blood before it could be stored. This loose, drooping apron of flesh always happened with the fat ones. Beady eyes looked out from swollen sockets, eyes that were once myopic and saw with the help of thick lenses, now accustomed to the blood-sight of the strigoi. His hair was salt pepper and hung in tangled curls about his head.

"You bastard. You bastard. YOU BASTARD!" he whined, thrashing hard enough to momentarily break free from Adler's grasp. But he didn't even try to attack Adler, no, he went straight for the elder, to his queen. "Oh no, oh no, no . . ." he breathed as he collapsed beside her. He tenderly touched the area around the knife, which was planted right between the milky orbs of her breasts, the skin there pure alabaster. The black sludge that wept from the wound stood out in dizzying contrast. "Need to elevate you, need to stop the bleeding, need to—"

Adler grabbed the sniveling thing by the hair and abruptly slammed him into the macabre throne of bone and wood that the elder sat upon with a crunch. The thing cried out as Adler brought him up and held the revolver to the strigoi's head.

"You tell me where the boy is, and I'll let you tend to your *bitch*," Adler growled, still sickened and jarred by the intense magic illusion he'd been forced to endure. "She can bleed a while yet."

"You poisonous creatures! You come into our lair, destroy our home! I won't, I won't tell you a goddamn—"

"You will, or she dies. And you know what happens when she dies, right?" Adler asked. The thing stopped squirming, its corrupted brain weighing the options. This one had been turned for a while. It acted and reacted more like a man than a beast. Was this the one named Charles? The cunning one who'd had the sadistic idea of the blood bank? Of that specially marinated cannibal's blood, which must've been like pure ambrosia to the strigoi elder.

"You promise to let me tend to her?" he asked.

"Bring me the boy, *alive*, and I'll even help you get the knife out. It's coated in a special anti-coagulating agent. You sound like you were a doctor once. Surely you know what that means. Run along now, before I put a bullet in both of you," he said, hurling the flabby thing down from the altar.

The man disappeared into the corruptive shadows, which even now were dissipating with the elder's grave injury. She wouldn't die from this injury alone of course. Fire was the only sure way to make sure this thing died the true death. But this lowly strigoi, no matter how clever, wouldn't know that. Sheer desperation drove him to do what he could to save his precious queen.

As he waited, Adler stared down at the elder, her flowing blonde hair hanging off the edges of the altar. She was nearly catatonic now, the silver tip only an inch away from her heart.

"Clever bitch you are. Thought you'd outrun us, coming all the way out here to the edge of the world," he said with a grin. "I bet Adolph helped with that clever little trick. Well, guess what? He's dead. So is all of your horde. Small numbers you keep. Wise, better to have a smaller, manageable pack. You're a smart one to have lasted this long, I'll give you that," he said, grabbing the dagger and roughly pulling it from her sternum, letting the obsidian ooze leak out with more fervor. She drew in a harsh, bubbling breath. Her mouth formed silent words. He knew she was trying to conjure, even in her near state of death, she was still fighting.

He grinned. *How admirable.* With one big hand, he grabbed those delicate cheeks and made a fist, squishing her beautiful face together, her lips pooched out into an almost comical expression, a bubble of blood welling up and popping from that scrunched O of flesh. Even still, those eyes, which he could see clearly in the darkness, penetrated him. He felt his grip falter ever so slightly, and he sharply looked away.

"Won't work on me dear. Nice try," he said, anger briefly boiling over as he tried not to think about the bits of flesh between his teeth. Tried not to think about how invigorated he felt, his injuries sustained in battle all gone, as if he'd supped from a truly nutritious well. No, he would refuse to acknowledge that that part of the illusion was real. Even if he could smell grilled flesh somewhere from this vast atrium, even if it was plausible that the sadistic madman Charles had devised the plan, to feed him human flesh while in the throes of the illusion, and thus corrupt the very virtue of his existence. To violate the most sacred tenet of The Order. To break this mighty warrior and shatter him mentally, if only to help overcome him physically.

He looked toward the ceiling, hoping Gunther was all right. If he wasn't, he would draw out the elder's death for a very long time. Days perhaps, letting his sanity slip away with her life. He knew how to do so, from the days of the inquisition, when they hunted the last of her kind from what they thought of then as the edge of the earth. There was no inquisition to be had however, no torture-for-information methodology here.

Adler would conduct the torture for his own sake, his own needs. His fingernails dug furrows into the elder's perfectly symmetrical face. How many innocent souls had she lured to unspeakable horror with that cherubic gaze? He wanted to pluck each blue eye from their sockets and stomp on them like rotten grapes, but he would not.

He would let the intelligent imp think he'd kept up his end of the bargain, until Gunther was in sight and unharmed.

"Are you scared, old one? To finally be facing death after so long eluding it?" he asked. She did not respond save for another bloody bubble that welled and popped, leaving a fine mist of blood against his already gore-caked fingers.

He heard the patter of bare feet against stone, heard a grunting sound. Not releasing his hold on the elder's face, he withdrew the revolver in his other hand and kept it trained toward the tunnel entrance he'd seen the deflated strigoi scuttle into.

A moment later, the cunning little beast shuffled in, a naked Gunther in tow. Adler could see the many crescent bitemarks marring the boy's pale, muscular body, and a thin grin pulled at his face.

"I see you tried to sample the boy. How'd that turn out for you?" he asked, knowing the answer. The Reckoning, by whatever infernal processes the body underwent during the transformation, had resulted in warden blood being repulsive, almost toxic to strigoi. Many enthralled who'd never encountered wardens before would attack with the bite, their instinctual first move, only for them to recoil, their chops twisted in disgust as the special ichor coated their teeth and burned lips. It appeared several tried regardless, perhaps starving from the extreme rationing evident in this particular thrall system, refusing to believe this thing that walked and talked like a man did not taste like that which they so sought.

"Alive, as promised," the flabby strigoi said, and shoved Gunther to his knees, his hands bound behind his back. He proceeded up the throne. Adler put out a hand to halt him.

"Free him," he commanded. The man looked at him, beady eyes, a mole's eyes really, blinked up at him, as if finally suspecting he might've been duped.

"But I—"

"Do it," he said, pulling the hammer back on the revolver. The thing sneered at him and then scuttled back down the altar, its body jiggling and its skin flapping as it did so. He went to the kneeling Gunther and pulled his wrists up to his mouth, ripping away the binding with his teeth.

"Get him, boy," Adler said as soon as he heard the bindings hit the ground. He turned back to the elder, the slit in her chest now readily drooling the ancient blood that flowed through her veins, hearing Gunther give his war cry, a high, piercing wail. This was the boy's true initiation. All wardens must learn to unlock the black rage within that allows them to truly harness the powers they'd been blessed with. A warden's virtuous rage was their true superpower, it was the thing that amplified all their augmented abilities, it was what gave them the true upper hand in battle. So much like the livid, enraged juggernauts of the Nordes, who fought with the strength of ten men thanks to heady hallucinogens and a belief they fought with the hand of Thor at their backs.

"No, wai—" the flabby strigoi cried out before Adler heard powerful blows landing against tepid flesh.

"YOU MONSTER!" Gunther screamed, and Adler smiled as he heard his once green protégé shed his boy-like naivety of the ways of the world, a snake molting its old skin. Adler nodded with pride as he heard a true warden being forged from the fires of that rage.

Adler slid two fingers into the gash, feeling the firm edges of her breast plate. Like peeling the shell from a boiled egg, he began to pry loose the boney shelf, holstering his revolver to dig into the ribcage, and pull out the black, terrible heart that still beat even as he pulled it from its organic housing, aorta and valves pulsating weakly as he held it in his hands. He hoped this was the last one, the final blight to walk upon this earth, though he knew deep in his own ancient heart there would always be more.

Whatever cruel thing had brought this world and universe into existence would always ensure there would be struggle. The scales must always be balanced.

He squeezed the organ in his hand until it ruptured. Behind him, the striking blows took on a wet, crunching quality. Adler pried the elder's mouth open and shoved the heart inside, and even on death-knell reflex, he watched as the fangs sunk into the gristle.

"That's for making me remember my mother's face," Adler said quietly, taking the silver blade and cleaning it against his pants, wiping the blood away. He proceeded down the altar, which would make the perfect pyre upon which to burn her, an effigy to evil itself, and found a hand-sized stone dislodged from the ceiling. He glanced over at Gunther, his fists a blur of glistening black, the clever strigoi now an unidentifiable pulp. He didn't stop the young warden. This was his baptism by blood. This was a holy moment. Adler would not interrupt it.

He stood at the base of this throne of depravity, this unholy symbol for all that should not be, realizing that the tanned leather bindings holding the wood and bone together were not animal hide. He saw the blemishes of birth marks and freckles, a tattoo here and there. All dry as kindling.

He struck the back of the blade to the karst, and sparks showered the first step of the throne. Immediately smoke rose up from where the sparks hit the wood and hide. Adler blew gently, small embers glowing orange as he fed them oxygen, until the crackling of wood and tanned human skin told him the fire had caught. It did not take long for the embers to blaze into a full-on conflagration.

"Come, Gunther," Adler said, gently touching the young warden's shoulder. Gunther started as if snapped out of a trance, and Adler knew it *was* a trance. Gunther looked down at what he'd done, as if in disbelief that he'd done it. "Our work is done," he said, helping the boy to his feet. He could feel the warmth at his back as the throne began to blaze. As the fire spread, the corruption waned, and the two could see clearly

255

as the flames rose. "Let's see if our horses stayed put. I'm sure you're hungry after that ordeal."

"Aren't you hungry, Herr Schmidt? I could hear you fighting through the caves," Gunther said, looking at his master, perhaps sensing the profound change that had taken place in the man.

"No," Adler said with a sigh, tasting that most forbidden fruit still clinging between molars and incisors. "I don't know if I will ever be hungry again."

AFTERWORD:

The undertaking of this novel was probably my most forward attempt at "historical horror" to date. Having been a life-long resident of these beautiful rolling hills, I'd always dreamed of setting a period-piece story against such a richly historical area, that is often overshadowed by its smoky cousins to the east when it comes to prevalence in American literary canon. There are several authors I'd like to thank here, whose historical texts provided invaluable insight into the complex geopolitical atmosphere of the Ozarks during the civil war:"

Vance Randolph's "The Ozarks – An American Survival Of Primitive Society" as well as his most well known book, "Ozark Magic And Folklore"
Brooks Blevins "A History Of The Ozarks" Volumes 1, 2 and 3
Robyn Burnett and Ken Luebbering- "German Settlement In Missouri"
James W. Erwin- "Guerilla Hunters In Civil War Missouri"

ABOUT THE AUTHOR

Richard Beauchamp is an author of horror fiction. He lives right on the eastern edge of the Missouri Ozarks, where he often uses his unique location between the rolling karst hills to the west and the alluvial flatlands of the Mississippi River Valley to the south as settings in his stories. He has been writing fiction since 2017, and his work has been nominated for both the 2018 Pushcart Prize and the 2022 Splatterpunk Awards, and his work has appeared in such anthologies as "SNAFU" from Cohesion Press, the "Negative Space" series from Dark Peninsula Press, and "Along Harrowed Trails" from Timber Ghost Press.

Richard lives at home with his wife, too many cats and a very good dog. When he isn't transforming this lush, verdant land into horrifying set pieces for his fiction, Richard can be found roaming the foothills, fishing the many clear streams and lakes that populate the area, and camping among white oak and short leaf pine.

MORE WORKS BY THIS AUTHOR-

"Horror In The Highlands- Collected Horrors From The Ozarks" (Bell Mountain Press)

"Triptych- Three Tales Of Frontier Horror" (Independently Published)

"Black Tongue & Other Anomalies" (D&T Publishing)

"Autonomous" (Independently Published)

Complete bibliography, current convention schedule and more information can be found at

www.richardbeauchampauthor.com

Made in the USA
Monee, IL
29 November 2024

71613637R00159